Sailing an Alien Sea

Library of Congress Control Number: 2 0 1 2 9 2 0 4 6 6

ISBN: 0-9885200-0-1
ISBN-13: 9780988520004

Cover photo "Still Sailing Meadowness" © KEIT
http://www.facebook.com/keitopolis

Sailing an Alien Sea

Cindy L Gold

Dedication

For Connie and Terry, who know me and like me anyway. You never gave up, so how could I?

Acknowledgments

Many were generous with their time, agreeing to slog through crude drafts and tolerating my incessant grubbing for compliments. I offer my sincere and alphabetical thanks to Dave Cato, Jim Fudge, Amanda Gold, Christopher Gold, Donna Hamilton, Sandy McGregor, Betty Sherriff and Rebecca Tarr.

I am especially grateful to Verna Wilder. Her editing and feedback were invaluable. More importantly, her love of my work convinced me to persevere.

As for my husband, Terry, I would not have started and surely would not have finished without his unflagging enthusiasm.

1956

1

A somber procession of four kids trudged down Apache Street, with six-year-old Stevie Hernandez pulling the Red Flyer wagon. His best friend, Mike Burke, walked next to him. Mike's little sister Angie and Nola Bradley brought up the rear. Though it was a mild autumn day, Nola was wearing her winter coat.

"Psssst! Here comes that new boy who lives down on the corner," Stevie said low so only the wagon crew would hear. "Get ready."

The new kid approached. He pointed to the wagon and whatever might be under the tattered green blanket that covered it. "Hey, whatcha guys got there?"

"Nothin'," Mike said, then inspired to add more drama, dragged the back of his hand across his cheek, pretending to wipe away a tear.

"Is it a dead bird? Is it a cat? Did somebody's dog die?" the new kid said.

Mike shook his head as if he were too choked up to speak.

"C'mon, guys, what is it? Show me! Please? C'mon, show me. Puhleeeze?" he said.

"Nope. Sorry. We can't do it. It'll make you sick," Mike said.

The new kid turned as if to leave, then must have changed his mind. He turned back to the wagon crew. "My name's David. I live down there." He gestured with his chin to the end of the block. "In that yellow house with the big St. Bernard in front." The crew's attention was momentarily diverted from the wagon's secret cargo as they looked down the block, scanning for the St. Bernard, wanting to see if it had a little barrel of brandy around its neck as they always had in the cartoons.

It was David's chance to strike. He lunged at the wagon, grabbed a corner of the blanket, yanked it off with a vicious snap. His eyes went wide and his high-pitched scream echoed down the block. An arm! A child's bloody, gauze-wrapped severed arm lay oozing in the wagon.

His scream was followed by the raucous laughter of the wagon crew as they snorted and pointed at their hapless, confused victim.

"You dummy! It ain't a real arm. Look here," Stevie said as he lifted up the ketchup-soaked gauze, revealing the prosthetic arm. "It's just Nola's fake arm."

"Who's Nola?" David asked.

"I am," Nola said, smiling, maybe feeling somewhat guilty now about traumatizing the new kid.

"How come you need that thing?"

Angie pulled back Nola's right coat sleeve, revealing Nola's tiny arm. It looked almost like a newborn baby's arm, except it had no elbow, no hand, and no wrist. There were only two fingers attached to the end of it.

Then David was gone, running full speed back toward that yellow house on the corner.

1967

2

I met Nola when I was thirteen and she was almost eighteen, her days of pulling pranks on the neighborhood kids long forgotten. If she'd told me the wagon story the first day we met, I don't know if I would have laughed. I like to think if I had known her when she was a little girl, I would have been part of the wagon crew, but who knows? Maybe I flatter myself. Maybe I would have been the screamer.

There wasn't much for teenagers to do in Santa Fe. My older brother Clint and I usually ended up at the bowling alley. He was fourteen, going on twenty-five, and a good guy to have around when you were somewhere you weren't supposed to be. Like the bowling alley. The day I met Nola, he and I had been shooting pool, laughing, swapping stories, and then he went outside for a cigarette. Fifteen minutes later he came back in, his arm slung around the shoulders of some girl I'd never seen before.

"Hey, Sylvie, I'm gonna take off now. You OK with that?"

No, hell no, I'm not OK with that, I thought. We'd gotten a ride to the alley with his friend Alan, but Alan was long gone. I had no idea how I was going to get home, but I knew that if I told him that, showed any sort of weakness now, got in his way of having fun, acted *like a girl*, he would never take me anywhere again.

I shrugged, did my best to sound nonchalant. "Yeah, no problem. I'll just finish this game and take off, too."

"You need any money or anything?"

"Nah, I'm good," I said, even though I had only 35 cents in my pocket.

They walked away, and I turned back to the pool table to finish the game. Two older guys who looked to be in their twenties were at the table next to me. I hadn't paid any attention to them before, but now every time I bent over to take a shot, I could feel their eyes riveted to my butt. I ignored them, which seemed to have the unintentional effect of making them crave my attention all the more.

I studied the table, calculated my angle of attack, and leaned over to take my shot. I felt a hand brush across my backside. I whirled around. The guy who touched me—the one missing his two front teeth—took a few steps back, grinned at me, and lasciviously stroked his pool cue. His buddy hung back, languidly chalked his stick, his eyes slowly making the trek down my body. He was not smiling.

I flung my cue onto the middle of their table, and the balls scattered. Bad-teeth-guy looked surprised, but the other guy looked mad. No time to back down now. "Why don't you take a picture, assholes? It lasts longer." I grabbed my army jacket off the coat rack and walked out of the poolroom, determined to look like I was in no hurry. I was rounding the corner, heading for the exit, before I turned to see if their eyes were still on me. They were. I turned to them, used both hands to flip them off, and then, stepping more lively now, I left the building.

I sat down on the steps at the bowling alley entrance, positioning myself so I wouldn't be taken by surprise if they decided to follow me out. I cursed Clint under my breath for stranding me. Our mom had instructed us, in no uncertain terms, not to leave the house while she was at work. She was always giving Clint, my older sister Emily, and me strict instructions about this or that. I always weighed the consequences against the risk, concluding (usually mistakenly) that the risks were small and the consequences bearable. Now, sitting on the cold steps, I was rethinking my previous calculations. If she found out Clint and I had snuck out to the bowling alley, I'd be grounded for a month and Clint would be sentenced to many weekends of hard labor helping our dad with yard work. Mom would be leaving work in an hour, so I didn't have much time.

I'd heard stories about horrible things happening to hitch-hikers, but Clint hitched all the time and nothing bad ever happened to him. He told me that hitching was a great way to meet cute girls or some dude who would get you a six-pack or maybe sell you some weed. He'd warned me though: never, ever, ever get into a car with a guy you didn't know, unless that guy's wife *and* kids were in the car with him.

There was no other choice. I walked out to Cerrillos Road, a four-lane drag that runs though the center of Santa Fe, and stuck my thumb out. Cars slowed, windows rolled down, drivers made astute observations in both English and Spanish about my butt. After ten minutes of harassment, I was convinced I'd be walking the eight miles home.

A swoopy blue Impala rolled to a stop ahead of me. I trot-ted up to it, leaned down to get a look at the driver.

"Need a ride?" the female driver asked.

I said nothing, my brain spinning, trying to make sense of all the contraptions on the steering column, unable to understand how a girl with no arms and no hands was capable of driving.

"Say, aren't you Emily Loft's sister?" she said. "You're Sylvie, right?" The shock of her knowing my name brought me out of my fog. "Yeah, that's right. How come you know my name? Are you friends with Emily?"

"Yeah, we hang out together sometimes. We've got a couple of classes together at school, too. Are you headed home?"

"Out toward Bellamah. You know where that is?"

"I do. I can take you there, no problem. Hop in."

I slid into the front seat, knew I should say something more to her, something that wouldn't be construed as rude or embarrassing, but as usual, every comment that came to mind was intrusive. What happened to your arms? What's that thing on the steering wheel? How'd you learn to drive? How do you get the car door open?

"Thanks for the ride," I said.

"I'm Nola Bradley, by the way."

Manners, manners, where are my damn manners? "Nice to meet you."

"Nice to meet you, too. I've been over to your house a few times, but I don't think I've ever been introduced to you. Have we met?"

Believe me, if we'd ever met, I would remember it. "No, I don't think so."

"Maybe you weren't around or were in your bedroom or something."

Very likely. When I was at home, I rarely came out of my bedroom. It occurred to me just then that Emily and Clint never seemed to have as much homework as I did. Why was that?

"Oh well, it doesn't matter. It's nice to finally meet you."

She was focused on changing lanes now, so I stole a long look at her. She had shoulder-length brown hair, flipped up at the ends, and black cat-eye glasses. Her hairstyle and her glasses were all the rage ten years ago but now were seriously out of fashion. She had the look of girls who have spent too much time in Home Economics class, sewing their own aprons and learning the proper way to starch a man's dress shirt.

She looked just like most of the girls my sister hung out with. Except for the arm. Or was it arms? I needed another look.

"What about you, what grade are you in?" she said.

"I'm in the eighth grade."

"Really?" She looked at me out of the corner of her eye. "You look older than that."

I slouched down a little on hearing this, thinking it made me look cool, more adult.

"What's that thing you're wearing around your neck?"

"This?" I held up my Maltese cross with the surfer in the middle of it. "It's a surfer's cross." It was unusual because it was gold and had a red plastic backing plate that made it sparkle, not like those crappy fake pewter ones from TG&Y. It cost me five bucks and I was extremely proud of it.

"A surfer, you say? Do you know how to surf?"

Santa Fe had no ocean, no lakes, not even a river. Unless you counted the stupid Santa Fe River, which usually had absolutely no water in it, just dirt. And weeds. And cigarette butts. Which made it an arroyo, not a river.

"No."

"Huh. Well, what does it mean?"

Nobody had ever asked me that before. Lots of kids at my junior high wore surfer crosses. A guidance counselor might hypothesize that the crosses signified a love of all things southern California: the Beach Boys, Gidget, woody station wagons, muscle cars, hanging ten— that they gave the wearer a sense of belonging. Then, as now, guidance counselors understood nothing.

"It doesn't mean anything. I just like the way it looks."

"And the army jacket? Do lots of kids wear those too?"

I shrugged. "I don't know. It's practical, ya know. Lots of pockets." And my mom would murder me if she knew I was wearing it, making it all the more precious to me. She was a proper lady and would never go anywhere without first spending an hour in the bathroom "putting on her face" and leaving a poisonous cloud of hairspray in her wake. This was in stark contrast to my utter disinterest in such womanly rituals. She was forever telling me, "For God's sake, put some shoes on. And would it kill you to run a brush through that hair? You look like a damn hippie!" I didn't necessarily want to look like a "damn hippie," but I was pretty sure that if she didn't like a particular thing, then that thing was probably cool.

"How about you? You got any brothers or sisters?" I asked with what I hoped appeared to be a casual glance, though she probably knew I was studying her face, struggling to resist the urge to stare at that strange little right arm, those metal extensions clamped onto all the levers.

"Nope. It's just me. I'm one of those 'spoiled only children' you hear so much about." She gave me a smile. "That's me— spoiled rotten."

I'd never met another girl who was so warm and friendly, at least none who treated *me* that way. It was a peculiar sensation. It emboldened me to take a closer look at her. She had no arm at all on her left side, just a couple of fingers hanging limply from the shoulder. On her right side she had an arm, but it was out of proportion to the rest of her body. It was only a few inches long and instead of having a hand at the end of it, the arm tapered down to two fingers.

Fascinated, I watched her drive. The extensions on the levers put them within her right arm's reach, but when her fingers were on the turn signal, things got trickier; to maintain control she pressed her shoulders against the steering wheel and used her chin and her knees to keep the wheel steady. If her demeanor had not been one of the utmost confidence, I would have been terrified.

I'd finally worked up enough nerve to ask her about all the gadgets on her car, but it was too late. We were turning onto my street, and I spotted my mom's Pontiac station wagon in our driveway. "You can stop here and let me off."

"Don't you want me to take you up to your house?"

"Nah, here's good. I can walk the rest of the way."

"Gotcha. I understand completely." She stopped the car. "Maybe I'll see you around sometime, huh?"

"Yeah, maybe so. Next time you come over, give a knock on my bedroom door."

"OK, I'll do that."

A few minutes later, I was slinking into my backyard. I took off my Maltese cross and put it in a pocket in my army jacket. Then I took off the jacket and crammed it behind one of the juniper bushes that grew below my bedroom window. As I walked in the house, I wondered if I'd see Nola again. I hoped so.

Finally, something interesting just might happen in this hick town.

3

A few weeks later, I was startled by a knock on my bedroom door. I opened it and found Emily and Nola there. Nola was smiling a welcoming smile. Emily was smiling too, but it was the kind of smile that usually meant, "You might get away with (fill in crime here), but you won't be so lucky next time, twerp."

"I'm going over to Nola's house to hang out," Emily said. "Nola said we should ask you if you want to come along. So, do you?" There was something in her eyes that made me think I was supposed to say "no thanks."

"Sure, that'd be fun. Let's go."

So it began. Amazing! A junior high girl getting accepted by a couple of high school girls. Sure, they might be a couple of Home Economics refugees, not exactly the "in crowd" by most kids' standards. Any kids' standards. But they had driver's licenses and they could sometimes get beer, and dammit, they were in high school.

I knew I had arrived the first time I found myself in Nola's bedroom. *I'm in!* I thought, resisting the urge to dance a little victory dance.

Emily plopped down on Nola's bed, obviously comfortable in this environment. Whatever there was to see here, she had already seen it many times. I, on the other hand, was almost giddy from the newness of this experience.

The first thing that struck me was her room's tidiness. No clothes on the floor or bed, no psychedelic posters on the wall, no automotive parts on the dresser. And somebody was obviously a fan of crochet.

I considered my own bedroom. Under my bed, I had a copy of *Sex and the Single Girl*. Due to the surreptitious late-night nature of my reading, a flashlight was also hidden there. In my desk drawer, hidden between piles of old algebra homework was an envelope with two weeks' worth of lunch money in it. I was saving up to buy the latest Doors album. And though I didn't know for sure, I suspected that unlike me, Nola had no clothes or jewelry hidden in the hedges underneath her bedroom window.

My bedroom was filled with secrets and dark urges and rebellion. Her bedroom was filled with—needlepoint. This was not the room of an angst-ridden teenager. This was the room of Aunt Bee on *The Andy Griffith Show*.

A tray on her dresser held cosmetics and cosmetic brushes. The brushes had Popsicle sticks masking-taped onto their handles. This seemed odd, but I didn't wear makeup and for all I knew, all sophisticated girls taped Popsicle sticks to such things. Other than that, it seemed to be a perfectly normal middle-aged woman's bedroom. Which would be fine and dandy, except she was only eighteen.

So what? She's nice to me; she even invited me over to her house. She drove me over here in *her own car*, for Christ's sake. Besides, it had never been easy for me to make friends (or keep them), and now here was Nola voluntarily letting me into her inner sanctum. Let's not reject her just because of a doily or two.

We were going to play *Monopoly*, a game I hated, but I'd made up my mind on the way to her house that if she wanted to slaughter chickens in the backyard for entertainment, by God, I would do it and like it.

She asked me to get the game from the top shelf in her closet. I pawed around on the shelf, pushing things aside, trying to find the game. As I pulled the game down, I noticed her clothes hanging from the rod.

"How come all of your clothes are sleeveless?" I said.

Silence.

"Hey, I asked you 'How come all of your clothes are sleeveless?'"

"I'm waiting for you to figure that out," she said.

I gave her a quizzical look. Emily was no help. She appeared to be studying her left thumbnail with intense interest.

Nola responded with an encouraging smile.

"Oh. Damn," the answer dawning on me.

She started to laugh. "You're such a goofball."

"While we're on the subject, I want to ask you something."

"While we're on what subject?" She arched an eyebrow.

"The subject of arms."

"Who said anything about arms?"

"C'mon. I want to know something."

"And what might that be?"

"I know that you were born with your arms like that, but what happened?" I wondered if Nola's mom was sick while she was pregnant with her.

"Nobody knows. People often ask me if my mom took thalidomide, but she didn't." I'd heard of thalidomide. It was a drug sometimes prescribed for morning sickness. An international scandal developed when a link was made between taking the drug during pregnancy and severe birth defects.

"My mom was very careful when she was pregnant with me. No smoking, no drinking, nothing like that. So, who knows?" She shrugged. "Sometimes things just happen and that's that."

"And your back? Were you born with it like that?" Her spine had a kink in it that made it impossible for her to stand up straight.

"Yes. I've got problems with my back and my hip sockets, too. When I was born, the doctor told my parents that I would never walk. I had five back surgeries at Shriner's Hospital and had to spend about a year in a body cast while I healed. They couldn't fix it, but it's a lot better than it was."

I pictured an infant with only one arm and a screwed up spine trying to crawl. How in the hell did she ever learn to do it? Or walk?

"How come you don't have some kind of artificial arms?" I said.

"Actually, I do have an artificial arm."

"How come you don't have two of them?"

She tilted her head toward her left shoulder, the side with no arm at all, just two fingers coming straight out of her shoulder. "These fingers don't work, so if I put an artificial arm on this side, it would be strictly cosmetic." Then she tilted her head toward her right. "On this side, even though my arm is small, my fingers work pretty good, so I could use them to control the artificial arm."

"Why don't you wear it?"

"It's heavy and awkward, so I need somebody to strap it onto me, which is a pain in the ass. And it looks all stupid and fake. And I can't do much of anything with it."

"Why not?"

"It's got a metal claw on the end of it. The only thing it's good for is pinching stuff and dragging small things around. I can do more with my own arm and fingers. Or I can use my stick." She pointed with her chin at a wooden dowel on her bedside table. The dowel was about two feet long and a half-inch in diameter. It had a small leather loop on one end and a thing that was sort of like a coat hook on the other end. "Hand it to me."

I gave it to her, and we sat down on the edge of her bed.

With her two fingers, she held the looped end of the stick. "See, I can take it like this and use it to help get my shoes on." She slipped off one of her loafers. Then she held the stick down to the floor and scooched the loafer into position. When she slid her foot into it, the back of the loafer folded down and got stuck behind her heel. She used the hook on the stick to push the back of the shoe upright so her foot could slide in.

"I can use it to get my dress off the hanger, too, like this ..." She went to the closet, held the stick up, and used its hook to work a dress off a hanger. The dress fell to the floor and she snagged it with the hook and then flipped the dress onto her bed. "See? Like that."

I studied the stick and nodded. I was impressed that she'd figured out how to use a 50-cent dowel to help her with things like getting dressed.

Then she told me the story of the wagon, and we rolled on the bed laughing until we cried.

We never talked about the artificial arm again.

I was always happy to be included in anything Nola was involved in unless it got too personal. Unfortunately for me, I learned that sooner or later, if you spent enough time with Nola, doing something "too personal" was inevitable. I could handle simple things like scratching her nose for her, adjusting her glasses or putting on her socks. Anything more demanding was embarrassing and awkward for me. Emily, on the other hand, seemed completely at ease doing whatever was required. Maybe it was because she'd had lots of "mothering" experience with Clint and me.

Like most teenage girls of that era, I was painfully shy about having anyone see any of my private parts. It's worth pointing out that in those days we had more private parts than we do now. I have vivid and horrible memories of changing clothes in junior high P.E. class. I would put one corner of my towel between my teeth and hold the other corner with one hand, trying to create a screen between me and prying eyes. Then, with my free hand, I would squirm out of my street clothes. Getting items like panties and bras off without exposing vast expanses of flesh was particularly demanding. It was all I could do to keep from dislocating my arm or chipping a tooth. Red-faced and sweating, I'd eventually get my gym uniform on. No matter how many times I was in that locker room, no matter how many times I dressed and undressed, I never got comfortable with my own nakedness. Or anybody else's.

Nola and I had been friends for months, but she'd never asked me to do anything even remotely intimate for her until one weekend when she slept over at our house. The morning after, I needed to get into the bathroom, but I heard someone in it. I knocked on the door.

"Hello?" I said.

"Yeeeeeesssss?" It was Nola.

"Can I come in for a minute? I have to get some toilet paper for the other bathroom."

"Sure, c'mon in."

She was combing her hair. "Sylvie, can you help me with something?"

Oh damn. Please don't let it be a tampon, please don't let it be a tampon. Please, oh please, don't let it be a tampon.

"I've got this dumb cowlick sticking up and I can't get it to lie down. Could you spray a little of your mom's hair spray on it for me?"

Oh. Is that all? Whew!

I got the hair spray and sprayed a little, then smoothed her cowlick down with my fingers.

"Great, thanks. That looks good. Now would you mind doing something else for me?"

Oh crap. The tampon.

"Would you spray some deodorant for me?"

Whew again! Spraying on deodorant was a rather personal thing, but perhaps I could handle it without dying of embarrassment.

"Sure. Where is it?"

She shrugged one shoulder in the direction of her bag. "It's in there."

I got the deodorant out of the bag. She lifted up her arm and waited. I stared at the area under her arm. Uh-oh. There was nothing there that I recognized clearly as an armpit. I didn't want her to know that I was confused, so I sprayed in the general vicinity of where I suspected an armpit might be, hoping to get lucky.

"What are you doing? That's not my armpit. Jeez! Go lower."

"I'm sorry, I'm sorry. I guess I don't know where to spray it. Sorry."

"Do it again. It's easy. Look for the hair. You know, underarm hairs." She shook her head back and forth in mock disgust. At least I think it was mock.

She lifted her arm again, waited. I studied underneath it, searching for the hair. Ah ha, there's a few. I sprayed again.

"Good. Now do the other side."

She turned her other side toward me. This was going to be a bit more problematic. There was no arm at all on her left side, just two fingers hanging from her shoulder. I would have to lift the fingers up. I wasn't afraid of touching the fingers. It wasn't like they repulsed me. It was just that it seemed so intimate. I didn't want Nola to think that I considered her body repugnant, because I didn't think that at all.

I gingerly lifted up the two fingers and gave a little squirt of deodorant. "Is that OK?"

"Yeah. Fine. Thanks."

"No problem."

I don't know if I had sprayed in the right spot or not. Probably not, but I suspect she had noticed how flushed and nervous I was and took mercy on me.

The next time I was called into action, she must have remembered this incident. She assured me not to worry about *her* being embarrassed about these things. "When you've been poked, prodded, probed, and pawed as much as I have, you cease to know the meaning of the word 'modesty.'" She laughed when she told me this, but I didn't think it was funny; I didn't like thinking about everything she must have been through at Shriner's. I cringed at the thought of strangers touching me, doctor or not. That was my phobia, though, not hers; if her shoulder itched and needed scratching, I don't think she much cared who scratched it for her.

In time, one gets used to anything, and after a summer of lounging around and frequent sleepovers, I had stopped ruminating about Nola's "situation." But I'd be lying if I said I was so comfortable hanging around with her that I'd forgotten all about her appearance and what she could not do. If you were her friend, there would be times when it smacked you in the head and you wondered not just how *she* could handle it, but how *you* were going to handle it. I hadn't fully appreciated this fact until I started going out in public with her.

My training ground was the Vic's Big Boy Restaurant where Emily worked. Our trips to the restaurant usually went something like this: I'd pull open the restaurant door for Nola (she was good at pushing doors, but not so hot at pulling them), and she would walk up to the hostess stand. Staff turnover at Vic's was heavy, so we frequently encountered a new hostess. Nola would say something innocuous to her like, "Good afternoon. Table for two, please." The hostess would invariably look at Nola as if she'd said, "I am an alien from the planet ZorBlax. I'm here to eat your brains." After a moment or two, the hostess would regain her composure and say, "Oh, yes, well … yeah … follow me please."

Nola had an odd walk. I think it was because she couldn't balance herself the way fully-armed people could. Her spine was twisted in an S-shape, so she listed to the right. She walked with a kind of rocking motion, dipping her right shoulder up and down with each step. Sometimes, when she was tired or in pain, the rocking motion was more pronounced. It reminded me of a pirate with a wooden leg that was a tad too short, clomping his way across a boat deck in a squall. Her walk alone might be enough to cause a fellow diner to glance up briefly from his or her plate to observe her passing by. Having once glanced up, though, conversation between dinner companions came to a halt. It seemed like every person at every table was staring at us. As we passed, I heard whispering in our wake, eyes burrowing into our backs.

Nola kept walking, never acknowledging that anything out of the ordinary was going on around us. She chatted the hostess up as we made our way to our table. By the time we were seated, the hostess had relaxed. Then the waiter or waitress would come to the table, and the tension ramped up all over again.

The first few times I experienced this I was a wreck. I wanted to scream, "What the hell are you people looking at? Why don't you mind your own business, you jackasses!" It was clear she was accustomed to slack-jawed gaping from bystanders and a panicked, disoriented staff, and I envied her power to take control in these situations. Luckily, after a few months of experiencing this kind of treatment, I hardened to it. I stopped worrying about how it made me feel and instead began to study Nola's tactics.

On our outings, I made mental notes:

Nola is indicating to the staff that she is mildly concerned with their well being. Why?

Odd. She's telling the waitress where she needs her glass of water and that she needs a straw. Isn't that obvious even to a moron? Oh. I get it. She's avoiding potential awkwardness, trying to put them at ease.

And what's going on here? That cashier just looked at her like she was the result of a gruesome nuclear accident, and yet Nola didn't spew profanity or threaten violence. Very, very interesting.

How did she learn these marvelous (and utterly foreign to me) skills? She told me that when she was a kid, she and the other neighborhood kids sometimes went door-to-door selling school crap. Sometimes she was in a wheelchair (due to one of her many back surgeries), but they didn't care—they'd fight over which one of them got to push the chair. They were happy to have her along, not just for the "sympathy vote" as Nola called it, but because she was the only one in the group who was not afraid to talk to strangers. I concluded that the rules she learned on the mean streets of Santa Fe hawking candy bars still applied. Make eye contact. Smile. Ask questions. I hoped that maybe someday I'd be able to pull that off. Maybe.

Sometimes, though, even she had trouble keeping her cool. One afternoon we were at the Piggly Wiggly standing in the checkout line. The woman ahead of us in line had a kid with her who looked to be about five years old. When the kid caught sight of Nola, his eyes opened wide and he shrieked, "You don't have any arms! Mom, Mom! Look at that lady!" He pointed to Nola. "Hey! You don't have any arms!"

Nola peered down at the kid, eyes narrowing, and said, "Noooooooo shiiiiiiit," deadpan, drawling the two words out, Texas-style.

The kid's mother gave us a snotty look. "Well! I'd appreciate it if you wouldn't use that kind of language to my child."

Nola ignored her. Out in the parking lot I asked why she hadn't made some sort of scathing remark to the woman. She said, "I was thinking of saying something like 'Oh, really? Well, I'd appreciate it if people like you would teach their little darlings some manners before taking them out in public.'"

"Oooo, that would have shut her up. Why didn't you say that?"

"I didn't want to upset the kid any more than I already had. After all, it's not his fault his momma lets him run wild, is it?"

Maybe she was right; maybe it was normal for little kids to act up like that, even though my own mother would smack the bejesus out of us kids if we ever created a fuss over somebody who didn't look "right."

Sometimes it was too much for me. I'd think, hey, I just don't feel like going out today. It's going to be too much of an ordeal. Let's stay home and watch TV or listen to music in my bedroom. Whenever I had these thoughts, I'd start to feel small. Cowardly. For Christ's sake, if she could hack it—and hack it every day of her life—the least I could do was find the guts to walk through a K-Mart with her.

4

It was the last summer Emily and Nola had before they graduated high school. From time to time, they allowed me to hang out with them, whiling away summer nights, sprawled out on Emily's bed talking about boys and daydreaming about the future. We loved to listen to music and to dance. When we heard a song on the radio that we liked, I'd jump up off the bed and holler "Dance, Dance, Dance!" Then Nola would jump up too, and we'd start flailing around like someone had jammed ice cubes down the back of our underwear. Sometimes Emily would dance too, but mostly she sat on the bed smoking, shaking her head, and laughing at our frantic gyrations.

If Emily was jealous of the friendship between Nola and me, I was oblivious to it. If the subject had ever come up, I would have scoffed at the idea. They were the same age, had gone to the same school, knew the same teachers and students and, I assumed, had shared adventures the likes of which I would never experience. As I saw it, my role in the threesome was primarily that of comic relief. This didn't trouble me; I was well versed in playing The Backup. Big brother Clint had shown me the way.

One summer, when I was eleven and Clint had just turned thirteen, we were banished to my grandmother's house in Roswell for a couple of months. The official reason for the banishment was that Emily had threatened to run away from home if she didn't get some relief from babysitting us while my parents were at work. My grandmother, less than thrilled at the prospect of having two rambunctious kids constantly underfoot, bought Clint and me memberships at the Roswell YMCA. The previous summer, Clint had had a friend with a season pass to the local pool, so he went swimming with him every chance he got.

I wasn't so lucky. The closest I ever got to having fun in the water was on those rare occasions when Robert Pacheco, a boy who lived a few blocks away from us, invited all the neighborhood kids to his house to play on his Slip 'n Slide. The past few summers always turned out the same way: some boy (and it was always a boy) launched himself onto the micron thin sheet of wet plastic and bruised his tailbone, cracked a rib, or sprained a wrist. Then Robert's mom would have to make an awkward and apologetic call to an alarmed parent and the Slip 'n Slide went in the trash. The first summer this happened, Clint and I snuck into Robert's backyard under the cover of darkness and dug the Slip 'n Slide out of their trash and took it to our house. All was well and good until my mom came home early from work one day and caught us playing on it in our yard. There was lots of explaining, a couple of whippings and the Slip 'n Slide went back in the trash, but this time, it had been savaged by a box cutter and would be neither slipped nor slid upon ever again.

The first few times Clint and I went to the Roswell YMCA, we played happily together. He taught me how to swim and how to dive down to the bottom of the pool. He liked to throw a penny in the water, and then dive down next to it, motioning for me to get the penny. I was afraid, but seeing him under the water, waiting for me, gave me courage to go after that penny, to hell with the consequences.

Some days we were at the pool for hours, so we passed the time challenging each other: who could dive down the deepest (Clint), who could swim the farthest without stopping (Clint), who could tread water the longest (Clint again, dammit). I was having a great time until one day a boy neither of us knew swam over to us and asked if he could join us in our penny diving competition. "Let's go on the other side of the rope, to the 6 feet," he said.

Clint and I exchanged a look; he knew that I was still terrified of the deep side of the pool. "You comin'?" he said, in a casual tone, as if me swimming on the deep side was a frequent pastime.

"No." Of course not, you idiot.

"OK. I'll catch up with you later," he said, and then he and the new boy swam under the rope, headed for the dreaded deep.

I looked around hoping to spot some other similarly abandoned little sister I might be able to glom onto. No luck. I spent the rest of the afternoon diving alone for the penny and swimming laps in what I now dejectedly realized was truly "the baby side" of the pool.

The next day, Clint asked me to go swimming again.

"What for?" I said. "As soon as some boy asks you to play on the deep side, you'll take off. I don't want to spend all afternoon by myself."

"You won't be by yourself. Besides, Donnie Ray probably won't even be there."

"Who's Donnie Ray?" Why everybody in Roswell went by two names instead of one, I didn't know. Donnie Ray. Suzie Jean. Bobbie Lee.

"He's that guy I met yesterday. Now stop being such a brat, and let's go."

"I'm not a brat. I just don't want to play by myself."

"You won't be by yourself. I promise. Cross my heart, hope to die, stick a needle in my eye."

After a few minutes of his begging, I figured he must be serious, so I relented. We went to the pool and fifteen minutes after we got there, stupid Donnie Ray showed up and off the two of them went, stranding me in the shallow water again.

Over the next few weeks, it happened again and again; please oh please Sylvie will you come to the pool with me, then Shaft City after we got there. Finally, I wised up, and then every time he asked, I refused, and he went alone. He must have not liked that because one day he surprised me by offering to give me a dollar if I went with him. I would have loved to have that dollar, but I still refused.

"What do you want from me?" he said, irritated.

"I want you to play with me. The whole time. And teach me some more stuff."

"If you want to learn some stuff, why don't you take some swimming lessons?"

"Grandma won't pay for lessons! She won't even take us to Dairy Queen unless we pull weeds all day for her."

Clint sighed. He knew I had him on that.

"You're acting like a baby. Why can't you find somebody else to play with?"

This was an excellent question, but one for which I had no answer.

"Take it or leave it," I said, using a well-worn phrase of my father's.

He agreed to my demands and I was secretly relieved. I was getting pretty sick of hanging around the house with my grandma, forced into helping her do housework in the mornings and then experiencing a slow death in the afternoons in front of the TV watching soap operas like "As the World Turns" and "Days of our Lives" as the whir of the window air conditioner in her tiny, dark living room lulled me into a coma.

On the drive over to the pool, I decided I would surprise Clint by proving to him that I could now swim under the rope that divided the pool and make it all the way to the diving board without stopping. I'd gained a lot of confidence on those afternoons when I was forced to swim alone. When I showed him that I could swim just as good as Donnie Ray, boy, was he going to be shocked!

At the pool, we lazily paddled in the shallow water while I silently psyched myself up for my upcoming performance. How was it possible to feel like you are sweating when you are up to your neck in cold water? I knew I had to stop stalling. Donnie Ray could pounce at any moment and my chance to impress Clint would be gone.

"Hey Clint, swim over to the diving board and then look back at me."

"Why?"

"I want to show you something."

"Why can't you show me right here?"

"No! You have to go over by the diving board. And watch me though, OK? Watch me!"

"All right, all ready, I'm going!"

He swam to the far side. He hung onto the edge of the pool and turned to look at me. I pointed at myself and he gave me a thumbs-up and I nodded back at him. I dove under the rope and swam toward him, pacing myself, not wanting to run out of steam too early. All went well until I crossed the nine-foot depth marker. The lane dividers on the bottom of the pool seemed very, very far away and I envisioned my body sinking lifelessly to the bottom. The vision ruined my rhythm, causing me to accidentally inhale a mouthful of water. Coughing, I had to stop and tread water for a moment to regain my composure.

I saw Clint in the water near the diving board, still hanging onto the edge of the pool. Next to him in the water was a girl who looked a couple of years older than him. She was wearing a two-piece swimsuit with red cherries printed on it. What they were talking about, I do not know, but Clint apparently found their discussion enthralling.

I swam toward them, my arms slicing into the water, my legs furiously kicking, each stroke resulting in a noisy explosion of water. I was exhausted by the time I reached him.

"You were SUPPOSED to be watching me!" I nearly shrieked, my chest heaving as I tried to suck down some much needed oxygen.

"I *was* watching you," he said, giving me a blistering look. I didn't care.

The girl looked around nervously, and then edged away from us.

"I'm getting out now." I pulled myself out of the pool, intentionally whipping my head, my ponytail flinging water in his face. I was almost at the locker room door when Clint came up behind me, thwacking my shoulder hard with his middle finger.

"Oww!" I whirled to face him. "What'd you do that for?"

"Why'd you embarrass me like that?"

"You mean in front of Cherry Butt?" I said, putting my hand on my hip and wiggling my hips while I rolled my eyes.

"Stop that; you look like you're having a seizure. And who's Cherry Butt?"

"That girl in the swimsuit. The one with the cherries."

He looked over his shoulder at her. She was out of the water now, sitting on the edge of the pool. He waved at her, but she seemed not to notice.

He turned back to me. "What's your problem?"

"I told you to watch me. You said you would, but you didn't. You're a big, fat, dumb liar."

"I *told* you, I was watching you."

"Nuh-uh. You weren't watching me at all. I coulda drowned out there."

He jerked his head in the direction of the lifeguard, whose attention was now focused on Cherry Butt. "You think I'd trust that doofus over there to keep an eye on my favorite little sister?"

"I'm your *only* little sister, and you *weren't* watching me and you're still a liar."

"Oh yeah? Well, how 'bout this? I saw you make it to about nine feet. Then something spooked you, and you had a coughing fit. Then, for some reason you started swimming like a killer shark was on your ass. Am I right?"

"Yeah, that's about right," I said, my eyes feeling extra-sting-ee now. Damn that chlorine!

He looked back at the lifeguard and the girl. "We OK?"

"Yeah... I guess so."

Grandma would be picking us up soon, so we agreed to meet in front of the building in half an hour. I was sitting on a bench near the front door when he came out. Cherry Butt was with him. I looked away and pretended not to hear as they said their hushed goodbyes.

The following week was our last in Roswell. Each day, Clint asked me to go swimming with him, and each day I declined. But now, he argued no more.

That last summer before Emily and Nola were launched into The Real World, I turned fourteen, about the same age as Clint was when he had fallen for the girl at the swimming pool. Then, as now, I saw myself as just The Backup, but I was content with that. Better to be The Backup and hope for adventure than to sit at home where there was no chance of it.

There's nothing quite like a Santa Fe summer night: warm, cloudless, still. At an altitude of 7,000 feet, we felt close to the sky. In the 1960s, Santa Fe was a small town with little light pollution, so a million stars blazed in the darkness. On those perfect summer nights, a young girl's thoughts would inevitably turn to love, longing, and possibly grand theft auto.

Emily and I would beg, borrow, and at times even steal, to go cruising, one of the few entertainments we had. We weren't criminals; we'd only take my parents' cars and we'd only do that if Nola didn't have her car. (Nola's parents were mystifyingly apprehensive about letting Nola drive her car. They'd tell her, "It's going to rain!" or "There's too much traffic on Cerrillos this time of day!" One night she asked for permission to take the car and they told her that it was "too dark.")

We had many opportunities over the summer to refine our technique. Nola's mom would drop her off at my house to spend the night. We'd wait until everyone was asleep; then Emily, Nola, and I would slip out to the garage. Carefully, quietly, I would raise the garage door. Emily would get behind the wheel, Nola in the passenger seat. Our house was at the end of a steep street, which was useful. Emily would take the car out of gear, and I would push it out of the garage and watch it glide silently down the street. Then Emily would start the engine and turn on the headlights. I'd close the garage door, run down the street, hop in the car, and off we'd go.

My dad briefly owned a Triumph TR3 convertible. We loved that car, though it was usually trouble. One night Emily was driving and I was riding shotgun. The car was essentially built for two people, so Nola recommended we put the top down so she could sit behind us with her butt on the trunk and her legs down in the space behind the front seats. We decided that was a fine idea. Garage door up, down the driveway, and away.

We made our way out to Cerrillos Road, the busiest road in town. When there was cruising to be done in Santa Fe, Cerrillos was the place to do it. We'd been driving barely twenty minutes when we heard a siren. Our heads swiveled around to see a cop car. I thought Emily must have been speeding or had run a red light.

"We're dead, dead, dead! I'm going to be grounded until Mom and Dad are too old to remember who I am!"

"Take it easy, Sylvie. I know how to handle this," Emily said as she pulled over. The cop stopped his patrol car behind us and got out. He walked up to our car and studied the three of us for a moment.

"License, please."

My sister flashed her best come-hither smile. "Yes sir, officer." She handed him her license. He studied it and then directed the fierce glare of his flashlight onto her face.

"You know why I stopped you?"

"Why, no, officer, I'm sorry, but I don't." I was afraid to look over at her, but I assume she batted her eyelashes.

He pointed his flashlight at Nola. "Your friend here shouldn't be riding up there on the trunk in her condition."

Nola indicated herself by shrugging her shoulder while lifting her arm slightly off her chest and holding it there. "Who, me?"

"Yes, you," he said.

"But officer, I'm not pregnant."

I studied my shoes, my lips pinching together hard, trying not to laugh.

"You know what I mean," he said.

"What?"

Now he was the one who looked nervous. "I mean you shouldn't be riding around up there. It's not safe."

We said nothing. I continued to study my shoes.

"I'm not gonna give you a ticket, but you girls need to be getting on home now. Do you understand?"

"Yes sir, officer. We'll head straight home," Emily said. She always knew what to kiss and when.

He walked back to his patrol car, got in, and sat scribbling something for a minute before driving off.

We erupted in giggles and snorts, and I mimicked the cop in an exaggerated way, getting Emily and Nola laughing so hard they pleaded with me to stop. When at last Nola caught her breath, she said, "Dammit! I could be running down the street stark-staring naked and the only thing people would say is 'Look at that girl with no arms!'"

5

The three of us had a great summer, but when autumn came, everything changed. Nola started her freshman year at The College of Santa Fe. There she made new friends, friends who, I was convinced, were more suave and sophisticated than Emily and me.

I realized that Nola was the glue that had kept her, Emily, and me together over the summer. Now that Nola was preoccupied with college, Emily and I saw much less of each other. She was still living in my parents' house, but moving out was imminent: she had met an older guy named Kevin. Kevin had been a regular at a restaurant where Emily once worked and it was there, I suppose, that their love bloomed over servings of bad coffee and greasy *huevos rancheros*. He had his own place and she spent every free minute with him, doing what, she would not say. She was never one to gush over her boyfriends and Kevin was no different. All I knew about him was that he was a high school dropout and that he worked at a rundown machine shop on Agua Fria, making things like metal chimney caps. With only these few scraps of evidence to go on, I concluded that Emily was too good for him and that he must be drugging her, turning her into some kind of redneck version of a Stepford Wife, the kind who would keep the fridge stocked with Miller High Life, always have a fresh can of Skoal at the ready, and be the first to tell him how bitchin' his Dallas Cowboys tattoo looked. Drugging her, yes, it was the only possible explanation.

I couldn't worry about her though. I had my own problems. I'd started high school and loaded myself down with an overly ambitious array of college preparatory classes. I had always spent a lot of time in my bedroom alone, doing homework or reading, and was, for the most part, quite content doing so. But this college prep stuff was killing me. I was beginning to feel like Alex in the novel *A Clockwork Orange*, strapped in a chair with his eyes mechanically pried open, forced to watch hour upon hour of violent movies. Except instead of watching movies, I was reading textbooks dense with formulas, theorems, and corollaries. Some nights, I wished I had one of those eye-prying jobbies to help me stay awake long enough to finish my work.

Just when I was on the verge of giving up, I made a new friend at school. Her name was Isabel Delgado, and she and I were the only girls in my physics class. She spoke her first words to me three weeks into the school year.

"What the fuck are you looking at?" she said.

Them's fightin' words. If a Santa Fe girl said that (and exactly that) to another girl, hair pulling and face scratching wouldn't be far behind.

It was the last class of the day and we were in the hallway by the lockers. I looked left. Nobody. I looked right. Nobody. Was I prepared to throw down, right here, right now, with a girl I didn't know, a girl who might be carrying a knife, a girl who probably had fifty cousins in town, cousins who would hunt me down and shank the holy hell out of me the next time I went to the bowling alley? Fighting words, yes indeed. I carefully weighed my odds.

"What do you mean?" I asked, trying hard to imitate a soothing, friendly tone, one like Nola used on idiots who asked her particularly offensive questions.

"I *mean*," she said, "you were looking at me in class and I'm asking you 'What the fuck?' that's *what*."

I had no recollection of looking at her at all. "I was looking at you because . . . " My voice trailed off as I struggled to come up with something even remotely plausible. What possible reason could I have for looking at her? I looked at her now. Her hair was straight, black, and ridiculously long. "Because you look like Cher."

She flinched in disbelief. "Like Cher? You're kidding, right? No way, not with that hatchet nose."

"It's not the nose. It's your hair." Nola always said you could catch more flies with honey than with vinegar, so difficult as it was for me to maintain a straight face, I said, "It's really pretty, you know, like Cher's."

Her eyes were dark, dangerous. Why stop now with the bullshit? I channeled Nola. "I wish I could grow my hair like that."

"It's easy," she said. "Just don't cut it."

I couldn't help myself. I laughed and quoted something from our physics teacher. "I guess that should have been intuitively obvious to the most casual observer."

"I.e., no shit, Sherlock."

The girl just said "I-E" and "shit" in the same sentence. I was really starting to warm up to her.

"You got a cigarette?" she said. I didn't but kind of wished I did.

"So," she said, and made little circles with her shoulders, loosening up. "We gonna throw down or what?"

"Only if you insist. But the way I see it, we need to stick together. We're the only 9th grade girls with the *cojones* to take physics."

"In 6th period."

"With Mr. Rodriguez."

"A technicality. We still rock."

After that day, Isabel and I spent many hours together working on physics and math homework and many more hours hanging out on her front steps, bored because we had no money, no wheels, and no boys to go anywhere with anyway. We'd both had a few dates, but the boys had turned out to be degenerates. After each bad experience, we swore off boys forever. "Forever" usually turned out to be about four weeks. By Thanksgiving, she had a new crush on Luke Cortez and I had one on Dale Thompson. We had never spoken to either one of them. Both boys were juniors at our high school, and Isabel and I seriously doubted that they had any idea who we were. The only thing Izzy (as I had taken to calling her) and I ever argued about was which boy was cuter. Oh, and which of us was going to get accepted first into MIT. When it came to boys and colleges, we liked to dream big.

One December night I was dragging the trash can out to the curb when I spotted a '66 Barracuda coming down the street. It stopped at our driveway and Clint got out. "See ya around, Dale." My gaze went to the driver. His baby-faced good looks caused my teenaged brain to flood with a potent concoction of hormones, adrenaline, and stupidity.

"Later," Dale said. He spotted me, jerked his chin in my direction. "Hey."

"Hey," I said.

Then he was gone and I was kicking myself for having missed my chance to make a move on him. But what could I do, standing there with the stupid trashcan and all, dressed like I was ready to drop a transmission? As I lay in bed that night, reliving that moment when Dale had spoken to me, I prayed that he had mistaken my near catatonic state for one of boredom and apathy (which would make me cool), instead of what it really was (which would make me a pathetic twerp). I wondered if I should talk to Clint about Dale. Maybe he could come up with something, preferably something not too obvious, which would get Dale and me in the same room together. As it turned out, a setup wasn't necessary.

Two weeks later, luck uncharacteristically came my way when I ran into Dale one night at The Pit Club, a local teen dance joint. Small talk, an offer of a ride home, a diversion out to a suitably deserted spot off Rodeo Road, steamy car windows— and then things took a predictable turn as Dale attempted to wedge his hand under the front of my bra. I locked my arms across my chest in an attempt to stop the pawing, but his hands just went lower, squeezing and rubbing me like a baker working a particularly sturdy hunk of dough.

My subtle blocking motions and gentle admonitions failed to dissuade him. The time was rapidly approaching when I would either have to give in to him or rabbit punch him in the kidney. I clamped my knees together. Baby-face or no, I'd had enough, so I pulled away from him. He reached a hand toward my breast and I slapped it away. "Stop it, goddamn it."

"C'mon. Christmas is the time for giving. So why don't you give?" he said, his eyes twinkling mischievously and his voice full of holiday cheer.

"Oh, ha, ha, ha. That's very funny. So funny I forgot to laugh."

"You don't think it's funny?"

"No, not at all."

"Then how about this? How about you get the fuck out of my car?"

"What?"

"Put out or get out, bitch," he said, with a playful wink, as if all girls understood how this game was played, so stop stalling already.

I yanked the car door open and got out, slamming it so hard that I felt something pop in my shoulder.

Dale stared out the window at me for a moment, perhaps pondering if there were any legal ramifications of leaving a girl ten miles from home on a deserted dirt road in the sticks on a cold December night.

He peeled out.

As I watched him drive away, leaving me in a cloud of dust, I desperately wished I had something substantial to throw at his car. Before I could search the ground for a rock, he was gone. "Good riddance, you stupid hick jerkwad!" I hollered. 'Christmas is the time for giving, so give.' What an asshole. I continued with these warm, scathing thoughts for a good mile before the anger ebbed and the cold started to creep in. Then, though I hated myself for it, I started wishing Dale would come back. I fantasized about what we would say to each other. He'd tell me he was sorry, but I would refuse to forgive him, and then I would grudgingly get back into his car and he would apologize all the way to my house. Just before I got out of the car, I would spit in his face. Or maybe he'd take me in his arms and give me a really sexy kiss. Hmm, what would be better—spitting on him or kissing him?

"You're disgusting." I said out loud, admonishing myself for thinking for even two seconds that Dale deserved another chance. Had I no decency? Had I no self-respect? Had I no mittens? *Man, it's freezing out here!*

Then came the self-recriminations. Wasn't it my own fault that this happened? Hadn't Clint always told me never to get into a car with a guy I didn't know? And let's be honest—I didn't know jack squat about Dale. And yet, I had hopped into his car and hadn't complained one bit when he drove out to a deserted spot and promptly commenced to ramming his tongue down my throat.

Nope, no complaints here!

What an idiot I am. No wonder I'm out here in the damn dark, walking down this damn dirt road, not knowing where in the damn hell I am.

Stop. Stop thinking such nonsense. It doesn't matter whether I made a mistake or not. Dale had no right to keep trying to dry hump me when I told him to quit. Period. It's up to me to take full responsibility for what I do, what I am. Where I am.

Next time. Next time, just you fucking wait. I dare some jerk to even so much as suggest I get into a car with him. That unlucky pervert is going to get it and get it good.

This line of thought comforted me. As I massaged my aching shoulder, I searched the ground for a suitable weapon, in case just such a jerk sprung out from behind the nearest juniper and ambushed me. How about a long, pointy stick? I could jab his eye out with it. No, I should whip him with it, use it like a car antenna and thwack him across the face. Witchoo! I spotted a length of broken rebar on the ground. I picked it up, slashed it around in the air, liked the heft of it, decided I'd keep it.

It was approaching midnight and the temperature felt like it had dropped ten degrees in the last hour. Shivering, teeth chattering, I trudged on another three miles, eventually forgetting all about Dale and anonymous attackers in the bushes, my brain transformed into a frozen blue-black slab of ice.

At last, I was off the dirt road and onto a real street with real sidewalks. The glow of porch lights and the welcoming shimmer cast by each living room's TV warmed me. I started to ease out of my stupor. I briefly considered knocking on someone's door, asking to use the phone to call for a ride. I hated the idea of asking strangers for help. I'd never done it before and didn't want to start now. Who would I call? Parents? No way—too many questions about what I was doing on Rodeo Road. Clint was never home on a Saturday night, so forget that. Izzy didn't have a driver's license, no help there. I could try to reach Nola or Emily. Nah, screw it. I didn't have far to go now. Besides, why let anybody know what a fool I had been?

A beam of headlights came from behind me. The lights belonged to a pickup truck that slowed as it passed and then came to a stop fifty yards ahead of me. The driver reached over to the passenger side and rolled down the window. Oh great. Another sex fiend, no doubt, wanting to take me out in the sticks and dump me. Just what I need. Well, screw him. I don't care if I have to walk twenty more miles. I slid the rebar up inside my jacket's sleeve, thinking I might need the element of surprise.

"Hey there. Where ya going? Do you need a lift?" the driver called out as I walked past the truck.

"No thanks, I'm good," I said. I kept walking, didn't turn to look at the driver, trying to remember what Clint said about being polite yet firm so as not to enrage possible serial killers. The truck crept along beside me. I had seen this technique before. It was only a matter of time before the male driver would say something like, "Why don't you come over here and see what I have in my hand?" And when he did? Rebar-o-rama, buddy boy.

"It's pretty cold out. And dark. Do you have far to go?"

"I told you. I'm fine." Phony-baloney concern. Just how dumb did this guy think I was?

"Well heck, you don't even have any gloves or a hat or anything. Here, at least take these gloves."

"NO!" I said, but still did not look at him.

A pair of gloves flew out the passenger's side window, landing on the sidewalk in front of me. I reached down and gingerly picked them up, using just my fingertips. Lord knew what was on those gloves. I flicked them in the general direction of the truck's bed.

"You are one stubborn girl, aren't you? Aren't you freezing?"

I whirled to face him. "Look—" I said, ready to tear into him, but stopped short. He had turned on the dome light instead of cowering in the shadows like most perverts. I was expecting somebody older, but I saw now that he was just a boy, my age maybe. He looked barely old enough to be driving, to say nothing of serial killing.

"Look," I started over, trying to knock the bitchy edge off my tone. "I've had a tough night and I'm not in the mood for any more bullshit." Crap. Still too bitchy. Try again. "I appreciate your concern and all, but I don't need your help, so why don't you just take off, huh?"

"Well, OK, if you're sure."

"I'm sure."

He studied my face a moment. "All right, if you're sure."

"Yes. I'm sure. Very, very sure. I can take care of myself. Now go on."

"Well, if you're absolutely sure. All right. Bye, then." He rolled up the passenger window and put his hand on the gearshift. He looked at me again, gave me one last chance. I pointed down the road and mouthed the word, "Go."

He drove off.

I was instantly filled with regret.

Our little interlude had made me forget about how much farther I had to walk, about how the tip of my nose, my ears, my hands were beginning to tingle in a scary, unfamiliar way. The rebar was starting to feel heavy, so very heavy, so I let it fall to the ground and wrapped my arms across my chest, putting my hands under my armpits for warmth. With grim, mechanical determination, I plodded along another mile when I saw a pickup truck stopped at the curb ahead of me, its red taillights glowing.

As I got closer, I realized it was the same pickup as before. Again, the boy rolled down the passenger side window. Something that resembled a marmot was hurled out the window. I got closer and realized it was a red and black plaid woolen hat, the kind Elmer Fudd might wear when he was thwacking that wascally wabbit. I picked it up.

The boy leaned over to the passenger window. "If you won't let me give you a ride, then at least put a danged hat on. Don't you know you lose most of your body heat through your head? I swear to you, it's a nice clean hat. Please, just put it on."

Still not trusting him, I held the hat close to my face, smelled deeply of it and then, convinced there was nothing disgusting on it, put it on. I pulled the earflaps down and marveled at how soft they felt against my raw, brittle ears. I knew I looked like a nut. But a toasty nut. I couldn't help myself. I smiled.

"There now, that's not so bad is it?" He smiled back at me, pleased, I supposed, that he had won this battle.

"Nah, it's not so bad." I smoothed the earflaps down, luxuriating in their wooly wonderfulness. "Quite cuddly, really. Thanks."

"Still want to keep on walking?"

"Are you kidding me? With a hat like this I could walk all the way to Canada."

"I just bet you could. But if you're going to walk that far, you're going to need some sustenance."

Hmm. He said "sustenance." Dale would never have used a word like that. I moved closer to the truck door.

He held up a package of Little Debbie cupcakes, seductively waved it at me.

Little Debbie. Cupcakes. Wait a minute. Wait just a diddly-dang minute.

"Orlando?" I said.

"You know my name?"

"Are you Orlando Chavez? Did you go to Gonzales Elementary? Did you have Mrs. Lavadie for second grade?"

"Yeah, I did. But how did you know that? Do I know you?"

I took off the Elmer Fudd hat. No recognition from him. I grabbed each side of my head and pulled my hair up into pigtails and started singing, *"Ay, ay, ay, ay! Canta y no llores, porque cantando se alegran cielito lindo, los corazones."*

"No way! Sylvie? Is that really you?"

I snugged the Elmer Fudd hat back on my head and took a bow.

"Oh, man, I don't believe it." He leaned over, opened the passenger door. "Stop being such a lunatic and get in here."

Orlando, Orlando. I hadn't seen him since the end of second grade when our class was forced to put on a school show, girls dressed in Fiesta dresses, boys in boleros, dancing and singing that ancient song, "Cielito Lindo." And now, thanks to that bastard Dale, here I was sitting in Orlando's truck, eating cupcakes and laughing, catching up on the last decade.

He'd been at St. Mike's, a private high school in Santa Fe. That explained why I hadn't seen him around my own high school. He was planning on going to the University of New Mexico in Albuquerque. I told him I was planning to go to UNM myself, but likely wouldn't go right after high school; I would have to work for a while to save up money for tuition.

I'd been enjoying the delicious coziness of the truck's cab, the cupcakes, and his company so much that I hadn't realized we were at my house. Shoot, just as I was starting to thaw out. I took off the hat and handed it to him. "Thanks for not giving up on me and leaving me to die. I really was freezing my ass off."

"The hat looks good on you. I think you should keep it."

His pickup rolled to a stop. "You know, I think I will. It'll remind me not to be blinded by good looking jackasses."

"Huh?"

"Oh, no, I don't mean you. I mean this other guy. Not that you're not good looking." Oops. Probably should not have said that. "The jackass I mean is the guy who kicked me out of his car tonight. The guy who—ah, never mind. Let's save the story for next time."

I got out of the pickup. "I'll make it to UNM someday, even if it kills me. Maybe I'll tell you the story then."

"Now I have an incentive. I'll be searching the campus for you."

As I walked up the sidewalk, I realized I believed him.

I opened my front door to find Clint lying on the living room floor, watching an old Boris Karloff movie in the dark. The rest of the family was in bed. "Hey," I said. "You know your buddy Dale? Well, he's a real dickwad."

"Dale? He's not my buddy. And yes, I know, he's a gargantuan dickwad. I can't stand that motherfucker."

"What the—? How come you were with him the other day, when he dropped you off at the house?"

"He dropped me off? When?"

"For Christ's sake, it was just a couple of weeks ago. How can you not remember?" Damn it, had he been hitting the reefer again?

"Oh wait, now I remember. Sammy Tso and me were hitching from The Pit Club. Dale's going steady with Sammy's sister, so I guess when Dale saw us, he felt like he couldn't leave us hanging. So he gave us a ride. That's all."

"Dale's going steady? With Teresa? Teresa Tso?"

"Yeah. What's the big deal?"

I told him what happened, about Dale pawing me, the whole "Christmas is the time for giving" thing and Dale thinking he was so funny, and how he left me on the side of the road like so much garbage.

Clint continued to stare at the TV and said nothing, as if he'd lost interest in my story. I was getting a little tired of the story myself, really. I grabbed a pillow off the sofa and lay down on the floor near him, and we watched Boris Karloff get his due as the inmates of Bedlam walled him up in the asylum, Karloff's terrified eyes peering out as the last brick was put into place, sealing him up forever.

A few days later, Emily and I were driving down Cerrillos Road, and I spotted Dale standing in the parking lot of the Tastee Freeze next to his beloved '66 Barracuda. He was shouting out a spectacular stream of profanity to nobody in particular as he pointed to the car and a deep scratch that went all the way from the front wheel well to the rear bumper.

Well whaddaya know? I thought. Christmas really is the time for giving.

6

For weeks I thought about Orlando and that night. I hoped I would run into him somewhere around town, but it didn't happen. I tried to act like Orlando's snubbing didn't bother me, but Izzy wasn't buying it. She suggested I just call him.

"Have you ever noticed how many people in the phonebook have the last name 'Chavez'?" I asked her. "There must be at least fifty! And it's not like *I'd* be hard to find—there are only two 'Lofts' in the book. If he wanted to call me, he would. But obviously he doesn't."

"I'm sure he wants to call you. He's probably just shy and needs a little encouragement."

"Yes, of course. I'm sure that's exactly what he needs."

"Lose the sarcasm and let me think."

The mathematician in her compelled her to get the phonebook so she could count the exact number of Chavezes listed. Next, she ran a time trial to see how long it took to dial a seven-digit number. This was followed by a comprehensive estimate of how long it might take to say, 'Is Orlando there?' and the reply. Said estimate took into account how many times I might actually connect to *an* Orlando, but not *the* Orlando. Her conclusion was that even if I called every single Chavez, it would take less than two hours. She was nothing if not thorough, and I admired her mightily for that.

"And if he's not listed?" I asked.

"Oh, I hadn't considered that," she said, obviously disappointed in herself. "So what? It doesn't change anything. Don't be such a drag! Start calling!"

I refused. She even offered to help me make the calls, but I wouldn't budge. As I walked home that night, I wondered if I had made a mistake, that I should have made those calls. By the time I got to my house, I had convinced myself that I'd done the right thing. Even though I'd spent less than an hour with him that night in his truck, I felt that I knew this about him: he was the kind of guy who, if he wanted to find me, now, two months from now, or two years from now, he would find me. And he wouldn't need my help to do it. Or Izzy's.

Eventually I gave up on ever seeing him again, grieved the loss of something we never had, and as the weeks turned into months, I forgot him. My attention was suddenly diverted to other things.

Emily, in a fit of insanity, married Kevin.

While they were dating, she'd said next to nothing about him. But as soon as they were engaged, his name came up a lot around the house, mostly in arguments between Emily and our parents. My parents never dared to hope their children would marry well, but Kevin failed to meet even their most meager expectations.

And what was the rush? It seemed like one day I had no idea who he was, and the next day Kevin and Emily were descending the front steps of the Methodist church while Nola and I stood near by, wondering what the hell had just happened.

While the photographer snapped pictures of the newlyweds and my grim-faced parents, Nola and I wandered away from the action and found a bench in the shade to sit on.

"What do you know about this guy?" I asked her.

She told me what I already knew: that he was almost 30 and worked in a machine shop. And, she added, he was dumber than a box of rocks.

"Then why is Emily marrying him?" I suddenly had a sickening thought. "Jesus! She's not pregnant, is she?"

"No." She cocked her head. "At least I don't think so. No . . . no, she would have told me about that, for sure. I think."

"What do you mean, you 'think'? Doesn't she always tell you everything?"

"She used to, but as soon as I told her marrying Kevin was idiotic, she didn't want to talk to me about him anymore."

Huh. Nola was usually the diplomat. If she'd said something brutally honest like that (in other words, something like *I* might say to Emily), then she must be really worried about her. Maybe I should be, too. Maybe Nola knew something that she didn't want to tell me.

"This makes no sense to me, no sense at all," I said. "You make him sound like some kind of reject from *Hee Haw*. If he was at least cute, maybe I could understand, but c'mon, look at the guy!" We turned to look at The Happy Couple.

My parents were sitting in folding chairs near the photographer, watching him set up to take the obligatory cutting-of-the-cake picture. Emily looked prettier than I'd ever seen her, her peacock blue dress shimmering in the sun. The photographer took a few pictures, and then it was time for the bride and groom to give each other a bite of cake. Kevin went first, pushing a generous hunk of cake onto his fork. He held it up to Emily's mouth. Just as she opened her mouth to take a bite, he brutally shoved it in, smearing her lips and face with icing. Blobs of the cake ricocheted down the front of her dress, leaving a greasy trail as it went. Nola and I gasped. My dad leapt up from his chair, his face blazing red, one angry eyebrow arched almost to his hairline. My mom, using both hands, grabbed the back of his suit jacket, jerked it, throwing him off balance enough that he plunked back into his chair. I could not hear what he said, but I could read his lips. "That little shit! I'll kill him!"

Emily tried her best to wipe the icing off her cheeks and shake the crumbs off of her dress, a strained, paralytic smile creasing her face. "Excuse me, please. I need to freshen up," she said.

"Go on, honey," Kevin said, beaming at the cleverness of his prank. "I'll be waiting for you!"

Nola's eyes were wide. "I'll be back," she said. "Help me out of this chair." I put my hand behind her back and give her a push. She headed toward the bathroom. An eternity later, she reappeared. I expected Emily to be with her, but she wasn't.

"Where's Emily?"

"Still in the bathroom. She needed a minute."

"A minute? You've been gone for half an hour. What the heck's going on?"

"Sylvie," she sighed. "Your sister just got married. It's a very emotional day for her. Can't you understand that?"

No, I couldn't. I thought when you got married everybody was happy and you danced and laughed and got lots of presents. Kinda like Christmas, except you got laid.

"Is she gonna be all right?"

"No."

"What?!" I said, alarmed.

"I don't know. Ignore me. It's an emotional day for me, too, so I'm talking nonsense. Everything's under control."

The photographer motioned for Nola and me to join the group in front of the camera. As we walked toward the photographer, I acted as though I had suddenly remembered something important I needed to do. "Oh, shoot! Nola, I'll be back in a sec! Go ahead and start without me." Before she could answer, I veered off.

I was wrung out, exhausted from all the small talk with Kevin's relatives and the wedding drama. Expecting me to now endure an idiotic photo session, well that was simply too much. I went looking for Clint, the master of escape.

A few months after the wedding, Kevin got a new job in Albuquerque, so this was Emily's big chance to finally get out of Santa Fe. They got an apartment near downtown. He spent his days selling car parts, and she spent hers working as a secretary at Blue Cross.

I was still in high school and working afternoons and Saturdays as a file clerk at St. Vincent's Hospital, so I didn't have a lot of time for cruising down to Albuquerque. And much as I hated to admit it, hanging out with Emily just wasn't as much fun as it used to be. The worst day cramming for exams with Izzy was less stressful than a day with Emily and Kevin.

A typical visit to their place went something like this: Emily would start dinner while Kevin worked on his car out in the driveway. I liked to sit on the kitchen counter (an act my mom considered uncivilized and never let us do at home, so I simply *had* to do it at Emily's). From my perch, I tried to get her to tell me something, anything, about married life. She was the only young person I knew who was married, so I wanted to know all about it. Is it fun sleeping together all the time? Isn't it great to never be without a date on a Saturday night? I bet you go out somewhere fun every weekend, don't you? Are you happy, Emily, are you?

If she answered, she was vague. Mostly, there was no answer. Instead, she would find an excuse to go outside to take Kevin something or other, or she would turn on the exhaust fan over the stove, making it impossible for us to carry on a conversation. It struck me that this young woman—in her powder-blue halter-top, white Capri pants, and two-dollar flip-flops—was capable of enduring even the most diabolical KGB interrogation without revealing a thing.

Dinner with them was excruciating. Kevin would take a bite of food, scraping his fork across his teeth, causing a spasm to shudder across Emily's face. He'd snort back some phlegmy wad of goo in his throat, and her fist would clench. He'd start a conversation and she'd squint down at her plate and give her meatloaf a vicious stab.

After a few minutes of trying to be sociable, the pace of Kevin's eating would ramp up and he would stop talking and start shoveling, as if he couldn't wait to get back to the driveway to finish his Hurst shifter job. Emily would spring up from her chair every few minutes to get this, move that, clean whatever. I'd end up sitting alone at the table, finishing dinner while she plunged into some inane household task like vacuuming the refrigerator's coils or meticulously scraping old wax off the linoleum with a razor blade. Something was wrong, but dammit, why wouldn't she tell me what?

I asked Clint about the situation. He shrugged and said, "Like I know anything about women." I called him a damn liar, said he knew plenty about women, so he better tell me what he really thought. He swore he was as mystified as me. Nola was no help. All she said was, "Emily tells me everything's great. Money's a little tight, but other than that, no problems."

A few months after the wedding, I was hanging out at Izzy's house. We were in the bedroom she shared with her little sister, Gloria. Izzy had banished Gloria to the backyard so we'd have the place to ourselves. The room was small, its floor a bare, institutional looking beige linoleum. The only furniture was a pair of twin-sized beds, two small, battered, flea-market dressers and a bookcase crammed with books ranging from Dr. Seuss to Carl Sagan. On the wall, two posters coexisted peacefully next to each other: one of Einstein, the other a Sesame Street poster of the letter 'G' (for "Gloria" I supposed, but it could just as easily have been Izzy's poster and the 'G' stood for "Gaussian function" or some equivalent mathematical nerd goop).

I sat on the edge of Gloria's bed, lazily swinging her stuffed Kermit the Frog doll around and around by its skinny green arm. Izzy sprawled out on her own bed and stared in the general direction of a water stain on the ceiling. Why she did this, I did not know, but over the last few months I had observed that she did some of her best thinking while focusing on that ugly splotch.

"I need to unload." I said.

"Go," she said, her eyes never straying from the splotch.

I complained to her about Emily, telling her that Emily was acting weird and didn't seem to want me around. If she didn't want me around, I was fine with that; I had my own thing and Emily had hers, so who cares? Still, I wanted to know *why* things between Emily and me had changed.

Izzy was like me. She believed at her core that there was an explanation for everything; you just needed skill and persistence to find it. Plus, she had three older sisters with six marriages and five divorces between them. Why, I asked her, did Emily marry

Kevin, and why would she stay with him, given he seemed to be making her so miserable?

"I've got three sisters, all of them bat-shit, so I've got some experience in these matters," she said.

"Well, what do ya think?"

"Tell me again, what's he look like?"

I told her. Reject from *Hee Haw*.

"Is he a smart guy, like is he going to be a doctor or engineer someday?"

I told her. Box of rocks.

"And how does he treat her? Is he lovey-dovey?"

I thought back on my visits to Albuquerque and was surprised to realize how difficult it was to recall any sort of affectionate gesture. "Sometimes he puts his hand on her shoulder and pats it when she's doing the dishes," I said at last.

"That's it?"

"Pretty much, yeah, that's it."

Izzy nodded. "Uh-huh, I see, I see . . . and you say Emily won't tell you anything about her and Kevin?"

"Nope. Nothing interesting anyways."

"Nothing at all?"

"I swear to you, nothing."

"And your mom, does she seem pissed off all the time?"

"Well, yeah. But she's always been like that."

"Your dad. Drinking more than usual?"

"I'm not sure. He spends most of his time in the garage working on the car or in the backyard, bashing hell out of one thing or another with a sledgehammer. He doesn't say much of anything to anybody, unless you want to talk politics, which nobody does."

"I know what it is." Izzy sat up on her bed, mirroring me, our knees almost touching, that crazy long black hair of hers hanging down almost to her shoes as she leaned in close to me, her expression one of dark certainty.

"What? What is it? Jesus, you're freaking me out."

"He's smacking her around."

"No way. That's crazy talk."

"It's true. Here's what went down. Emily married Kevin because she was positive she'd never find anybody else to marry her and he's smacking her around now 'cause he's pretty sure she'll put up with it. And, I'm just speculating here, she's afraid of what he'll do to her if she tries to leave him."

"Where the heck did you get that from? Have you ODed on soap operas?"

Izzy sighed and shook her head, as if to say, "Poor, innocent child. You have no idea what goes on behind closed doors, do you?"

"Besides, Emily's not like that. She'd kick Kevin's ass if he tried to pull anything like that," I said. "She'd say something. She'd do something."

"You know Jeannie?"

"Sort of." Jeannie was Izzy's oldest sister. She'd been married twice, divorced twice. She lived in Las Cruces, so I never met her.

"She married this guy, Louie. He was a lawyer down in Cruces."

Lawyer, eh? I nodded appreciatively. Jeannie had done all right for herself.

"I know what you're thinking," Izzy said. "But hold on. Jeannie didn't say shit to anybody about anything," she said. "Until one day my parents drove down to Cruces to surprise her and she was laid up with a broken collarbone."

"Seriously?"

"Oh yeah. Dead serious. They brought her back home with them, and it was really bad around here for a while. Every time the phone rang, somebody was hollering about something. At one point, I was convinced that my dad was going to buy a gun, drive down there, and shoot that bastard Louie right between the eyes.

"My mom and Jeannie slinked around, always going out to the patio to fight or whisper or whatever. I guess they thought that the rest of us kids were too young to be told what really happened to Jeannie. I can't stand all that secrecy, you know?"

Yes, I did know. It was maddening.

"So, one day I hid by the patio door and listened to Jeannie and my mom. That's how I found out what happened to Jeannie's collarbone. And that's when I heard her say she married Louie because she didn't think anybody else would ask her."

"Well, maybe Jeannie would do something like that, but that's not Emily. Besides, why wouldn't she tell me or Nola about it?"

"Maybe she did tell Nola, but she told Nola not to tell you."

Damn those two and their secrets!

"Why wouldn't she want me to know?"

"Because she thinks you wouldn't understand. Or she's embarrassed by the situation. Or both."

"Embarrassed? That's the stupidest thing I've ever heard."

"See, you don't understand."

"How can I understand something that's STUPID? Why the hell would Emily think she couldn't marry somebody better than Kevin? She's cute and nice and, damn it, I don't believe you. It can't be like that. It just can't."

"If you say so." She lay back down on her bed and stared at the ceiling, crossing her arms across her chest.

I swung Kermit by the arm, launching him at Izzy's head and missing. "Yeah, I say so," but there was a sick quivering in my stomach.

Proof, I needed proof. How could I ease "Is Kevin beating you?" into a casual conversation and what answer could I reasonably expect to get in response? A more subtle approach was called for, so instead I repeatedly asked Emily how she was doing. The answer was always the same. Everything was hunkydory. Kevin was fine, she was fine, every little thing was fine, diddly-ine.

Phase two of my plan: look for physical evidence. Each time I saw Emily, I surreptitiously studied her face and arms, looking for bruises or scratches. I saw none. Perhaps I wasn't giving Kevin enough credit; maybe he was a sneaky bastard and only hit her where the marks would be hidden. So, on several occasions, I suggested to Emily that we put on our swimsuits and sun ourselves in my parents' backyard. The first time I made the swimsuit suggestion, she snorted and asked me if I'd lost my mind.

"Since when do you lay out in the sun?" she asked, her voice tinged with suspicion.

"People change."

"Not you, Sylvie. You never change. Once you've made up your mind that something is *asinine*, that's it."

"So, do you want to lay out or not?" I said, peeved.

"Nope. I gotta get home before Kevin does and make dinner."

As she walked toward the door, she shook her head and muttered, "Sunning. Hah! Right, *you* sunning! That is *too* funny."

Clearly, sunbathing was a no-go. Now what? Short of pouncing on her while she was in the shower, I was out of ideas.

Over the course of two months of intense investigation, I found nothing to indicate that Kevin had been doing anything terrible to Emily. So I stopped looking for evidence and stopped interrogating her. I wasn't positive that Izzy's theory was wrong, but I was now convinced that I would never get at the truth.

Emily and Kevin rarely came to Santa Fe to visit. I'm sure they hated doing it, since it had become obvious (even to that lunkhead Kevin) that my dad merely tolerated him, and my mom out-and-out detested him.

One night I got a taste of *Life with Kevin*. He and Emily came to my parents' house for a visit. There was the usual strained conversation around the dinner table. My dad loved cars, so he must have figured that he could break the tension if he and Kevin swapped stories about their most recent car projects. It worked; Kevin started blathering about that dumb Hurst shifter and didn't shut up for half an hour. It was more car talk than even Dad could take, so as soon as he finished his last bite, he excused himself from the table and beat a hasty retreat to the bathroom, turned on the fan, and just for good measure, locked the door.

In a burst of energy, my mom and Emily leapt up from the dinner table and started clearing the dishes and scrubbing and scraping in a wild, noisy frenzy at the sink, leaving Kevin and me sitting at the table in an awkward silence. He was using his plate as an ashtray, so he took one last drag off his cigarette and stubbed it out in his mashed potatoes.

I fought back a gag.

"So, you want to go see it?" he said.

"See what?"

"The shifter. I'm done, and is it ever cool. It looks like it's S.E., man, it really looks good."

"S.E.?"

"Standard equipment, man. Like factory. Ya wanna see it?"

No, you dimwit, I definitely do not want to see it. I shot Emily a look that I hoped she knew meant "Get me out of this, for God's sake."

"Heck yeah, you should go see it," she said as she pushed me toward the front door. Dammit—had Nola told her what I'd said about Kevin?

We went outside and Kevin got into his GTO and motioned for me to get in on the passenger side. I slid into the bucket seat, intentionally leaving my door hanging open for a quick escape.

"See this?" He caressed the shifter, proud of his handiwork. The chrome sparkled under the dome light.

"Yeah, I see it. What's the big deal?"

"What's the big deal? What's the big *deal*? Didn't you hear a word I said to your dad? The Hurst kicks ass!"

"Uh, OK—if you say so—I guess I just don't understand why a shifter would make any difference."

"Let's go for a ride and I'll show you."

Aw, crap. Emily, I'm going to strangle you for getting me into this.

"Nah, sorry. I can't. I've got homework due tomorrow. I need to get to it."

"Ten minutes. You got ten minutes, don't ya? C'mon, let's go," he said, turning the key in the ignition, firing up the engine.

My intuition told me to fling myself out of the car and make a run for the house. But there was a part of me—a sticky, sappy, irrational part—that compelled me to root for the underdog. And Kevin was the under-est. Loathed by his in-laws, ridiculed by his wife, and cursed with the I.Q. of a cactus. Pitiful, wretched Kevin. He must have been going insane sitting around my parents' house, counting the minutes until he and Emily could get out of there. Guess it wouldn't kill me to go for a quick spin with him.

I closed my car door.

He revved the engine, gave me a stern look, and told me to hang on. Unfortunately, *to what* he failed to specify. He floored it, simultaneously yanking on the infamous Hurst shifter as if he was trying to rip it out of the console. The GTO tore away from the curb, tires squealing. I slid back and forth on the slippery vinyl seats, trying to get a grip on the dash, the armrest, anything.

We came to the end of the street, and as he rounded the corner, he downshifted with a vengeance and our heads lurched forward and then whipped back from the savagery of it. The car fishtailed around the corner, and I scrambled to find my seat belt. There was none.

The GTO hurtled out to Rodeo Road where there would be little traffic and lots of opportunity for him to show off. What followed was more of his crazed shifting, lots of neck-whipping, dash-grabbing, and sphincter-clenching. After fifteen hellish minutes of this punishment, he brought the car to an abrupt halt. He rolled down his window and stuck his head out, sniffed the air, looked concerned. "Do you smell something?"

"Just burning tires and possibly vaporized transmission fluid," I said, rubbing my stinging eyes.

He ignored me. "Huh. Wonder what that smell is ..." He sniffed again. "Guess we better head back." He gave a disappointed little pout, rolled up the window. He must have suspected there was something wrong with the car because this time he gently put it in first gear, eased away from the curb, and continued at a sensible speed instead of driving as if we were fleeing the scene of a bank heist. I released my death grip on the passenger door's armrest and clenched and unclenched my hands, trying to get the feeling back into my fingers.

"Well," he said, putting his hand on my thigh, "What do you think of Hurst shifters now?" He slid his hand up closer to my crotch.

I reached down, encircled his wrist with my thumb and forefinger, and gave his hand a vicious, snapping flick back into his lap. My eyes narrowed to murderous slits. "Here's what I think. I *think* you are a married man. And I *know* if you ever touch me again, I'm going to tell Emily. Take me the hell home. NOW."

I decided I didn't care if he lost it and kicked my ass out of the car. I'd walked home from Rodeo Road before, and sooner or later I'd probably do it again. Do it, I thought. Kick me out. I dare you. Do it.

He looked confused for an instant, but then his face contorted into a scalding rage. He rammed the shifter into gear and crushed the gas pedal to the floorboard. The tires shrieked, the GTO gave a jolt, and we heard a loud *thunk!* from underneath us. The car rolled to a stop. Kevin flung his car door open and walked around to the back, bent down, surveyed the damage. "Fuck! Sunuva goddamn bitch!" He stood up and gave the tire a spiteful kick.

I got out and looked under the car. The rear axle was broken. My hand flew to my mouth so he would not see me smiling and then bludgeon me with a tire iron.

We had a very tense 30-minute walk back to the house.

Emily greeted us at the front door. There was that evil glint in her eye again. "Did you two have fun? How was the ride?"

"Thrilling," I said, my voice flat, betraying nothing.

She squinched her face up in disbelief. "Really?"

"We broke the goddamn axle," Kevin said, his face still red with rage. "I'm gonna call a tow truck." He pushed past her and went in the kitchen to make his call.

While he was gone, I told Emily that he'd driven like a maniac and scared the holy crap out of me. She liked hearing that part, proving that misery does indeed love company. Then, I told her, he got carried away with the whole Al Unser Indy 500 fantasy thing and broke the car. She didn't like that part at all. Money was tight, she said. Real tight. We overheard Kevin say, "Just for a lousy tow? It's only five miles to the garage. That's crazy!"

Emily's attention was on the kitchen now, listening to the phone call. I touched her arm, bringing her back to me. "It's partly my fault. Why don't you let me chip in to get it fixed?"

"Why is it partly your fault?"

"Because he was showing off for me. You know how he is."

She nodded. Yes, she certainly did know.

"So, c'mon—let me give you a few bucks to help out."

She argued with me, but eventually relented. I gave her a hundred dollars and made her promise not to tell Kevin. I suggested she use the money for groceries. That way, he wouldn't have to find out about it.

It was a week's pay for me, but it was worth it. She was the new underdog.

1973

7

While Emily was enduring whatever private hell she was in with Kevin, Nola was having the time of her life at The College of Santa Fe. College did for her what years of cruising down Cerrillos Road had not—it got her a man. His name was Todd. He was an electrical engineering student and looked exactly like what one would expect an electrical engineering student to look like. Only more so.

Nola was still living with her parents, and Todd lived in the college dorm, so on those rare occasions when we all got together, it was usually at Emily's apartment in Albuquerque. Todd and Kevin tried to make small talk with each other, but it never went well. Kevin had convinced himself that Todd was an electrician, not an electrical engineer. He'd ask Todd for advice on how to wire up a new speedometer in the GTO or for insight into some other automotive quandary. The last time Kevin asked for advice, Todd admitted he didn't know anything about wiring cars but cheerfully offered to discuss at length the principles of acoustic microscopy. This witty comment was lost on Kevin, who, now that he understood the scope of Todd's uselessness, slipped out alone to the garage, leaving Todd to happily hang around us girls in the kitchen.

Two weeks after Nola and Todd graduated, I found myself once again at a reception eating wedding cake, but this time instead of a sense of impending doom, I felt only joy.

Todd seemed a nice enough guy. Dorky, yes, but he had a funny sense of humor and he seemed to adore Nola. He was always doing things like helping her into the car, putting on her cape (which she wore instead of a typical winter coat), making sure she had everything positioned just so at the dinner table. Very gallant. I missed the old days of chasing boys and stealing cars and running amok, but we were all grown up now and had adult things to do. It was high time we settled down and got on with whatever it was that adults were supposed to get on with. Granted, I was still in high school and legally not an adult, but I sure wanted to be one, so in my mind that counted.

After they were married, they moved to Albuquerque. Nola got a job working for a small accounting firm and became the primary breadwinner for the family. This was because Todd had inexplicably ended up working as a department store clerk at the mall. I desperately wanted to understand how this had happened. I would soon be starting my freshman year at the University of New Mexico and hoped to get an engineering degree myself, and I sure as hell didn't want to end up working at some dumbass mall. When I asked Nola about this, she told me that the market for electrical engineers was flat and as soon as the economy picked up, he'd start searching for a better job. Why can't he start looking now, I wanted to know. This question was met with a chilly stare.

Nola had lived an orderly childhood and carried that order-liness, and her famous eye for detail, into her marriage. She ran the household, made sure the bills got paid, arranged servicing for the cars, and scheduled furnace filter replacements exactly as recommended by the manufacturer. And Todd? He helped with the shopping and the laundry, I suppose. I don't know what else he did, but it seemed like he relied more on her than she on him. She seemed content with this arrangement; I never heard her complain about their relationship.

But so what? Evidently "not complaining" about a marriage meant nothing. I found this out the hard way.

One weekend, I came home from work and was surprised to find Emily at my parents' house. Several of her suitcases were in the foyer. She and my mom were out on the patio smoking. Emily's eyes were clumped up with wet gobs of mascara and my mom looked like she wanted to strangle somebody but couldn't decide who to start with. I looked outside and noticed Emily's car. Its backseat was full of things—dishes, linens, record albums, potted plants. I realized that this time there would be no going back to her Albuquerque apartment. Ever.

And still Emily would not tell me what had happened. Maybe she spilled her guts to our mom about what the final straw was, maybe she told every single juicy detail to Nola, but all I got out of her was, "It just didn't work out."

Kevin was in. Then Kevin was out. Just like that. Once their divorce was final, it was as if he never was. Even though Kevin was a Neanderthal, even though Emily seemed to have never had a happy moment with him, I still felt sorry for him and more than a little uneasy about how he was so cleanly and completely excised from the family. I concluded that if and when I ever got married, I had better watch my back. One minute I might be sitting around the Christmas dinner table, surrounded by my husband's loving family, my mother-in-law ooo-ing over the Baccarat crystal vase I'd given her, and the next minute that very same family would be gathered around the fireplace, pulling all of my pictures out of the family photo albums, throwing the pictures in the fire as they bitterly discussed the impending divorce, inventorying all the bitchy things I had done to their darling Reginald. "Fuck them and fuck Reginald, too!" I thought.

Emily hated Santa Fe more than she dreaded living in the same town as Kevin, so as soon as she could arrange it, she moved out of my parents' house and into a new place in Albuquerque. I felt bad that her marriage hadn't worked out, but now that the divorce was final, I hoped she would find some happiness.

While Emily's married life was in ruins, Nola's marriage was still going strong. I don't know if Nola gloated over that fact, but if she did, it wasn't for long. The third summer Nola and Todd were married, an old friend of Nola's came to visit. Her name was Sara, and she and Nola had met as little girls at The Children's Hospital, where Nola had gone for back surgery. Sara was there to have a badly damaged knee repaired, the result of a nasty tumble down some stairs. She and Nola had something very important in common—Sara's arms were almost exactly like Nola's. Neither of them had ever seen anyone "like them" so they were thrilled to meet each other and became close friends during what turned out to be very long hospital stays for both of them.

Sara lived in Nebraska, so after she left the hospital, the girls carried on a long-distance relationship through letters and rare visits. Sara wanted to come to Albuquerque to see Nola's new home and meet Todd, so she flew out to spend a few weeks with them.

It was funny to hear Nola talk about Sara. Nola obviously considered Sara a wimp. She said that even though Sara had higher functioning arms, she was content to let people wait on her. She was unemployed and lived with her parents. Nola said I'd see for myself when I met her.

It was near the end of Sara's three-week stay and I had yet to find the time to go over for a visit. I had just gotten home from work when the phone rang. It was Emily.

"You're *not* going to believe this," she said.

"What? What???"

"Sara's gone."

"You mean she had to cut her visit short and go back to Nebraska?"

"No. I mean she's *gone*."

"Gone where?"

"Todd's gone, too."

"What do you mean 'Todd's gone, too'"?

"I mean he's GONE! They're both gone."

I couldn't grasp what she was telling me. What was she so riled up about? "Maybe they just went shopping or something," I said.

"No, no, no, oh hell no. Shut up! Listen. Nola just called me. She said after she got home from work tonight, the three of them were supposed to go out to dinner together, so she was expecting that they would both be there. They weren't in the living room or the kitchen, so she called out for them. Nobody answered. So she started checking each room. Sara's luggage and stuff were gone from the guest room. Then she walked back into their bedroom to call Todd at work to see if he knew what was going on. She noticed one of the closet doors was open a little. When she went to close it, she saw that all of Todd's clothes were gone."

I sat down. Christ. Oh Christ. This is gonna hurt. This is really, really, really gonna hurt.

Oh, and hurt it did. Nola never saw that bastard Todd or that bitch Sara again. She never saw them, she never talked to them, no phone calls, no letters, nothing. She did, however, talk to her ex-mother-in-law, who told her that Todd didn't want to talk to her about *anything*. Period. Nola had to go to an attorney and sue for "abandonment."

There were a lot of tears and a lot of "whys." I didn't have the answers. What could I possibly understand about men? I'd had a few boyfriends in high school, but they always freaked out whenever things got "serious." And I'd never been married. How was I supposed to know why he would act like such a cretin? She admitted that she had worried from time to time that he might leave her for someone "normal," but she never imagined he would leave her for Sara. "Dammit!" she said. "Sara can't even drive!"

8

Emily screwed up. Nola did, too. Maybe they would recover, maybe they wouldn't. One thing for sure, though: I was determined not to end up the same way. Keep my priorities straight. Get out of Santa Fe. Get into college. Don't marry an asshole. So far my grades were good and I'd managed to save a little money. I'd even had some moderate success in minimizing the number of assholes I dated. My determination was paying off, but not as handsomely as Izzy's.

We were in her bedroom, me on her little sister Gloria's bed, she standing up in front of her bookcase, looking for something, her back to me. "What are you looking for?" I asked her.

"My yearbook, the one I just got. I want you to sign it. You bring yours over next time so I can sign yours, too."

"I didn't get one."

"Liar. Everybody gets a yearbook."

"Not me."

"Well, you've got your senior school pictures, though, right? Let me have one of those."

"Sorry. Don't have any."

"Stop being *pinche*. Just give me one."

"I don't have a year book, I don't have any pictures, I got nothin'. I always ditch on picture day."

"Why? It's not like you're ugly or anything. I think you're a real sex kitten." She came at me, pretending like she was going to scratch me.

"No. Hellcat." I hissed and fake-clawed back.

"Sex kitten," she said again, and we continued with our fake-clawing and name-calling until I gave her a rough push on the shoulder and she fell back on her bed.

"Gimme the picture," she said.

"I told you. I don't have any pictures. I hate having my picture taken and I especially hate anybody forcing me to have my picture taken. I hate anybody forcing me to do anything."

"Gee, I never noticed that," she said and rolled her eyes. She went back to her bookcase, found her yearbook, and brought it over to me. "Fine, forget it. Just sign this."

"I never know what to write in those stupid things." Actually, nobody had ever asked me to write anything in a yearbook.

"How about 'Dear Izzy, MIT will never be the same after you get there' or something like that."

I felt like I had been kicked in the sternum.

She and I had always talked about going to the same university. Last year, when her parents took her out of public school to send her to Santa Fe Prep (a private college preparatory school), it became painfully obvious that she and I were not in the same league. My parents could not afford to send me to private school. Izzy's parents couldn't afford it either. But unlike me, Izzy was a brilliant student and that, combined with her financial need, got her a full scholarship at the prep school. Yet, despite all evidence to the contrary, I had maintained my precious delusion that she and I would start UNM together. Now this.

"Well? Jesus, say something. Do *something*."

"Get me a pen."

"I didn't get a free ride, but almost," she said. "I lucked out on my SAT, so I'm getting some scholarship money, but I'll probably still have to work part-time." She was babbling now, trying to fill this new space between us with her words.

"That's great news, Izzy, really great," I said. "MIT. Wow, wow, wow."

Was she really that much smarter than me? I thought, not without bitterness. Had she simply studied harder than I did? Were her teachers more attentive than mine? Her parents more supportive? Was her first lucky break going to kindergarten when she lived in Sacramento? My parents never enrolled any of us kids in kindergarten! While Izzy was busy in school studying her A-B-C's, finger painting, and learning "Which one is not like the other?" Clint and I were stealing Slip 'n Slides out of garbage cans, sneaking into the old gravel pit near our house to play "army" and watching cartoons all day like a couple of heathens. Damn kindergarten! That must be it! I never stood a chance!

She gave me a pen. My hand hovered over the yearbook as I tried to unclench my jaw and struggled to think of something encouraging and sage to write. Maybe quote Madame Marie Curie or Helen Keller. Or I could just go with my gut and write, "Go to hell, Izzy!"

"You have to write *something*. Please," she said, with very un-Izzy-like tenderness.

I scrawled, "You go where I cannot follow. But it doesn't matter—I'll never forget you." I handed the yearbook back to her.

She read it. "You might end up at MIT someday, you don't know. It could happen."

"Yeah, I *do* know." She knew it, too. "It won't happen."

"You could get a scholarship or a grant or something."

"It's not just the money. It's my grades, my test scores. They're just not good enough."

"You could take the SAT again."

"Stop it, will you? You know I can't get into MIT. It's too late for me." The kindergarten-ship had already sailed.

"No it isn't, Sylvie! It's never too late. You could come with me to Cambridge and get a job and save money. We could be roommates. I'd tutor you at night and then you could re-take the SAT and apply next semester."

That might actually work, I thought. Then I remembered she would be working, going to school and dealing with her own classwork. Expecting her to tutor me as well was too much to ask of her.

"Thanks, Izzy, but I can't do it. Not right now anyway." Which meant never.

She lay on her bed and stared up at her old friend, the water stain on the ceiling, our silence sucking the oxygen out of the room.

At last she spoke. "I'll be back for Christmas break, and summer too. And we can write. You'll write me, won't you?" She continued to stare at the ceiling.

Clint came to mind. He'd left the previous year for North Dakota; his friend Sammy told him there was a fortune to be made in the oil fields. Clint and I had promised to write each other. OK, *I'd* promised. The first few months, I sent many letters, and all went unanswered. As time went on, my letters dwindled to nothing, and if he noticed, he never said so.

Izzy turned on her side and looked at me. "Well, are you gonna write me or not?"

"You write me first," I said.

That autumn, I left for the University of New Mexico in Albuquerque. I got a state government job as a warehouse clerk. I worked all day and took classes at night. It seemed each day ended the same way: me alone in my squalid downtown apartment, doing homework until my back ached and my eyes bled. But I felt free, free, free!

One Saturday morning, I was sitting at a table in UNM's library. The table was littered with empty coffee cups, textbooks, and papers. I was staring down at my trigonometry book contemplating a homework question:

From a helicopter hovering 400 feet over a floating space capsule, the angle of depression of the water line at the bow of the recovery ship is 77°. How far is the capsule from the bow?

My trig class was essentially a review of what I'd learned in high school, so I should have been able to work the problem with ease, but all I thought now was, "elementary" trig my ass.

"Is this seat taken?" I heard a male voice say. I ignored it. I came to the library for solitude and quiet, not to be pestered by some dumbass trying to make a move on me.

"Excuse me, *miss*. I asked if this seat was taken." The guy said "miss" the same way most people would say "bitch." That got my attention. I looked up from my book, ready to set the surly schmuck straight.

It was Orlando.

"May I?" he said, this time with the utmost politeness.

He sat. We talked for a few minutes before getting shushed, so we left the library for the student union. It was an hour before I got back to my homework. He had to get going so he could pick up his girlfriend, Aubrey, for a date.

Oh. His girlfriend.

When he got up to leave, we hadn't made any firm plans to see each other again. UNM was a big school, so it was entirely possible that we would never run into each other. I wanted to say something, tell him I was at the library almost every Saturday because my upstairs neighbor liked to listen to Foghat all hours of the day and night, tell him we should get together sometime. But I didn't get the words out; I let him walk away. Dejected, I turned my attention back to my trig book.

I glanced up and saw him walking back to my table. "Hey, Sylvie, I forgot to ask you this. I'm taking trig, too, with that British guy, Taylor. You know him?"

"Yeah, I have him for calculus."

"I'm sure he knows what he's talking about, but that accent . . . blimey, I can't understand half of what he's saying. So, anyways . . . I noticed you've got the same text book as me, so maybe you wouldn't mind us working together on some of this stuff."

"I'm not exactly Richard Feynman. I don't know how much help I'll be."

"At least you've heard of Feynman. That puts you way ahead of most of us."

We agreed to meet at the student union the following Saturday to study together. After he left, I told myself so what if he's dating Audrey or Aubrey or whoever? It doesn't matter. I like him. He likes me. The scene in *Casablanca* when Rick says, "I think this is the beginning of a beautiful friendship" came to mind.

Yeah. Like that.

He showed up the next Saturday and many more after that. When the homework was particularly brutal, we were all about cosines and arctangents. If the workload was light, we'd relax, talk about our worst professors or commiserate over some situation at our jobs. Aubrey's name came up once in awhile, but not enough to annoy me. I missed Izzy, but Orlando was a pretty good replacement. His knowledge of math and physics couldn't compete with Izzy's, but his good looks made up for whatever scholastic shortcomings he may have had.

I was glad to have him as a friend because I could tell him stuff that I couldn't tell Emily or Nola. They'd both been pretty tight-lipped about their divorces and who knew what when, so I didn't completely trust them. Also, I'd discovered that if I told Emily something in confidence, she sometimes spilled it to Nola, and vice versa. Those two loved gossip more than Española loves low-riders. Something told me that Orlando would keep his mouth shut no matter what. It was an endearing quality.

One afternoon he came to my apartment to pick me up. We were going to have lunch and then go to the library together. He evaluated the limited seating options in my living room, made his decision, and sank down into my creaky, bottomed-out brown velvet Barcalounger. Tall and lean, he seemed too big for the chair, his long arms and legs sprawling out of it.

"Don't get too comfy," I said. "How 'bout we hop in the car and go down to Lotta Burger, maybe get us a couple of green chile cheeseburgers, then hit the library?"

"Why don't we walk down to the grocery store and get the stuff and make some hamburgers here?" he said.

"That'll take all afternoon. Why don't we drive to the store and get the stuff?"

"Walk."

"Drive."

"Walk. C'mon. It'll do us good. Sunshine, fresh air, exercise. It's not that far, and the weather's perfect. Seriously, you need to get outside once in a while, take a break from the books."

This was the same guy who, when he found out I was going to get my driver's license renewed, spent two hours trying to convince me to sign up to be an organ donor. He'd won that argument, so it was highly unlikely that I'd win this one.

We began our trek to the store, and it was pleasant enough except for me occasionally tripping over the heaved-up sections of the sidewalk and Orlando grabbing my arm to keep me from falling down, saying now he understood why I didn't want to walk anywhere, that obviously walking was a challenge for me.

"Shut up, stupid. I know how to walk."

"Clearly you don't."

"Maybe I've got something heavy weighing on my mind."

"Like what?"

I'd wanted to tell him about Nola and Todd, about how Todd met a woman with the same kind of arms as Nola, and that he'd run off with the hussy. It was such an unbelievable story. I'd been itching to tell it to somebody. On the other hand, it seemed disloyal to Nola, to turn her painful story into gossip with Orlando, a stranger to her.

"I don't know if I should tell you."

"No problem. Don't tell me."

"All right, I'll tell you."

"Then tell me, already."

As we continued our walk to the store, I learned that unlike me, he was a good listener, and he allowed me to tell the tale without interruption. When I was finished, he said, "*That* is some heavy stuff."

"It's unbelievable and outrageous is what it is."

"I'm really sorry for your friend. I can't imagine what it must have been like to be blindsided like that."

"She's taking it pretty hard. I think she believed the two of them were going to have a long, happy life together. Heck, even I believed that, and I never believe that kind of sappy stuff."

"It's good that you and Emily are helping her get through it."

"I don't know how much good we're doing. I think what she needs right now is a new guy to take her mind off that loser. Nothing will mend a girl's broken heart faster than a new guy."

"Whoa, there. You aren't trying to set me up with her, are you?"

"You? No way."

"Really? And why not? Are you saying you think I'm too shallow to go out with a handicapped girl?"

"Are you too shallow for that?"

"Well, yeah. Of course I am."

That made me laugh. He was the least shallow person I'd ever met. "Don't worry. I'm not trying to set you up with her."

"Good. I hate it when people try to set me up."

"Say no more. But, hey—don't call her handicapped."

"How come?"

I told him Nola attempted to school me on this matter. Early in our friendship, I'd asked her if there were any other "handicapped kids" in her swim class. This was apparently an insult. She explained that she considered herself a person "with a handicap" or "with a disability." Not a "handicapped person."

"Guess I never thought of it that way. Makes sense," Orlando said.

"Well maybe you ought to explain it to me because I don't get it at all. I mean, what's the difference?"

"She's saying that even though she has a handicap, it doesn't define who she is."

I didn't know what it meant for something to "define you." Sounded like some sort of touchy-feely *I'm OK, You're OK* crap.

"Whatever."

"I think she means something sort of like this. Let's take you for example. You've got that ugly scar there on your leg, right?" he said and looked down at my calf. I got the scar years ago when Clint got his first motorcycle. He was giving me a ride on the back of it when he got a sudden urge to impress me by popping a wheelie. When the front wheel left the ground, I fell off the back of the bike, skimming my bare calf across the muffler as I tumbled to the pavement. The burn hurt like holy hell but taught me two very important lessons. One, don't wear shorts on motorcycles. Two, don't get on motorcycles.

"Yeah, what about it?" I said.

"When I think of you, I don't think of you as 'that burned girl.' I think of you as that smart, cute, funny girl who is some-times tough, sometimes neurotic, and sometimes both at the same time. See? Like that."

Well, whadaya know? He thinks I'm funny. But I never realized my scar was that noticeable. Now I'm all self-conscious about it. Gee thanks for nothing, Orlando!

"Hmm. I guess I get it. Sort of," I said, deciding that I could follow the "handicapped rule" without understanding it. "Well, anyways . . . the main thing I'm worried about is I don't know what's going to happen to her now that she's alone. She's pretty good at taking care of herself, but I have a bad feeling that she's going to go back to Santa Fe and live with her parents for the rest of her life."

"What's so bad about that? Wouldn't it be good for her to be at home and have her mom and dad around to take care of her?"

I snorted. If Nola had been there and if she were capable of smacking him, she definitely would have.

"What's so funny? What'd I say?"

"One day you'll meet her and you'll see for yourself."

9

Nola was living alone in the house she and Todd had rented when they first got married. The logistics of it were turning out to be a lot more complicated than I had anticipated. I would not have considered it possible to underestimate Todd's role in Nola's life, so it came as somewhat of a surprise to me that as independent as Nola was, there were more than a few things that she simply could not do. Anybody who gets divorced has to readjust, but most don't have to figure out new and creative ways to get dressed or fed or have clean clothes.

Between her parents, Emily, and me, we had most of the bases covered, but we were logging a lot of miles trying to make things work. Nola was grateful for the help but annoyed at the same time about having to accept it. Something would have to change.

I didn't want her to leave Albuquerque and return to her parents' house. I knew our friendship wouldn't be the same if she did. If she moved back to Santa Fe, it would be an admission of defeat; it would tell the world that a girl "like her" couldn't make it in on her own in The Big, Bad World. Even if she was able to handle that defeat, I couldn't.

She dropped in on me while I was making dinner, and the subject of her leaving came up again. I was desperate to present an ironclad case for her to stay in Albuquerque. Where to begin? Maybe I could appeal to her practical nature.

Tourism is Santa Fe's main industry, providing the area with primarily low-paying service industry jobs. I couldn't imagine

Nola doing work like that. I told her if she went back to Santa Fe, she'd have a hard time finding something that paid a decent wage.

"You'd be wasting your time there. You'd have a much better chance in Albuquerque. Maybe at Kirkland Air Force Base or Sandia Labs," I said.

"Oh, I don't know about all that military stuff. Maybe I could get a government job in Santa Fe."

Santa Fe is New Mexico's capital city, so there are lots of civil service jobs there but not nearly enough to go around. Competition is fierce, I told her. So far Nola had been protected from the cold, cruel world of public service. I hadn't been so lucky, so I figured it was my duty to warn her.

As I made salsa for the tacos, I told her about "The Bro System." I don't know where the expression came from, but in the 1970s, its principles were in full force in New Mexico. The Bro System had two primary directives. Directive Number One: Do as little actual work as possible. Directive Number Two: Get as many of your friends and relatives into The Bro System as you can. The better job you do on Number Two, the easier Number One would be.

"Why do you do it that way?" she said.

"Do what what way?"

"Make your tacos like that. Wouldn't it be easier just to use store-bought taco shells, cook the meat in a skillet, and fill the tacos?"

"Are you listening to me here? I'm trying to talk to you about your future."

"Yeah, I'm listening. But I've never seen anybody make tacos like that."

"My mom makes them like this, so that's how I make them. Watch, start like this." I took another corn tortilla, smeared a thin pancake of ground beef on it. "Don't put too much meat on—it'll fall off if you do." Holding one edge of the tortilla with my fingers, I dipped it part way into the hot oil. When the tortilla began to soften, I folded the top half over. "I don't know why, but they taste better like this. You oughta try making them this way sometime."

"I don't think I want my face that close to a skillet full of hot oil. Not without wearing a welder's mask."

"Ah, good point." I slid another tortilla into the oil. "Sure you don't want to try one? There's plenty."

"No, I already ate dinner, but thanks. Now, where were we?"

"I was saying that somebody like you would have a terrible time working for the government in Santa Fe."

"What do you mean somebody *like me*?"

"Educated. Smart. Conscientious. Hardworking."

"What's wrong with that?"

"Nothing inflames a Santa Fiend more than some smarty-pants girl waltzing into the office and acting like she's better than everybody else. Behind your back, they'll mock you. They'll say, 'Who the hell does she think she is, trying to make the rest of us look bad? Thinks she's so hot because she went to college. Stuck up bitch!'"

"Did you say 'Santa Fiend'?"

I ignored her question, went on with my tirade, telling her sure, nobody would dare say anything blatantly offensive to her face. They'd be afraid that badmouthing her would cause them to wind up in their supervisor's office getting lectured on affirmative action policies, quotas, and blah, blah, blah.

"Maybe they wouldn't actually *say* anything to you, but you'd know," I told her, "you'd definitely know. Every day you'd be faced with those backbiting hags—" (and it was invariably the women who excelled at making others miserable) "—following you with their mascara-encrusted eyes, not bothering to hide their jealousy and loathing. True, they'd know you can't get fired. They'd also know *they* can't be fired. So they'd carefully walk that line, being as unhelpful, insulting, and belligerent as possible without risking a written reprimand."

"Have you been practicing this little speech?"

"Maybe. A little." A lot.

"I see. So, enlighten me. What's a Santa Fiend?"

"It's a person who thinks the world owes him a living and is in a state of chronic indignation because he doesn't think he's getting his fair share."

"Indignant, huh?"

"Yeah. Very."

"Huh. You don't say. Are you a Santa Fiend?"

"What?" My mouth flew open in surprise. "Me? No, of course not. Why would you say that?"

"Well, you seem pretty indignant about a lot of stuff. I was just wondering . . ."

"Thanks a lot for nothing. I'm *not* a Santa Fiend."

"All right, all right. Take it easy, Sylvie. I'm just yanking your chain." She laughed.

"I'm trying to be serious here."

"Believe me—nobody knows better than me how serious this is. I don't want to move back to Santa Fe, but if that's what I have to do, then that's that. I do it. I get over it. I move on."

"Yeah, but . . ."

"Stop, please? Let's relax and enjoy the guacamole. Scooch the bowl over here."

Get over it. Move on. Eat guacamole. It wasn't much of a plan, but it would have to do.

Ultimately, it was Emily who saved the day. She scoured Albuquerque's northeast Heights until she finally found two adjacent apartments for rent. Nola could live in one, Emily in the other, allowing Nola to have some autonomy and yet Emily would be right next door to help her if she needed it. I lived only about fifteen minutes away, so I could help, too. Together, the three of us might be able to make it work.

Still, sacrifices had to be made. The most noticeable one came a month after Todd left. One day Nola had long hair, styled like Emma Peel in "The Avengers." The next day it was shaved off super short like Twiggy's. Emily and I were shocked at the transformation. I imagined myself in that salon chair, watching as hanks of my long hair fell to the floor. So I blinked back a tear the first time I saw her with the new haircut. It didn't seem to bother her, though; she said her new hairdo was "liberating."

Before the divorce, Nola dressed as she pleased; if there was something she wanted to wear but couldn't manage to get on by herself, Todd was always there to help. Now, no Todd, so no slacks, no shorts, no socks, and definitely no stockings. Instead she had to wear simple dresses she could pull on over her head. No zippers, no buttons, no snaps. Because of her divorce, almost everything she did in her personal life was changed—from the way she got ready for work in the morning to the way she made dinner at night.

I had confidence—maybe too much confidence—that Nola could handle the changes. From the moment I met Nola, that day she picked me up hitching when I was 13, I was astonished by her courage and sheer will. There were more astonishments, big and small since then. She had very nice handwriting. She could type. She knew how to swim (how scary must that have been to learn?). She even knew how to ride a bicycle.

Emily and I learned about Nola's bicycle riding when we were all still teenagers. Emily and I were cleaning the garage and Nola was keeping us company. Nola spotted Emily's old bike and said, "I used to have a bicycle."

Emily and I stopped sweeping and stared at her. Huh? How could she hold on to the handlebars? If she leaned over to reach them, she'd be staring at the ground, so how could she see where she was going? With operable fingers only on one arm, how could she possibly steer? She explained that her dad modified her bike, putting a stiff piece of rubber tubing that fit over one handle bar end and then arced up and fit over the handle on the other side. So, instead of leaning all the way over to the handles, she just leaned forward, rested her upper body against the tubing, and twisted her shoulders this way or that to turn.

The engineering aspects of it fascinated me, but it still sounded dangerous. I asked, "How did you learn to ride without killing yourself?"

"Same way as every other kid. Training wheels."

Oh. Duh.

"I haven't been on a bike in years. Hey, Emily, how about giving me a coast?"

I looked down the driveway. The scary steep driveway.

"How 'bout I go down to the end of the driveway and you get on there?" Emily said.

"Sounds like a plan," Nola said.

A stupid plan. Emily was never one to think an idea all the way through to its tragic, inevitable conclusion.

Emily rolled her bike to the foot of the driveway and got on. Nola sat behind her on the coaster, sidesaddle. The hairs on the back of my neck were standing on end. I silently calculated how long it would take for an ambulance to get to the house.

Emily and Nola took off down the street, with Nola leaning hard against Emily's back, hanging onto her blouse—hanging on as well as one could hang on with only two fingers. The street was a straight downhill shot, and as they gained momentum, I heard them laughing and screeching. Suddenly, the rear wheel slewed and Nola lost her balance and fell to the pavement. It was a terrible sight to see: with no way to break her fall, one knee took the brunt of the impact, followed by her shoulder and then her face. I sprinted down the street, not knowing what I would do when I got to them.

Emily helped Nola stand and then brushed the pebbles and asphalt crumbs off Nola's raw, skinned knees and forehead. Nola was breathing shaky-like, making little snorty noises, trying not to cry. "Ow, ow, ow. Damn, diddly, damn-DAMN, that HURT." Then she started to laugh. Emily, who had been on the verge of tears, could hold them in no longer. She started to laugh and to cry. I turned away from them, knelt down, and pretended to examine the bike, waiting for the catch in my throat to subside.

True, after that bike ride she wasn't eager for another. That was because she was smart, not because she was a coward. No, no way would anybody ever accuse her of being a coward! I was so used to Nola being able to handle whatever came her way that I figured she would just "handle" her divorce too. She cried plenty over Todd, but I thought it was the usual "You broke my heart, you worthless son-of-a-bitch" kind of crying. Not "You broke my heart, crushed my soul, ruined my life, and utterly destroyed whatever tiny shred of normalcy I might pretend to have, you worthless son-of-a-bitch" crying.

She and Emily commiserated with each other in a way that was beyond me. Nola and I would screw around and do wacky stuff and try to be *fun* girls, but whenever Emily and Nola were together, things seemed more serious and mature. Who knows? Maybe when I wasn't around they discussed things like term life insurance or how to avoid mildew on the shower walls. And now, besides being best friends, they shared this awful thing called divorce. I was barely out of my teen years when their lives were falling apart, so I'm sure I didn't grasp all the social and financial ramifications of it. But I did understand this: Todd taught her that someone you loved and trusted, someone you believed you could depend on, anytime, anyplace, could suddenly—and seemingly without any provocation whatsoever—leave you without a single word of explanation or apology. He taught her that. He taught me that, too.

1975

10

Most tourists coming to Santa Fe put the Plaza on their must-see list. Never make the mistake of referring to the Santa Fe Plaza as "the town square." Doing so will immediately and irrevocably ruin one's chance of passing for a local. The fact that it actually *is* "the town square" is irrelevant.

The Plaza is the ancient hub of the city, dating back to the early 1600s. It's made up of a small park surrounded on all four sides by shops, restaurants, and museums. We went there to buy our school clothes, and if fortune shone upon us, we might pop into TG&Y for a Frito pie and a look at the parakeets and tropical fish. We also enjoyed the escalator at Sears, which was the closest thing we ever got to an amusement park ride.

The Plaza is also home to Santa Fe's annual festival—Fiesta. As part of Fiesta, the streets surrounding the Plaza are closed to vehicles. Street vendors take over, selling tamales, Indian fry bread, cotton candy, and other astoundingly unhealthy treats. Mariachis and flamenco dancers perform on the bandstand, music blares, and people dance and sing well into the night. Then, as now, Fiesta is primarily an excuse for hordes of people to swarm the place and get drunk on their collective asses.

For a young girl, it is a chance to show off her new Fiesta dress. When I was a kid, Fiesta dresses were typically homemade and slathered in lots of rickrack, ribbons, and lace. The sparklier the better. Under such dresses, girls wore a gigantic petticoat or—what the heck—several petticoats. Why not? It was Fiesta! I was a tomboy, but wearing a dress like that was enough to make even me start twirling in front of the mirror, feeling like a movie star. "Raul, bring me my castanets!"

In addition to the party on the Plaza, Zozobra (also called "Old Man Gloom") is burned. Zozobra is a scary looking 50-foot effigy that resembles Eddie Munster, if Eddie Munster snorted angel dust. He looks like he is wearing a white robe with black cuffs and a black collar and, inexplicably, a prissy little black bow tie. Cables on a giant metal framework suspend him. When he is set on fire, the cables are pulled to make his head move and his arms thrash around, as if he is writhing in agony from the flames. At this point in the proceedings, terrified children either fall into a stunned, saucer-eyed silence or start screaming their heads off.

There is a point to this brutality, of course. Zozobra represents your troubles. Legend has it that when he is burned, your troubles are destroyed with him. I don't think it is Zozobra's burning that frees the revelers of their worries; rather, it is the copious amounts of liquor and pot they consume during the festivities.

The pyrotechnics involved dictate that Zozobra's burning take place a safe distance from combustibles. So he is constructed on a ridge near Fort Marcy Park. Parents pile the kids (and the beer and pot baggies) into their cars and drive to the park, where a huge dirt lot has been designated for parking. Most people sit in, or on, their cars and watch the fireworks fly and Zozobra get torched. When it's over, there is always a huge snarl of traffic as thousands of people leave at the same time. This is good because it gives drivers a chance to sober up before getting out on the road.

My parents hated the whole production, so the only time we went was when relatives from out of town came to visit and wanted to be entertained. As kids, my brother and I looked forward to going because we liked the fireworks. And even though Zozobra's menacing features scared the hell out of us, we were quite enamored with the whole idea of setting crap on fire.

Though Orlando was born and raised in Santa Fe, he had never been to Zozobra. When I found this out, I knew I must convince him to go. Usually he resisted getting dragged off to see schlocky tourist stuff, but I preyed upon his generous nature, telling him that Nola also had never seen Zozobra and that she would like to go. He wanted to know why she and I didn't go by ourselves.

"Santa Fe. Darkness. Liquor. Two girls. All alone," I said in an ominous tone.

"You got a problem with a bunch of drunk guys leering and slobbering all over you while you try to enjoy a simple night out with your friend?"

"Yeah, you could say that. Something about walking to the ladies room and having to run a gauntlet of hammered, horny guys catcalling things like 'Hey, baby. Where's your boyfriend? Have a beer with us, *essa*. Come over here to see what I have to show you! Don't you want to sit in my lap?' that cramps my style."

"Take Emily with you. 'Safety in numbers' and all that."

"There is no safety in three girls instead of two. Most guys would say that it just improves the odds. Besides, Emily hates Zozobra. Says it gives her nightmares."

"What about me and Nola? What about our nightmares?"

"You do this for me and I'll bring you some green chiles. Roasted and peeled. Enough to last a month." Or two weeks, if he ate it on everything the way I did.

That sealed the deal. I called Nola and told her Orlando had agreed to come with us and that he'd pick me up first and then we'd swing by her place. She was excited about going and wanted to know all about "this Orlando Guy." I always had trouble convincing people that he and I were just friends. Maybe Nola would get it.

I could have told her about that night when Dale dumped me out on Rodeo Road and Orlando gave me a ride home. But that story didn't show me in the most flattering light. Maybe it would be better to start at the beginning, when I first met Orlando.

I was in the second grade, I told her. Orlando and I rode the same school bus. He got on the bus before me, so when I got on, I passed his seat. I had to be careful. If anyone saw me show the slightest interest in him, horrid chants of 'Orlando and Sylvie sittin' in a tree, k-i-s-s-i-n-g' would erupt and all bets would be off—he would never, ever, speak to me. So as I passed him, I allowed us only a nanosecond of eye contact and a hint of a smile. He retuned my smile with a solemn, subtle nod. At least I liked to think it was a nod; he may have just been looking at a piece of lint on his pants.

One day during class, my teacher, Mrs. Lavadie, caught me whispering to the kid who sat in front of me, and punished me by sending me to the cloakroom. The cloakroom was a long, narrow closet that ran across the length of the back of the classroom. A row of coat hooks were screwed into the wall and a shelf above the hooks held the kids' mittens and lunches. "Sylvie, I told you NO talking!" the mean teacher said to me. "Get in the cloakroom and don't come out until I tell you to."

I slunk to the back of the classroom, red-faced, head hanging down, trying to avoid eye contact with the other kids. Once in the cloakroom, I sat on the linoleum floor, my knees pulled up to my chest, elbows on knees as I cradled my face in my hands.

I snorted in short little breaths, my chest heaving. I was determined not to cry—I didn't want to come out of the cloakroom with a tear-stained face and boogers running out of my nose and have all the kids stare and snicker. I needed to find something to take my mind off my troubles.

I noticed all the lunches on the shelf. Some lunches, like mine, were in brown paper bags. Others were in metal lunch boxes decorated with cartoon characters. I knew what I would find in the paper bags: a baloney sandwich made with gummy white bread slathered with mayonnaise and a lone, limp piece of lettuce embedded in one of the pieces of bread. Probably a mushy apple in there, too. If the kid was lucky, there might be a bag of chips. Likely as not, there would just be some carrot sticks wrapped in wax paper. Maybe a dumb ol' box of raisins. I also had a pretty good idea what was in those nice lunch boxes. Chips, *always* chips. And Dolly-frickin'-Madison cakes, or—ooo-ooo—Little Debbie cakes!

I started salivating, dreaming of Hostess fruit pies and Cheetos. The temptation to rampage through those fancy-shmancy lunch boxes, pillaging every damn bag of chips, every Moon Pie, every—

Next thing I knew, Orlando was standing next to me, rubbing an eye with his fist, lower lip quivering.

I stood, wiped the dirt off the back of my dress, tried to make myself presentable. "How come you're in here?"

"I talked back to Mrs. Lavadie. She asked me if I had my spelling homework and I said 'No' and she said 'Why not?' and I said 'Because spelling is stupid,' and everyone laughed except her and then she told me to get in the cloakroom."

Wow. In two years, I'd never heard him say more than three words to me. Now he was spilling his guts. I was in love.

I had to play it cool. He sat down on the floor. I sat down close to him, maybe too close (he may have been the kind of boy who suffered from a deadly fear of "girl cooties"), but he didn't seem to care.

"Which lunch is yours?" I said.

"Why do you want to know?"

"Just tell me—which one?"

"That one," he said, pointing to a big grocery bag cut off at the top to make it look more like a store-bought lunch sack. His name was written on it in pencil, and the grease seeped through, smearing the writing.

Ah. Not a fancy-lunch-box kinda guy. Excellent.

"Do you like Little Debbie cakes?"

His eyes lit up. "Oh, those chocolate cup cakes! I like to pull the wad of icing off the top first and let it melt in my mouth."

"Me too. Wanna see if we can find some?"

"You mean steal 'em out of somebody's lunch?" He looked confused.

"I don't know—I was just thinking, that's all," now feeling ashamed of my Little Debbie lust.

We discussed the pros and cons of rifling through the lunch boxes, but before we could decide what to do, Mrs. Lavadie was at the door. "All right you two! Stop that talking right now! And get up off that floor!" she hissed, grabbing my arm and jerking me to my feet. "Get back to your desks, and I don't want any more nonsense out of you two today," she said, drilling us both with her cruel eyes.

Orlando and I walked out of the cloakroom, both of us oddly relaxed, and frankly, a tad annoyed at having to return to our seats. This was not the demeanor our fellow classmates expected. They eyed us suspiciously as we took our seats. *Exactly what went on in that cloakroom?* After the cloakroom incident, I hoped that Orlando and I would now be friends, but he never said much more than hello to me for the rest of the school year. Then I skipped ahead in my story, to our encounter that day at the library.

"That's amazing!" Nola said. "He was in your second grade class and then, after all these years, he runs into you at UNM. Maybe he's your destiny!"

"Oh yeah, that's it. Orlando is my destiny!" I said, sarcastically.

"He won't be with that kind of an attitude."

I sighed and blew out an exasperated breath.

"How come you never talked about him before?"

This was a tricky question, one that deserved careful consideration. The truth of the matter was that I never introduced anybody to Nola unless I was absolutely positive that the person wouldn't act like an idiot. I was now sure of Orlando. I must answer Nola's question with the utmost diplomacy and delicacy.

"I dunno," I said and shrugged.

She eyed me suspiciously.

"Look, do you want to go see Zozobra with Orlando and me or do you need to see his tax returns for the last five years first?" I said.

She had no further questions or objections.

A few weeks later, Orlando and I pulled up to her apartment building. An unexpected pang of doubt hit me, and I worried that Orlando would get weirded out. But when he saw Nola coming down the stairs from her apartment, he got out of his truck and hurried around to the passenger side to open the door and help her up into the cab. He was cool and relaxed, which was a relief, especially since the three of us would be crammed into the front seat of his pickup truck for the hour drive to Santa Fe, with Nola in the middle.

It was just starting to get dark when we arrived at Fort Marcy. Orlando found a good parking space and backed the pickup into it. We got out and he put the tailgate down and threw a few blankets on top of it so it wouldn't be so uncomfortable to sit on. The three of us hopped up, with Nola needing a little help to keep her upright as she got up on the tailgate.

"I've got some good news," Nola said, and she smiled a smile that could only mean one thing.

"Who is he? How did you meet him? What's his name? What does he do for a living? How old is he? Is he cute? What's he—"

"If you'll stop grilling the holy dog crap out of me for five seconds I'll tell you everything. Now shut up, will ya?"

"What are you two talking about?" Orlando said.

"Nola met a guy. Or she's going to meet a guy. Or something," I said.

"Do you want to hear this or not?"

"I do!" Orlando said. "I've always wondered about what girls say about guys when we aren't around. So, shush up, Sylvie."

I made a zipping motion over my lips.

"That's more like it. I met him through a personal ad," she said.

I drew my hand across my mouth again, unzipping it. "What? Have you lost your mind?"

"I know, I know. You think I'm pathetic. But listen; this time I really think it might work out. He was so nice on the phone, so easy to talk to. How could I not take a chance and meet him?"

"Agreed to meet him? You agreed to meet him? Are you crazy?"

"What's so crazy about it? It's not like I told him, 'Hey, let's meet at midnight behind an abandoned warehouse.' We met at the coffee shop in the Federal Building at 8:30 in the morning."

"Still—you should hear some of the stories I've heard. My friend, Mike—he's got all kinds of wild stories about personal ads. One woman he met had hair coming out of the top of her blouse, right at the neckline. The whole time they were eating lunch, she kept tugging on her neck hair. Another girl stood him up at the restaurant, said she was going to the bathroom, and never came back. And this other girl he met, she—"

"Sheesh. You're the crazy one," she said.

"What's the matter? Don't you believe me?"

"I believe you all right. I just don't care. I've already met him. I like him. I'm going to continue to see him. And that is pretty much THAT."

Well, hell. She'd just ruined a perfectly good tirade.

"C'mon, now, don't pout. Just listen to me. He's really sweet. And cute," she said. "Real cute."

"Yeah, that's what they said about Ted Bundy, too. 'He was so nice, so polite, so well groomed. Handsome, too!' Next thing you know, they find a half-naked, mutilated body in a car trunk somewhere."

"For God's sake—must you always go right to the most grisly thing imaginable?"

"Yes, she must," said Orlando.

"Worst case is he's just a jackass, not a serial killer," Nola said.

"You need to be careful answering personal ads. People lie about all kinds of stuff," Orlando told her, but he was staring at me. Probably because my "Mike" story was made up. There was no Mike. It was Orlando who was abandoned at the restaurant. Orlando was the guy who met the hairy-necked girl.

"You don't need another jackass in your life. You've had plenty already," I said.

"Who answered whose ad?" Orlando asked.

"He answered my ad. I put one in that little newspaper, *Valley News*. You put an ad in and then if somebody is interested in you, they call this special phone number and enter the code associated with your ad. Then they leave you a voice mail. It's cool. That way, if you don't like the way the guy's message sounds, you don't have to call him back."

"Did you get a lot of voice mails?"

"A few. Most who did leave messages for me sounded like telemarketers, like they were calling every single girl who placed an ad, hoping to get lucky. But this guy—he sounded like he had his act together. It was as if he knew exactly what he wanted to say, like he actually put some thought into it before he dialed the phone. I was impressed. So I called him. We hit it off right away."

The first wave of fireworks went off and a huge shower of red and gold sparks fell from the sky, casting Old Man Gloom in an eerie light.

"Did you ask him whether he was married or not?" I was trying not to sound snotty, but probably did anyway.

"Yes, of course I asked him. Jeez, I didn't just fall off the turnip truck. He said he was married once but he's been divorced for about a year. No kids, which makes things a lot less complicated."

I wondered if Nola told the guy what she looked like before he agreed to meet her, how she might have approached such a delicate subject. "Did you exchange pictures or anything like that before you met each other?" I asked.

"No. We just talked on the phone. And talked and talked . . . " She had that dreamy expression on her face, the one she always got whenever she met a new guy. "But I did tell him I have a disability. I didn't tell him exactly what the disability was; I just asked him if he thought that would be a problem for him."

I snuck a sideways glance at Orlando, whose focus was now directed at the fireworks, his expression betraying nothing. He was probably questioning his decision not to bring a six-pack along.

"So, you didn't mention in your ad that you have a disability?"

"Nope."

"Why not?" I asked.

"Because I want people to get to know me a little first. If I just blurt out 'I have a disability. I don't have any arms!' then that might dim my prospects a bit, don't ya think? This way, I can try to win them over with my sparkling personality. Have a fighting chance, you know?"

Her approach seemed dishonest, but I couldn't argue with the logic.

"So what happens next? When are you going to see him again?"

"He said he has to go out of town for a few weeks and he'll call me when he gets back. I'm so nervous and excited. Every time the phone rings, I just about jump out of my skin. Call me, call me, call me. Arrrrrrgggggghhhhh! Call ME!" she said, swinging her legs and bouncing up and down on the tailgate.

I'd seen her this way before. I didn't like it. When two people first meet, they size each other up, trying to figure out who in the relationship will be getting the better end of the deal. You want to be sure that it's you—not the other person. If a guy gets involved with Nola and decides he's the one getting the better end of the deal, I damn well want to know why.

This hadn't been an issue lately. Guys drifted in and out of her life, usually before I got a chance to meet them. But she'd been in a long dry spell, so I was afraid this new guy might make her do something reckless. The problem was, how could I talk about this with Nola without making it sound like I meant, *What could he possibly see in you?*

"Don't do anything stupid," I said, and then noticed her arm was moving up and down in my general direction. "What's that? What are you doing?"

"I'm flipping you off," she said.

Orlando laughed and pointed at Nola. "I like this girl."

"I know how you can get carried away sometimes. I worry about you."

"Oh? Is that so? Well, you get carried away, too. What about what's-his-name—Nick?"

"You mean Rick."

"Rick? Who's Rick?" Orlando asked, suddenly taking an interest again.

"Nick, Rick, whatever. You got all gee-whizzy over him and then he dumped you and I had to listen to you flog yourself for two months after that. The way I figure it, it's my turn again. So, relax. I'm a big girl. I can handle myself."

Orlando turned to me. "Who is this Rick guy?" Then he turned to Nola. "I never heard about any Rick. Who's Rick?"

I smacked him on the shoulder. "Will you forget about Rick?"

"What's Mr. Wonderful's name?" I asked Nola.

"Travis."

"Travis, as in 'tra-ves-ty'?"

"Just for that, when he calls, I'm asking him over for dinner and you're going to have to help me clean house."

"If he calls."

"And take me to the laundromat," she added.

I figured I'd better quit while I was ahead. If I kept pushing it, I was going to end up waxing her car.

The three of us gazed skyward as a round of fireworks lit up the night with a spectacular ball of blue and green that exploded into a canopy that rained pink sparkles all around us. The air was heavy with the smell of gunpowder, alcohol, and marijuana. Zozobra's massive head was now slowly turning, and it seemed as if he was looking right at us, his arms jerking up and down. A cloud of gray smoke began to swirl around him, until the only thing we could make out was the glint of his eyes and his oversized scarlet lips.

"Just burn the damn thing already," I said.

11

The average standard of living in Albuquerque in the 1970s must have been a lot lower than now, because back then lots of people went to the laundromat, not just homeless people. The apartment buildings that my friends and I could afford did not have luxury items like washing machines.

Going to the laundromat had its advantages. Because of the wide variety of people going there, it often made for some excellent people watching. You would think that as much as Nola was gawked at, she would have no interest in staring at anyone else, but there you would be wrong, very wrong. She'd had a blast at Zozobra, sitting on the tailgate of Orlando's truck, watching the constant stream of people who walked (or stumbled) on their way to the Port-O-Potties. The only part that bothered her was the occasional extra-super-loud boom of some of the fireworks. She had no way to cover her ears to muffle the noise. By the time Orlando or I realized that the sound was hurting her, it was too late for either of us to reach over and cover her ears.

The laundromat people-watching couldn't compete with Zozobra, but Nola thought it was better than sitting around the apartment alone all day.

Nola sometimes took her laundry with her when she went to visit her parents in Santa Fe. Her mom, though she spoiled Nola in some ways, expected her to do her own laundry when she visited. At home, she used her stick to pull the clothes out of the washer and put them into the dryer. At the laundromat, though, either Emily or I transferred the clothes from the washer to the dryer and put the coins in the coin slots for her. Nola did the folding.

It was the start of my second year at UNM, and school was getting off to a rough start. As hard as I had to work the previous year, this year was starting out even worse. In order to keep up, almost every spare moment I had was spent on homework. Going to the laundromat with Nola was great because she usually volunteered to proofread whatever paper I was working on, as long as it had nothing to do with math or computer programming. Proofreading must have been mind numbing for her, but it was a good way for her to pay me back for helping her.

On this day, we were at a laundromat that just opened the week before, so it was clean and modern. We were both a little excited about going there, which is indicative of how boring our lives had become.

"Swanky," I said, walking into the place and spying all the shiny, scum-free equipment.

"There's a bunch of washers in that row. Let's go over there," she said, pointing to them with her chin. After a few more trips to the car, our battalion of laundry baskets was in place and I was ready to start loading quarters.

I noticed one of the washers already had clothes in it, but they were finished washing. Nobody was nearby, so I figured I would take the wet clothes out and move them into one of the metal baskets that the laundry provided. I reached into the washer and started to pull them out. Next thing I knew, a woman was standing next to me. "What do you think you are doing? Those are my clothes," she said as she snatched them out of my hands.

She was middle-aged and had a weathered face that she'd tried unsuccessfully to soften by troweling on a generous layer of makeup and painting her lips with a slash of bright scarlet lipstick. Some of the lipstick was stuck on her teeth. Her mousy brown hair sprang out from her head, scorched and brittle from too many home perms and dye jobs. She reeked of cigarettes.

I was pretty sure I could take her.

"Sorry. I didn't know who they belonged to," I said, trying to burn a hole in her forehead with what I hoped was a steely gaze.

"You shouldn't be hogging all of these washers. Other people need to do laundry, too, you know. You're not the only one with better things to do than hang around here."

"They're not all for me. I'm helping my friend with her laundry, too." I turned to look at Nola. The witch turned to look, too.

Nola had been listening to this little exchange. "Hi," she said, exuding good cheer, and then gave a little wave, as if to say, "Delighted to meet you, neighbor!"

The witch's expression of indignation and outrage was immediately replaced with confusion, then shock, then shame— all in the space of two seconds. "Oh . . . uh . . . hi," she said to Nola. "I, uh . . . didn't realize you were . . . doing . . . " her voice trailed off. "Sorry," she said and then quickly gathered up her wet clothes and moved off to the other side of the laundromat.

I sat down next to Nola.

"Oh, brother," she said. "I bet she's got a dildo with a kick starter on it."

"Must be high time for her to take it out for a spin, too. She seems wound a little tight, doesn't she?"

"Yeah, tight."

"You think I could have taken her?"

"Of that, I have no doubt," she said, "but I bet we wouldn't be allowed back in here. We don't want to wear out our welcome before we've even had a chance to try out the new dryers."

"Or check out the bathroom."

We'd done the public bathroom scene many times. Nola had her own system of ranking them. Much hinged on the placement of the toilet tissue. If the bathroom was a bad one, through the stall door I'd hear her say something like, "I get so sick of having to bend down and practically give myself a swirly just to get a frickin' piece of toilet paper." She'd come out of the stall and say, "Why the hell does everybody seem to think the only disability a person can have is to be in a wheelchair?"

Our expedition to this bathroom would have to wait. I wanted to get the scoop on Travis. "What's the plan for the weekend? Did Travesty call you?"

"Stop calling him that. His name is Travis. Tra-vis. And yes, miss smarty-pants, he did call me. And he's coming over." She wiggled her eyebrows at me, Groucho Marx style.

"Ooooo, do tell."

"He called last Tuesday. We talked for hours; it must have been midnight before we hung up. I had a terrible kink in my neck the next day." Probably because the only way she was able to hold a telephone was to clamp the receiver between her ear and her shoulder.

"I bet," I said, reaching over to give her shoulder a little massage. "Where's he taking you?"

"Taking me?"

"Yeah, where's he taking you? You know. For dinner. Where?"

"I'm going to make him dinner at my house."

"You're going to make him dinner? Why? Why don't you go out?" I was trying not to visibly cringe. I'd eaten her cooking. From a culinary standpoint, she was a disgrace to our New Mexican heritage. Instead of whipping up delicious, colorful, spicy dishes, she usually made bland, gummy concoctions that always involved noodles, cans of cream-of-something-or-other soup, and canned tuna fish. A ripple of fear shuddered across my stomach just thinking about the glop.

"He said it would be cozier to eat in. Then we could talk and make dinner together and whatever."

"And whatever."

"Yes, whatever." She gave me a suspicious look. "What's got your knickers in a twist?"

"Seems risky to me, inviting some stranger over to your place."

"Well, how do you think I'm going to get to know him if we don't do anything together? That's what dating is for, silly."

"You think there's no way this guy can turn out to be some sort of craven, depraved nut job?"

She let out a long sigh, exasperated with the way the conversation was going.

"Just what do you think he's going to do to me?" she said.

"I don't know. If he's a nut job, well, I suppose he'll do some kind of, well, nut-jobbery on you."

"Nut-jobbery."

"Yeah. Nut-jobbery. It has a hyphen in it." I considered this. "Yes, it is definitely hyphenated."

"Oh, for Pete's sake. Contrary to what you might read in the papers, the world is not overrun with serial killers and perverts."

"Just be sure you tell him lots of people know he's coming over," I continued. "Oh, and make him touch a bunch of stuff too."

"Why on earth does he have to do that?"

"Fingerprints, fool, fingerprints."

"Bah!" She waved me off.

"My point is—ah, to hell with it. You're going to do this thing no matter what I say, aren't you?"

"Yup," she said, with an emphatic nod.

Our washers stopped, and I noticed that witchy woman was giving me the evil eye, outraged that I hadn't immediately leapt up to put my clothes in the dryers. I got up.

"Wait," Nola said. "You'll help me, won't you? Come over and help me get ready?"

No, I thought, absolutely not. I refuse to be a party to this insanity.

She was smiling now, looking expectant, nodding her head up and down, up and down, up and down, as if to say "Yeah, yeah, yeah—do it, do it, do it!"

"Why can't Emily help you?"

"I think she's a little bugged with me right now. My car was in the shop last week and she had to drive me to work three days in a row. I've kinda worn out my welcome with her."

"Oh, all right, already. I'll do it. What time should I be at your house?"

I noticed witchy woman still glaring at us, so I turned to face her. She must have seen something in my eyes that made her think better of saying anything to me because she bent her head down and studied her freshly laundered dish towels. Lucky for her. I definitely could have taken her.

12

Over the next few days, I called Nola several times, but her line was always busy. After about the tenth time, I finally got through. Just as I thought, she'd been yammering with Travesty pretty much nonstop. Ten seconds into our conversation, she told me she needed to get off the phone; he might be trying to call her. Well, he can just wait a few frickin' minutes, I incorrectly believed.

Try as I did to engage her in conversation, it was all for naught. If she could have worn a watch, she would have been checking it. Constantly. We set a time to meet that night, and she said, "'Kay. 'Kay. Fine. Yeah, fine. Bye." Click. Now I knew how bill collectors felt.

By the time I got to her house that night, I had recovered from my hurt feelings and was ready to throw myself into the game. As promised, I took Nola to the grocery store. Then it was back to her apartment, with me lugging everything up two flights of stairs, while she trailed behind me. At her door, I struggled with the bags, my purse, and her keys, trying not to drop anything. She caught up to me at her landing and stood close behind me while I fumbled with the key, trying to unlock her front door.

"Hurry up," she said, pushing against my back with her shoulder.

"I'm trying, all right? Just hold your horses."

"I have to pee. For Christ's sake, hurr-REEEE UP!"

"Damn it! Have you ever tried to open a door with two fingers?" I said, as I struggled with the lock.

"Many a time," she said. "Maaannnny a time."

I cocked my head, thinking about that for a second. "Yeah, I guess you have."

"You've got the wrong key, anyway, goofy. It's the silver one."

Oh.

At last I got the door open and Nola zoomed past me to the bathroom. I took the bags in the kitchen and started unloading them. I considered putting stuff away, but I wasn't sure what she needed out for dinner. Plus, I knew that things needed to be put away "just so." Not only because she needed things a certain way so she would be able to reach them but also because she was awfully particular about stuff in general. She would want the macaroni to the left of the tomato sauce, not to the right, just because that's the way she wanted it, and she would set you straight if you screwed that up. The pressure was too much for me, so I took the sissy's way out and just left the groceries on the counter and waited for her.

She came out of the bathroom a few minutes later and took command of the kitchen. I asked if she needed any help with the food preparations, and she said yes, I could open some cans for her. She had an electric can opener she could use to open them herself, but things would go faster if I could open them before I left. No problem. Anything else? Yes, actually there was something else I could help her with; I could shampoo her hair.

"You mean like in the sink or what?" I said. I had never given her a shampoo before.

"No, in the shower."

Uh-oh. Wretched flashbacks to high school P.E. classes ripped through my brain. She sensed my hesitation. I'd done

plenty of toilet-paper retrieval, back-scratching, eye-drops insert-
ing, nail-clipping and Band-Aid sticking for her, but I had never
seen her naked.

"Please? It won't take five minutes, I promise. I just want
to look as good as I can for Travis. Purty please with a cherry on
top?"

My brain scrambled to invent a plausible reason why I
could not possibly shampoo her hair. No words came out.

"I'm an only child, you know, and Sylvie—you're the closest thing I've got to a little sister. I'm all alone in the world." She
squinted her eyes and sniffed, pretending she was about to cry.

"Do you pull that 'only child' crap with Emily, too? It's
only going to work for you so many times, then you're going to
have to come up with some other way to bend us to your will."

More eyelash batting.

If I didn't do what she wanted and things went bad between
her and Travesty, she'd blame it on her greasy hair and it would
be all my fault and I'd never hear the end of it.

"Fine, let's get this over with. But if I'm like a little sister
to you, you better leave me something in your will when you die.
And not that hideous crocheted orange afghan, either. It better
be something good."

"Will cash do?"

"Yes, quite nicely, thank you."

"Done. I'll contact my attorney first thing tomorrow, start
the paperwork."

I was satisfied with the deal and followed her down the
hall. In the bathroom, she asked me to help her off with her
dress, and as I pulled it up and over her head, I was startled to
discover she was naked underneath. She stood before me, her face
the picture of cheerful anticipation. I'm sure she had no idea how

embarrassed I was by all this. When she was growing up, legions of doctors and nurses had examined every part of her extraordinary anatomy, from her strange arms to her twisted spine to her socket-less hips, leaving no bone, no organ, and no mucosal surface un-prodded. When I was growing up, even my own sister made sure her bedroom door was locked each night before changing into her spectacularly unrevealing nightgown.

It took all of my focus to keep my voice from quavering and squeaking. Must try to look relaxed . . . Must not freak out . . . Must not stare. Wait! Must look at some stuff or she'll be insulted. Just not the wrong stuff, but which stuff is the wrong stuff? Must . . .

"Turn the water on and let it heat up, would you?" she said, interrupting my internal blathering.

I leaned down, turning on the tub faucet and then the shower. I tested the water with my hand, made sure it wasn't too hot. When I thought it was right, I moved out of the way. "Now get the shampoo, the green bottle—right there," she gestured with her foot. "Wait a minute till my hair is good and wet." She dunked her head under the water, shaking it back and forth, and then moved it out of the water. "OK, I'm ready." She closed her eyes.

I squirted some shampoo on my hand. At 5'9" she was a few inches taller than me, so I had to stand on tiptoe to reach the top of her head. I gently massaged the shampoo into her hair. "Harder," she said. "Get in there and really scrub."

"I don't want to hurt you."

"I'll let you know if you're hurting me, don't you worry about that. Go on."

I rubbed harder, frothing up a huge head of lather.

"Yeah, yeah, like that," she said, enjoying this way more than I believed possible. Suds oozed down her face and she sputtered her lips. "Help! Help! Someone's drowning me!" she said.

"Crap, I'm sorry. Wait! Let me get a washcloth." I got a cloth and wiped the lather off her face. "How's that? Ready to rinse?"

She was, so she dipped her head down in the spray and I rinsed her head until all of the shampoo was out.

"My back, my back, do my back!" she said, sounding almost giddy.

All this nakedness and touching was pushing me to the verge of a nervous breakdown, but damn, this seemed to be making her so happy. I lathered up her back and began to wash it. I studied the long scars that ran down her spine, the result of her childhood surgeries. The holes where the sutures had been were still plainly visible, even after twenty years.

We were both quiet, her enjoying the back rub, me thinking about those months she'd spent as a child in a body cast.

"That's good. You can go now. Just hang the washcloth here on the rack so I can reach it."

"You sure?"

"Yeah, I'm good. I can do the rest. If you want, watch some TV or something while I finish up. Oh, and thanks, you're a good shampooer. Very thorough, excellent scrubbing action." She nodded appreciatively.

"Hey, what are friends for?" I said, but silently prayed she wouldn't call on me again for shampoo duty.

I pulled the bathroom door almost closed, went to the living room, and sat down. Suddenly I felt like crying but didn't know why. Maybe it was just the relief of getting out of the bathroom. No, that wasn't it. I closed my eyes and tried to figure out how Nola would take a shower by herself. First everything would have to be in its place before she even got started. Washcloth here. Soap there. Towel right there. She'd probably use her foot to turn the water on. But how could she do much more than just rinse off? It was mind boggling to think about all the obstacles she had to contend with just to get ready for work in the morning.

I recalled a particular daiquiri-drenched night that she, Emily, and I had spent together, right after Todd and Nola split up. The liquor had put me in an uncharacteristically philosophical mood. I asked her what she regretted most about not having arms. She said she didn't think about that sort of thing much; she'd never had arms so didn't really know what she was missing out on. There must be something, I'd said.

I expected her to say she wished she could lift and carry things like groceries or laundry. Or say that if she had arms, people wouldn't always stare at her or think she was retarded. Or that it would be easier to get dressed, to drive, to get a job.

"Hugs. I miss hugs. I'd love to be able to hug people, especially my husband. Oh, and babies," she said.

"You wish you could have babies?"

"No, I don't mean that. I can have kids any time I want. And believe me, I don't want. I mean I wish I could hug a baby. Cradle it in my arms like you do when you're giving it a bottle. I think that would feel really, really nice."

I held a sofa pillow to my chest and patted it gently. "You mean like this?"

"Uh-huh, exactly like that."

I didn't believe her. It was too much of a TV-movie-of-the-week kind of answer. Hugging? Holding babies? What sentimental drivel. But now that I had helped her with a shower and seen her reaction to being touched, it didn't seem so sappy.

Fifteen minutes later, Nola came out of the bedroom, dressed now, radiant. She twirled around. "What do you think?"

"You look fabulous. It's about damn time you got that greasy hair washed. I've been meaning to talk to you about that for weeks. Frankly, it was starting to smell a little."

"Oh, shut up. Next time I want your opinion, I'll beat it out of you," she said, but she was still smiling.

She asked me to set the table, mistakenly believing I could manage such a simple task. Instead, she found it necessary to school me in the proper positions for the silverware and such, remarking (as she often did) that I must have been raised by coyotes—coyotes with red neckerchiefs, if she really wanted to insult me.

I helped her get some spaghetti sauce going. We listened to the stereo and sang along. All those years of singing in school choirs had given her a singing confidence that I would never have. I sang low and quiet, she loud and with feeling. There was head bobbing and humming and a little dancing as we worked together in the kitchen, her joy and her excitement about her date rubbing off on me.

We were done and it was time for me to go. At the door, I said, "Good luck tonight. Call me tomorrow and tell me all about it."

And this I left unsaid—Travesty better not turn out to be a jackass.

She didn't call. Not that day, nor the one after, so I called her. I was thwarted yet again by a constant busy signal. It was starting to wear on my nerves. How could anybody talk that much? Or listen that much? Maybe he had murdered her. Or worse, maybe she was hurt and sprawled on the floor by her night table, the phone's receiver dangling from its cord as she lay helpless inches away from it, unable to put it back in the cradle.

My phone rang, rudely startling me out of my catastrophizing.

It was Nola. She told me about the date, that Travis loved dinner, and they had talked long into the night. They'd been talking to each other almost daily since then, and he had spent the whole day with her the previous Sunday.

Sounds serious, I told her, but was wondering how anybody could enjoy so much talk and so little action.

"He's so warm and funny and considerate. Things are going so great I don't want to let myself believe it. And guess what?"

"What?"

"I think I'm going to ask him to go to Santa Fe with me to meet my parents."

"Your parents? How come you're going to introduce him to your parents? You haven't even introduced him to me yet."

"So?"

"So? So why haven't you introduced him to me yet?" This wasn't a complaint; I hated meeting new people. It was too damn much work not to be me.

"Well, I guess I didn't want to introduce you two until I was sure he could handle you."

"Handle me? What's that supposed to mean?" Wait—this was beginning to sound a lot like the conversation she and I had when she wanted to know why I hadn't introduced *her* to Orlando.

"Oh, nothing," she said sweetly. "Stop being so paranoid."

"What about Emily? She hasn't met him either. What's your excuse for that?"

"Actually, Perry Mason, when Travis came over on Sunday, he and I went next door and rang her doorbell. We were going to invite her over for dessert. She didn't answer."

Oh.

"Still—how can you introduce him to your mom and dad after only a few weeks?" I was worried. Things were going too fast. "You don't want to scare him off, do you?" I said, while silently praying that she would.

"If he's not scared off by now, my parents sure as hell aren't going to scare him."

There was that impeccable logic again. "Maybe he'll think you are more serious than he is, like you want to be 'exclusive' or something. Maybe you ought to wait a few more weeks, till you're more sure of him."

"Nah. No guts, no glory, I always say."

"I've never heard you say that."

"Well, I'm saying it now."

"Fine," I said, a smidge irritated.

"Fine," she said, with finality.

"Fine," I said again.

We were silent for a moment.

"I think you should slow down, that's all. Get to know this guy a little better," I said.

"Like you're the expert."

If Emily or Clint said this to me, my response would have been swift and scathing. And laced with profanity. I let my retort sizzle, unsaid.

"I'm sorry," she said, "You shouldn't worry so much about me. I promise I won't do anything dumb. I'll call you in a few weeks and let you know how it's going. I gotta go now because Travis will be here any minute."

She hung up. I sagged down in the Barcalounger and brooded over her "expert" comment. I wondered if I should call the *Valley News*, put in a personal ad of my own. What could I write about myself that wasn't a bold-faced lie? "I've been told I'm weird. You probably wouldn't like me, and I probably wouldn't care."

Nah. What for?

I called Orlando instead.

13

"How's Aubrey?" I asked him. "I didn't tell you? Aubrey dropped out of school and went back to California."

"She *did?*" I had a moment of panic. "You aren't thinking of moving to California, are you?"

"Why would I do that?" he said.

"To be with Aubrey."

"I don't want to be with Aubrey. That's why she went back to California. I want to be with Jackie."

Over the last few months, I'd resigned myself to the notion that Orlando and I someday, decades from now, would be exactly where we are now, except we'd be in nursing homes, talking to each other on the phone, reminiscing about the time his fifth wife threw his suitcase out the window onto the piazza below in Rome. But just now, there had been a split second—that second between him mentioning Aubrey and him mentioning Jackie—that I thought I might be The One for him. Or at least The Next One of Many. It was a thrilling second, but it was over now. Let's hear what Jackie's got that I don't.

She was beautiful, of course. I had expected that. She also had money, which I hadn't expected. I believed there weren't any women who had money in New Mexico. Their husbands or their fathers may have money, but the women? Nada. Dead broke. Not Jackie, though. She was a real estate agent for a company in Santa Fe that specialized in luxury properties. Orlando explained to me how commissions worked and pointed out that one didn't need to sell very many million-dollar properties to make a killing.

Santa Fe's a popular hangout for celebrities and the rich. When these super-privileged interlopers buy property here, they inevitably tire of eating fancy dinners at The Compound. Next, the novelty of ordering burritos "Christmas-style" wears off. After that, it doesn't take long before they realize there is nowhere else to go, nothing to do, the schools are terrible, local government a quagmire of nepotism and corruption, and most everyone in town despises them for their wealth. Then it's *hasta luego, baby!* as they board a private Gulfstream jet back to New York or Chicago. The rambling hacienda is back on the market and everybody's happy.

Real estate agents love property churn. Jackie had sold one particular million-dollar-plus house three times in 18 months.

I decided I detested her.

I wasn't so thrilled with Orlando, either. How could he allow his head to be turned by a pretty face, a fabulous body and a pile of money?

"She wants to go to Mazatlan together. I'm pretty psyched. I've never seen the ocean before! It's going to be great!"

"But what about school? Won't you miss classes?"

"We're going over spring break."

I'd forgotten about spring break. Difficult to believe a college student could "forget" about spring break, but since I worked full time and went to class at night, it wasn't a big deal.

"Sounds perfect," I said, absentmindedly hurling a sofa pillow across the room.

"I hate to cut it short, Sylvie, but I gotta go. I need to make plane reservations."

"Sure, sure, I understand." I didn't, of course. I'd never been out of the state, never been on a plane, never gone on vacation. Unless you count trips to Roswell, which no one in their right mind would.

He hung up, and I looked at my trusty Barcalounger. "Well, I guess it's just you and me again, buddy." I picked up my statistics textbook, sat down, and turned to the section, "Statistical Hypotheses." It stated:

A statistical hypothesis is an assumption or statement, which may not be true, concerning one or more populations.

I muttered, "Yeah? Well, I hypothesize that Jackie is a nutcutting bitch and that Orlando *will* be sorry."

Minutes later, all thoughts of Aubrey, Jackie, and Orlando were gone, mental images of them submerged and ultimately drowned by the synaptic demands of calculating variances, partial derivatives, and confidence intervals, the symbols and the solitude lifting me to the heavens.

Maybe I couldn't go to Mazatlan, but I could go to Pancho's. Pancho's is an Albuquerque restaurant that serves cheap cafeteria-style Mexican food. One of its major draws is that each table has a little flagpole. You raise its flag if you want something like a drink refill or more sopapillas. And you *always* want more sopapillas. It's the kind of place no self-respecting Santa Fe local would be caught dead in. I love their green chile stew. And those silly little flagpoles. So much for self-respect.

Emily and I were in Pancho's serving line when I was surprised to see Nola ahead of us. I nudged Emily. "Hey, look who's here."

"What's she doing here? Without us, I mean."

"Maybe she's with her mom. Go catch up to her. Maybe we can sit with them."

"Keep an eye on my tray till I get back." She slipped out of the line and made her way up to Nola.

A few minutes later, Emily was back. "They want us to join them. They're going to get a table over by the fountain."

"Who's 'they'?"

"Nola and Travis."

"Travis is with her?"

"Yup."

"What's he look like?"

"You haven't met him yet?"

"Nope. Never even seen a picture. So, tell me! What's he look like?"

"Ehh," she shrugged. "He's ok, I guess. You'll see for yourself soon enough."

We made our way down the serving line. Emily was quiet, probably thinking about what Travis would be like. I was focused on checking for health code violations.

We paid for our food, then wandered over to the fountain and spotted Nola. When we got to their table, Nola said, "Hi! What are you guys doing here?"

"Buying shoes," I said.

"Wise ass," she said. "See, Travis? She's the one I told you about—the sassy one."

"At last we meet," I said, arching one eyebrow and unintentionally sounding like James Bond when he ultimately meets the villain, face-to-face.

"You must be Sylvie. I've heard a lot about you. I'm Travis." He stuck out his pudgy hand, which I reluctantly shook.

"Travis? Oh, I thought you were Ted. Didn't you say you were coming here with some guy named Ted?" I said, making what I intended to be a sly reference to Ted Bundy. I hoped Nola picked up on it.

Nola looked at Travis. "Told you. Sassy."

I got more squinty.

"And this is Emily. The sweet one," she said.

"Groovy," he said, now shaking hands with Emily.

Groovy? Did he just say "Groovy"?

Emily started the interrogation. She was good at it; she had many of hours of practice on my dates. Where did you go to school? Do you have any brothers and sisters? What part of town do you live in? How did you and Nola meet?

While they talked, I studied him. He looked about ten years older than Nola, which made him close to 40. Positively decrepit. He was a few inches shorter than her—5' 7" perhaps. Hair and sideburns on the longish side, especially for a man of his advanced years. He wore glasses with heavy gold frames on his round flabby face. His watery blue eyes appeared wavy and distorted behind the magnification of the thick lenses. He wore a western style shirt open at the neck one too many buttons, exposing a generous patch of repulsive chest hair. I was sure that he was wearing cowboy boots, the pointy kind—the kind so pointy you could kick a snake's butt with them. On one wrist he wore an expensive-looking watch, on the other, a chunky gold chain. Bracelets like that were always, always, always a bad sign.

I checked his left hand, searching for the telltale tan line of a temporarily removed wedding ring. No luck there—he was too pasty to have a tan line. This meant he didn't work outside.

I tried to get a good look at his teeth, which was my secret technique of sizing up a guy. A man who didn't take care of his teeth probably couldn't—or wouldn't—take care of anything else. No luck there. Even when he smiled, his scraggly mustache somehow managed to hide his teeth.

Emily was going too easy on him, wasn't asking him anything I wanted to know. Where was that hard-driving brutal technique she always used on my boyfriends? "Where'd you go to college?" I demanded, playing the part of the bad cop.

"College? College wasn't my bag," he said.

My bag? I hadn't heard that expression in ten years. Hated it then. Hated it now.

"Oh. I see," I said, not hiding my disdain. "Where do you work?"

"Work?" he asked, as if mulling over a particularly perplexing ethical dilemma.

"Yes. Work. You know. For money. A job. J-O-B?" I felt a painful pinch on the side of my thigh, Emily's signal to back off.

"I'm a loan officer at The Bank of Albuquerque." Now he was the one doing the squinting.

"Loan officer" sounded like an important job, which meant that either I was mistaken about what a loan officer did, or he was lying about being a loan officer.

"I used to work at that bank," Emily said. "I was a teller at the branch on north Lomas a few years ago. Which branch are you at?"

"The one on San Pedro." Then they started talking shop about banking and such. Nola sat there grinning, as if she was thinking, "Isn't he just the dreamiest?"

I studied her now, the way she looked at Travesty, the way she leaned on his shoulder in the conspiratorial way that lovers do. The situation was obviously out of my control. Might as well raise the little flag and get some more sopapillas.

14

Summer was upon us, and I decided this would be the year I would force myself to ride my bicycle to work. Albuquerque was not exactly a bike-friendly town, but I was determined to find a route, make it work, and to hell with the catcalls that would be coming my way.

It was ten miles to work, an hour bike ride from my apartment to the office. My route was mostly on the shoulders of busy streets, and even if I hadn't been deluged by catcalls, it would have been nerve-wracking. Some drivers delighted in flicking lit cigarette butts out their car windows at me. One guy even opened his passenger door as he passed me, hoping, I suppose, that I would hit it. Most lacked even the most rudimentary knowledge of physics because their ejected debris frequently missed its target.

Albuquerque still had quite a few farms and ranches scattered around town, though they were getting sold off at an alarming rate to make room for new subdivisions and strip malls. I was happy to find Oglala, a mile-long stretch of dirt road that connected two major streets. As soon as I turned onto Oglala, I felt my body relax. The noise level dropped noticeably, as few cars traveled it. The road had a couple of farms on each side and one ranch, which had cattle. On a nice day, I smelled the hay and the corn in the fields. On not so nice a day, I smelled the manure and maybe the stench of a road-kill skunk.

My morning rides were usually cool, even in the middle of summer. If the weather had been dry, Oglala was smooth, making it an easy ride. The occasional car rumbled past me, its wheels throwing up dirt and small rocks, stinging my bare legs and leaving me temporarily blinded in a cloud of dust. After a rain, the road was worse; it transformed into a muddy quagmire that eventually dried into a bone-jarring washboard that bounced me around so hard I could barely keep my bike upright.

Halfway down Oglala was an old farmhouse that sat back from the road. With its weathered powder-blue clapboard siding and its metal pitched roof, it was out of place in Albuquerque, as if a tornado had plucked it from a Kansas cornfield and dropped it here. A huge cottonwood tree stood in the front yard with a tractor tire swing hanging from its low branches. Sometimes I'd see a few chickens pecking around under the tree.

And there were dogs. Three of them. The first few weeks I rode by the farm, at least two of the dogs would zoom around from the back of the house, bounding toward the fence. Once at the fence, they'd bark their heads off until I was well past the house. The fence struck me as flimsy and much, much too low. I was pretty sure that given the proper enticement, the dogs were capable of jumping it.

I tried to figure out a way to protect myself. I could carry a big stick; maybe strap it to my handlebars somehow. No, scratch that. I was so inept, I'd fumble it trying to get it off the handlebars, then the dogs would pounce on me and tear my face off and with my one good eye, the one they'd neglected to claw out, I'd watch the biggest dog trot down the road with my stick in its mouth.

I didn't want to stop going down Oglala; it was my favorite part of the whole ride. Maybe I could make friends with the dogs. I considered throwing them little snacks but nixed the idea, figuring their owner would come out and ream me, accuse me of trying to poison them.

At last, I had a plan. Slowly, slowly I would get them accustomed to having me around. If a dog could get used to a collar on its neck, surely it could become accustomed to a person riding by on a bike a couple of times a day. I tested this theory, riding on the far side of the road so they wouldn't be threatened, but when they came into view, I stopped and called out sweetly to them. "Puppies! Puppy dogs! How are you today? Good doggies, aren't you such good doggies?" The first few weeks I did this, they still barked the whole time I spoke to them and looked ready to lunge at me. By the fourth week, they barked as they came around the side of the farmhouse to investigate the noise, but as soon as they heard my voice, they quit barking and stood at the fence, eyeing me suspiciously. By the sixth week, they barked no more and instead whined at the fence as if they wanted me to come over. Eventually I got up the nerve to approach the fence and stuck my finger through a hole in the wire mesh, giving each dog a little stroke on the muzzle.

When the ride was monotonous, I'd pass the time inventing names for the dogs. I chose "Molly" for the black and white Border collie. The long, sleek dog that was part Weimaraner I named "Auckland." I liked this name not because it necessarily suited the dog but because the name Auckland conjured up the idea of getting the hell out of New Mexico and going to some exotic far-away land. (In my mind, any place with trees and flowers and water was exotic.) The other dog was a mutt, perhaps part German shepherd. Of the three dogs, I judged it to be the most likely to chase me down and rip off my arm. So I gave him a name to help diffuse the fear I felt when I saw him. I named him "Cupcake."

With the dogs now under control, my mind was at ease. Most days, I enjoyed the sublime solitude of the ride. Other days,

I thought about Izzy and wished she were with me. It had been months since I'd heard from her. The last time I saw her, she'd come home over her Christmas break. It was an unseasonably warm late December afternoon, so we sat on her front steps just like in the old days.

She told me all about MIT. As she spoke, an evil worm of jealousy began to burrow into my heart. Yes, oh, yes, I was very happy for her, but damn it, she was already a sophomore and digging into the juicy stuff like artificial intelligence, and here I was, still a freshman because I had to work full time, taking worthless idiotic classes like Medieval Renaissance History because it was the only thing offered at night that fit my schedule. Charlemagne, schmarlemagne! Izzy was going to have her frickin' Ph.D. in nuclear physics or some damn thing and I'd still be slogging along in night school.

I had a tough time coming up with anything to say about school without sounding bitter. Maybe MIT was a blast, but what about Massachusetts? Maybe it sucked—yeah, I'll ask her about that.

"It's so cold in Cambridge, I can barely stand it!" she said. "When it snows, it's not like when it snows here. It doesn't melt! They scrape it off the roads and still it doesn't melt, it just turns into this big petrified pile of filthy stuff that lasts all winter. And don't get me started on the humidity!" I had no idea what "humidity" felt like, but it seemed to be something that everybody hated. Excellent! I took off my sweater, basking in the luscious Santa Fe sunshine, just to rub it in.

"What do you do for fun?" I said.

"Oh, there's all kinds of things to do: museums, the symphony, art galleries, and all this historical stuff in Boston like old boats. They call them 'tall ships' I think."

The only museum I'd ever been inside of was the Palace of the Governors on the Plaza. A "palace" sounds interesting and exotic, yes. But The Palace of the Governors is not interesting or exotic. New Mexico was once part of a vast Spanish territory and The Palace of the Governors was home to some of its bureaucrats. The building looks less like a palace and more like a Department of Motor Vehicles. I'd been there on school trips as a child and was occasionally coerced into going there when my parents wanted to show out-of-town visitors all the enchantment Santa Fe had to offer. If pottery shards, arrowheads, and conquistador crapola excite you, you'll love it. Otherwise, you're better off moseying across the street to TG&Y for a Frito pie and a stroll down the parakeet aisle.

Obviously, comparing cultures would be a waste of time.

I could brag about having a boyfriend, if I had one, which I didn't. Izzy knew Orlando and I had reunited at UNM, so maybe I could exaggerate a little and claim that he was my boyfriend. The fact that he was sleeping with Jackie didn't mean that he didn't like me, too. Except he and I weren't sleeping together. Or dating each other. All right, scrub that idea.

Barring the weather (and maybe the food), whatever Santa Fe had to offer no doubt paled in comparison to the glamor and sophistication of Massachusetts. Forget school, forget culture, forget boys. Still, there had to be something I could deride.

"Are you going to start talking 'Boston,' you know, saying stuff like 'Let's go to the lee-kah stoh-ah and get some bee-ahs' or whatever?"

"Don't be ridiculous. I would never talk like that."

"No?"

"No way. I'd say, 'Let's go to the lee-kah stoh-ah and get some bee-ahs, *pendeja*.'"

We laughed then, and I laughed again now, recalling it as I rode down Oglala. I wanted to hang on to that memory of her, but something was happening to it. Izzy's voice in my head was still perfectly clear, but I couldn't quite remember what that moment had *felt* like. It was as if the real feeling had decayed and in its place was something else, something subconsciously invented. Maybe she was experiencing the same thing; I hadn't heard from her since Christmas.

I pedaled on a few minutes, and then something occurred to me. Even if I saw her over the next school break, she wouldn't be the Izzy I knew, the one who cussed and got in fistfights and stared at the ceiling when she needed to think. The Izzy who ate tamales with her hands, hated to wear shoes, and fell in and out of love with boys so fast they never knew what hit them. The next time I saw her, her long hair would probably be cut fashionably short, her manners would be impeccable, and she would have much to say about the sorority she just joined, the crisis in the nation's nuclear energy program, and her new Ph.D.-candidate boyfriend.

Izzy—*my* Izzy—was already gone.

15

Santa Fiends love to talk about green chile peppers: where to get the best chile, how to roast them so the skins come off easily, who sells the hottest ones, was Hatch chile as good as everybody said it was. People make green chile stew with it, of course, but in Santa Fe we also put it on hamburgers, mix it with scrambled eggs, slather it on pizzas. Chopped green chile was on my family's dinner table at almost every meal.

These days you can simply go to the neighborhood grocery store and buy the chiles already peeled and roasted, but when I was growing up, you bought them fresh from roadside stands and roasted them at home.

Preparing chiles often turned into a weekend-long production, so if someone offered you help, you took it. And if you had daughters you could shame into helping? That worked too. So it was that I found myself that beautiful fall day trapped in my mom's kitchen, the wonderful smell of green chile permeating the air and the oil from the chiles setting our raw cuticles on fire.

We had been roasting and peeling for hours and were exhausted. It is grueling work. First you roast the chiles. Then, one chile at a time, you pull off its skin. Next you scrape the stem and the seeds out. Then you chop up the meat of the chile and freeze it for later. Actually that's not quite the right order—I left out the most important step. *First* you take out your contact lenses. *Then* you start handling the chiles.

At day's end, we'd prepared enough chile to last through winter. Mom set some aside for me, filling a Styrofoam cooler with the precious stuff so I could take it back to Albuquerque. If Emily found out I had a cooler full of chile and had hoarded it all for myself, there would be hell to pay, so I decided to swing by her house on the way home so we could divvy it up. Maybe I'd surprise Nola with some, too. She'd helped me with my taxes but refused to take any money for her troubles. A few packages of chile would let her know how much I appreciated the help.

Over the last few months, Travis had become a regular fixture at Nola's, so I had tried, really tried, to like him. It didn't work. Every encounter with him only served to reinforce my loathing and mistrust. As I stood at Nola's door, I prayed he'd be elsewhere: at work, out of town, or in jail.

Travis answered the doorbell.

He stood in the doorway, giving me the once over the way he always did. Was it an expression of craven lust? Or was he smarter than I thought he was and had figured out how I truly felt about him and was scanning me for weapons?

"What's in the cooler?" he said.

"Just ice. I'm here to collect your organs for donation," I said, my voice flat, funereal. He was holding a beer. "Oh, wait—I see it's too late for that. Your liver is obviously defiled and will be of no use to us."

"Smart ass," he said, stepping aside to let me in, then suddenly thrusting his foot out in front of me, trying to trip me.

"Hardee-har-har! See, I can be funny, too!" he said. His watery blue eyes met mine.

My right shoulder imperceptibly recoiled as my left leg stepped back into position, a fist formed . . .

Nola appeared behind him. "Whatcha got there?" she said, unwittingly saving Travis from having an Igloo cooler slammed into his skull.

"Green chile," I said, relaxing my grip on the cooler. "My mom and I peeled a bushel this weekend, so I brought you some. It's the least I can do for your help with my taxes."

"You didn't have to do that. I wasn't expecting anything."

"Hey, you protected me from the ignoramuses at the mall." She had taught me to never let those back-alley tax preparers anywhere near my W-2s.

We went in the kitchen, leaving Travesty on the couch to watch *The Dukes of Hazzard*. I took some chiles out of the cooler and she showed me where to put them in the freezer. "Over there. No, next to the peas. Now move the pork chops over. And put the sausage patties to the right of the chops." Finally everything in the freezer was arranged according to her master freezer plan.

We spoke to each other in our own silly version of New Mexican Spanglish, something my friends (Anglo and Latino alike), sometimes did.

"Any chiles for him, *esa?*" I said, pointing with my chin toward the living room.

"*Eee-jolé.* The gringo—he is a sissy. No chiles for him."

"*Bueño, esa.* More for us, *qué no?*"

"*Sí, mi hita,*" she said, and we giggled.

"What are you gals doing in there?" Travis called out.

"Nothing, sweetie, nothing at all."

We walked back into the living room and she sat down next to him on the sofa. I sat in a chair opposite them. I noticed Travis had his beer can on a coaster. His feet were up on the coffee table, but his boots were off. Good—he was making himself at home, but not *too* at home. Maybe things weren't totally out of hand. Yet.

"Emily and I need to go to Santa Fe next weekend. Want to ride up with us? We can take you over to your mom's for a visit," I said.

"Thanks for the offer, but I can't. Travis and I are going shopping."

"Shopping? For what?"

Travis took a swig of his beer, in what I'm sure he believed was an extra-studly way. "A big, red shiny truck."

"And why do *you* have to get dragged along on this exciting shopping excursion?" I said.

"He wants to make sure I like it, too."

"Why? It's his truck. Why should he care if you like it?"

"Because it might be her truck, too," Travesty said, taking another swig. "Yup. Nothing like a brand new, bright red, air-conditioned Dodge Ramcharger with a 318 V8 and full-time four-wheel drive, to get a girl hot and —"

"What possible use could Nola have for a truck?" I said, cutting off his caterwauling.

"It even has an ice chest built into the console," he said. "If you get the deluxe interior, that is, which we would. For Nola."

"It'll be handy for moving," Nola said.

I eyed them both suspiciously. "Moving? Moving what?"

"Stuff," Travis said, enjoying this little game.

"What kind of *stuff*?"

"I might be moving in with Travis. Or he might be moving in with me," Nola said.

"Or maybe nobody is moving in with anybody," I said, trying to hide my irritation.

"We haven't decided yet. We're just talking about it."

If I voiced my objections, she'd think it was just my usual jaded, cynical, overly protective crazy talk and she wouldn't listen. I wasn't any good at manipulating people. What would Emily do in a situation like this? Hmm. Got it—I can make her parents the bad guys. "Your mom and dad are going to flip out," I said.

"Nola's a grown woman. She can do whatever she wants," Travis said as he slipped his arm around her shoulders, pulling her closer to him.

Nola was smiling, happy to have her man next to her. Maybe she was thinking, "He may be a nimrod, but dammit, he's my nimrod." I'd have to attack this problem another day—a day without him there, working his pointy-toed-boot, hairy-chested, chunky-ass gold-bracelet-wearing voodoo on her.

A few weeks later I dropped in on Nola again. We took glasses of ice tea onto her tiny balcony, enjoying the warm September afternoon. We settled into a couple of rickety hand-me-down lawn chairs.

"Where's Travis? I thought he'd practically moved in with you." *And why not, what with the free food and beer and all.*

"He had to drive down to Los Lunas for work."

"How come he always comes over here and you never go over there?" *What's he hiding?*

"Because it's more comfortable for us over here. I've got all my girly stuff here. It's kind of a pain for me to pack it up and go over there."

Crap. That made perfect sense.

"How'd your little-red-truck search go?"

"It was a lot of fun. Travis sure knows how to work the car salesmen. It was interesting to watch him in action," she said.

I bet, I thought. He has car salesman DNA.

"We found one that he really likes. I think he's going to buy it. You know, he really does need a more reliable car. He has to drive all over northern New Mexico, and if his car should break down on him out in the toolies, it wouldn't be good. Did I tell you that he got stuck in Cuyamunge a few weeks ago and had to wait hours for a tow truck to come along? Poor thing. If anybody needs a new car, it's him."

Well, boo-fucking-hoo for him, I wanted to say.

"I'm a little bugged by something though," she said.

"What? Is it his preposterous sideburns?"

This remark was met with a cold stare. "Quit it. I'm serious now. Behave for ten minutes, can't you?"

"Sorry."

"He wants me to lend him some money for the truck."

"He WHAT???"

"He wants me to lend him $4,000 so that he can buy the pickup truck."

"You must be joking. Please tell me you're joking."

"He's got part of the down payment, but he needs more so he can get his monthly payments down. He had some savings when he was married, but his ex-wife took him to the cleaners. When they got divorced, she got the house, the good car, all the furniture, and most of their savings."

"She got the mine, he got the shaft?"

"Exactly."

"Why is it that every divorced woman I know says *she* got screwed in the divorce settlement and every divorced guy I know says *he* got screwed?"

"Just one of those little mysteries of life."

"Why is it your problem that his ex-wife screwed him? If the guy doesn't have the money to buy a new car, then maybe he shouldn't get a new car. I mean, hey, look at what I'm driving." I pointed down to the street, where my 1971 Volkswagen Beetle was parked. My dad had rescued it from the junkyard and fixed it up for me. In winter, I drove with an ice scraper in my lap, for those occasions when I needed to scrape the frost off the *interior* of the windshield. It wasn't much of a car, but I hadn't leeched off anybody to get it. I paid for it and I paid my dad for working on it.

"I know, I know. But it's not like he's asking me to *give* him the money. It's a loan."

"Why are you trying to talk yourself into this? He's a *loan officer*, for Christ's sake. Why doesn't he get a loan from the bank?"

"He told me his credit is terrible, that his ex-wife hosed it all up for both of them."

"Man, I don't know . . . Where would you get that kind of money?"

"My savings. I've got almost $10,000 saved up for the house."

I was stunned. I never imagined it possible for a young single woman to amass such a vast fortune! She'd been talking about buying a house ever since she got her divorce settlement, and now I knew it was more than just talk. Travis must know about it, that gold digging deadbeat!

"Did you tell him that?" I asked, but I already knew the answer.

"Yeah, I told him. He was pretty excited about it. He said, 'Wow, you can loan me the money and still have some left over for our house. Cool.'"

"He said 'our' house?"

"Yeah, isn't it great?"

"No, not cool, definitely not cool. Things could get messy if it doesn't work out."

"Oh, believe me, I know. But I feel like I have to trust the guy. I mean, isn't that what love is all about?"

"Todd. That's all I'm going to say."

"Thanks. Thanks for bringing him up. What's your deal anyway? I know you don't like Travis, that you've never liked him. Why not? What's he ever done to you?"

"For starters, I don't like the way Emily and I almost never see you anymore. We have to practically make an appointment to do anything together. And he's always around. He's like a piece a gum stuck on your shoe. A dirty, yucky piece of gum. With a chunk of hair on it."

"Easy there. That's my boyfriend you're talking about."

"If he needs money, why doesn't he sell off some of his dumb-ass *Lost in Space* crap?" He was always bragging about how much his "collection" was worth. "Who knows what he might be able to get for that space pod model or that nifty lunch box?"

"I already asked him that. He said he needs to hang on to it for at least five more years so he can get the best value for it."

"Give me a break. He's being idiotic. I mean, seriously, I don't see how you can date a guy who isn't as smart as you are."

"Being smart isn't everything."

I took a swig of my ice tea, briefly considering the possibility that Nola might be right, that if you want to find true love, you must be willing to take a chance, let your guard down, be vulnerable.

Nah. That's asinine. "You deserve better," I said.

"You're beginning to sound a lot like my dad."

"Sorry. Who am I to give you financial advice? I'm not the one who's figured out how to save up $10,000. But if he cares about you, he won't ask you to give—I mean *lend*—him money. He needs to pull himself up by his own jockstrap."

"Nice one," she said.

"Thanks. Feel free to use it."

We watched the sun going down over the Sangre de Cristo Mountains, the sky full of towering, frothy clouds turning surrealistic shades of pink, both of us lost in our thoughts. She thinking of love and romance, me thinking of the smog and the high level of particulates in the atmosphere.

16

Orlando was coming over for Halloween, which was a relief. I liked handing out candy to the little kids trick-or-treating, but the fun was overshadowed by my fear of opening my door to strangers. If Orlando was here, I figured I'd be safe. Plus, ever since Jackie sunk her claws into him, I'd gotten no more than an occasional brief phone call from him.

It was still light outside when my doorbell rang. I didn't have a peephole, so called out, "Who is it?"

"Ted Bundy." Damn it. Orlando knows me too well.

I opened the door to find him standing there with a brown paper grocery bag over his head. He'd made cutouts for his eyes and mouth and taped an unruly wad of purple fringe around the top of it for hair.

He thrust out his open palm. "Trick-or-treat!"

I put a tiny bag of candy corn in his hand.

"Witch's Teeth! Oh, I love these." He took the paper bag off his head, ripped open the package and stuck two pieces of candy under his upper lip, then pranced around with his little orange fangs. "Rrrrrawwrrr! Rrrrrawwwwwrr!" he growled until the candy fell out of his mouth onto the floor. "Aww, heck." He bent down and picked them up. "Oh, well, it's Halloween!" he said, then crammed them into his mouth.

"I had no idea you were so crazy about candy corn. I would have bought more."

He shook another handful of the candy into his mouth and chewed happily. Until he saw my TV. "Is that your only TV?"

"Yeah. Why?"

"What is it, twelve inches?"

"I don't know. Why do you ask? Are you mocking my TV?"

"Black and white?" He looked worried.

"Of course. Whatdaya think I am, a Rockefeller?"

"Well, jeez, how are we supposed to watch *Young Franken-stein* on that?"

"I bought you some beer."

"Well, thanks, but I don't really see how that's going to help."

"You will. Let's just eat and worry about it later."

"Yeah, but . . . "

"Keep it up and you aren't going to get any more candy corn."

"Witch's Teeth."

"Whatever."

"Where's Nola? You said she was coming over, too, didn't you?"

"Yeah, but she said she was going to be late so we should start dinner without her."

Though it was October, the weather was still nice, so we grabbed our bowls of green chile and took them outside to the patio, which faced the street. I told him we'd hang out there and if we spotted any trick-or-treaters, we could dash back inside to meet them at the door. Or maybe we could just fling candy over the railing at them.

Orlando was halfway through his chile and on his second beer before he got to what was really on his mind. "You know that girl Jackie I told you about, the one my cousin works with over at Hernandez Real Estate?"

"You mean the gorgeous one who lives near the Plaza and wanted you to go to Mazatlan with her for a week?"

"Yeah, her."

"Nope, sorry, don't remember a thing about her."

"I can see that. Well, anyways, I want to dump her, but I'm worried about how she's going to take it. When I told her that I was coming over here to see you and Nola, she blew a gasket."

Be cool, I thought. Let him tell his story.

At first everything with Jackie was great, he said. But now money was becoming a problem. He said he believed when a guy first starts dating a girl, sure, it's fine to expect the guy to pay for everything when they go on dates. But after you've been dating a few months, shouldn't the girl have to pay for stuff once in a while? At least offer to pay? Especially if the girl makes more money than the guy?

Well, yeah, I told him, I thought that expenses should be split. Unless there's a huge discrepancy between what the two people make. But I also told him that I'd met very, very few women who thought the same way I did about that. Or anything else, for that matter.

She's really jealous, too, he said. If she called him after work and he wasn't home, she wanted to know why. Whenever he had a baseball game to play, if she couldn't make it to the game, she'd give him the third degree about it later, wanting to know exactly when the game ended and where he went afterward. At first, it was kind of endearing, but now it was really getting on his nerves.

He'd told her that they weren't "exclusive" and she'd cried for an hour. (*Wait, what? They weren't exclusive? Why didn't he tell me that before?*) He'd tried to comfort her, but she got mad and threw him out. Then she called him at 2 a.m., drunk, and called him every name in the book. He'd thought, *Yay! It's finally over!* But the next day, she'd called him at work (which he hated) and apologized and wanted him to come over after work for something "special."

"What? What was it?" I asked him.

Orlando looked down at his sneakers, fiddled with one of the laces. Took a drink of beer. Tore off a piece of his tortilla. Rubbed the top of his head.

I thwacked him on the shoulder with my finger. "Well, are you going to tell me or not?"

"Not."

"Not? Not? Why'd you bring it up if you aren't going to tell me?"

"I wanted you to understand that Jackie can be very persuasive when she wants to be. Extremely persuasive."

As usual with him, just when things start to get juicy, he has to be a gentleman. Figures. Or maybe he expects me to read between the lines or somehow intuitively just *know* what he means by "extremely persuasive." Jeez, you'd think by now he'd know that I am utterly incapable of intuiting anything from anybody.

"Fine, I get the picture," I said, deciding it was OK that I didn't get the picture at all. "So now what's going on?"

A few weeks after Jackie's crying jag, he said, he met a girl named Fiona. She was the anti-Jackie. She worked at a plant nursery and lived in a little house on the south side, had a garden, practiced yoga. And, unlike Jackie, she didn't seem to care much about money.

Dammit all to hell. Just when I thought Jackie was out and I was in, some granola head ruins everything. I tried to stop myself, but failed. "You mean she's an old hippie? Some sort of

pot-smoking, commune-loving, incense-burning earth mother?"
I said.

"Hmm, let me think about that . . . well, she actually does like incense. And she's been known to smoke a joint every now and again. Not sure about the commune thing."

"Oh. I see." I nodded, knowingly.

"Cut it out, now. Fiona's a really sweet girl, and after being with Jackie, it's just so relaxing. Man, that Jackie . . . I just don't think I can take much more of the drama."

"Does Jackie know about Fiona?"

"Are you kidding? She'd gouge my eyes out if I told her I was interested in somebody else! That's exactly my problem. I'm pretty sure I want to break it off with her, be a man about it, tell her the truth, but I can't figure out how to do it without her exploding. I don't know what to do."

The sun was down now, and the trick-or-treaters were beginning to make their rounds. A few kids were coming up the sidewalk. Two of them looked to be about six years old and had ragged bed sheets over their heads, pretending to be ghosts. The third kid, a boy who was about ten, was dressed as a vampire. His cape was an old bath towel safety-pinned around his neck. He was having trouble keeping it in place and his plastic vampire fangs were making him drool. The towel was turning out to be pretty handy.

"Gotta get this," I said and went inside to greet the boys. I gave them some candy and was extra generous with the vampire.

Back out on the patio, I told Orlando, "I've been thinking about your dilemma."

"And?" he said, giving me a hopeful look.

"You're pretty well screwed."

"Well, gee thanks. Thanks for nothing."

"Sorry, man." I gave a helpless shrug.

We finished our chile in the darkness and then stood up to go in and watch the movie. As I turned to open the patio door, Orlando said, "Uh-oh. I think that Mustang over there is Jackie's!"

"Really?" I said, and craned my neck out over the patio railing, trying to get a better look. "Where? Over there? Is that it?" I pointed to a white car parked directly across from my apartment building.

"Oh crap. I can't believe she followed me over here."

"Maybe she hasn't seen us," I said, helpfully.

The Mustang's door opened.

"Fuck, fuck, fuck!" he said, as he tried to shrink back into the shadows of the patio.

I wasn't scared before but was now.

A woman I assumed was Jackie strode across the street, her black leather pumps making an ominous clicking sound on the pavement. She was wearing her real estate company's signature outfit: a blue blazer with massive shoulder pads and a hideous yellow neckerchief. I noted that she was carrying a purse roomy enough to hold an impressively sized handgun.

Before Orlando and I could flee for the safety of my living room, she was upon us. She hefted her purse up on the railing and it made a ponderous thud.

"So," she said, as if that told us everything.

"Jackie, what are you doing here?"

"'The question is, 'What are *you* doing here?'"

Usually he had a somewhat slouchy posture, but now he straightened up. "No, that's not the question. You have no right to follow me around town, spying on me. We need to have a serious talk about this. But not here. I'll call you tomorrow. Now, I think you need to leave."

"Is this *her*?" She gave me the once over. "Is this the whore I heard you talking to on the phone the other day?"

I was on my feet, my hand on the railing, ready to vault over it and strangle her with her repugnant yellow scarf.

Orlando deftly stepped between the railing and me.

"OK now, OK, let's all calm down and take it easy. Jackie, please, I'm asking you to just go back to your car and go on home. I'll call you tomorrow."

"I will NOT calm down. I want to know what the HELL is going on here, and I'm not going home until I find out. Who is this BITCH?"

My hand was pressing hard on Orlando's back now, but it was he who made the decision to go over the railing. In one graceful motion, he was over and had taken Jackie's hand in his. "C'mon now, it's not about Sylvie, so just leave her out of it. Let's go back to your car now, all right?" he said in a soothing voice.

"No, I don't want to!" she said and yanked her hand away from him.

A blue Impala pulled into the parking lot next to my apartment. The driver's leg appeared, pushing the car door open. Nola! She got out and walked toward us, swaying back and forth in her typical rocking fashion.

Jackie was facing her, and even in the darkness, Nola's strange gait grabbed her attention.

"Hoo-hoo!" Nola called out cheerily as she came up the sidewalk. "Whatcha guys doing?" Her eyes went to mine, then to Orlando's. What she saw there, I don't know, but she turned to Jackie.

"Hi, I'm Nola." She waggled her tiny arm up and down in an exaggerated way that I'd never seen her do before. "Are you a friend of Orlando's? I hope you don't mind if I borrow him for a few minutes. I've got a big pumpkin in my trunk. The clerk at the Piggly Wiggly was kind enough to load it in the car for me, but as you can see —" there was more of her strange arm waggling "—I'd have a bit of a problem getting it out of the car by myself. So what do ya say, Orlando, can you give me a hand?"

Jackie was riveted.

She turned to look at the Impala, then back at Nola. Perhaps she concluded that if she was going to go on a killing spree, maybe it could wait until tomorrow after all.

"Jackie? Can I walk you to your car?" Orlando offered once more.

"Forget it," she said, snatching her purse off the railing. She gave me a hateful look, then glared at Orlando. "Call me. Tomorrow." Then with military precision, she pivoted on one spiked heel and crossed the street to her Mustang.

Orlando and Nola walked over to her Impala and she handed him her car keys so he could open the trunk. Nola turned to look at Jackie, who was now in her car, the engine idling. Nola waved at her and hollered, "Bye-bye now! Have a nice Halloween!"

The Mustang burned rubber.

Orlando peered into the trunk. "Hey, there's no pumpkin in here."

"Nope. No pumpkin." She shrugged and smiled. "Guess I'm just a big, fat liar."

They both laughed and Orlando draped an affectionate arm over her shoulder. "You're really something, you know that?

You just saved me from getting kicked in the *cajones* and Sylvie from going to prison for assault. Boy, do I ever owe you."

"Aww, 'tweren't nothin'."

"If you knew Jackie, you'd know that's not true."

I nervously glanced down the street, straining to see if Jackie had changed her mind and was stopped at the end of the block, revving the Mustang's engine, preparing to gun it, come hurtling down the street, mow them both down.

"Want some Witch's Teeth?" he said, checking his pocket to see if he had any left.

"Do I!"

"Are you two going to stand out there jawing all night or are we going to watch *Young Frankenstein*?" I hollered.

Orlando leaned over, whispered something to Nola, and they laughed. She opened her mouth and he delicately placed a piece of candy corn on her tongue.

An unexpected and almost imperceptible twinge of jealously gave my brain a tiny jolt, but before I could grab onto it, hold it in my hand, autopsy it, the feeling was gone.

17

Memories of Witch's Teeth, she-devils, and phantom pumpkins faded, trampled by Christmas carols blaring incessantly, a constant crush of traffic between Albuquerque's shopping malls and Santa Fe, and high anxiety over finding the perfect gift, serving the most delicious feast, throwing the best party.

Ah, the lovely Christmas holiday season in Santa Fe, "The City Different," where, as with most holidays in that town, saints were celebrated, beer was consumed in massive quantities, and more than one wife or girlfriend was going to get punched by a loving husband or boyfriend by the time we rang in the New Year.

My family had a tradition of driving around town to look at Christmas displays, but now that we were older, only Emily and I kept the tradition alive. It seemed to be the only one we had left. Clint, still in the oil fields of North Dakota, had called yesterday and said he wasn't coming home for the holidays. Emily, Nola, and I were at my parents' house when he called and I practically jerked the phone out of my mom's hand.

"What do you mean you 'can't make it'? Who's gonna watch *Twilight Zone* reruns with me? Who's gonna make fun of Grandma's crocheted gifts with me? Whose gonna puke up eggnog and Southern Comfort with me?"

"I don't know. Emily?"

Right. He knew damn well that Emily liked crochet. Eggnog, too.

"But why? Why can't you come?"

He had a girlfriend, he said. They were going over to her parents' house in Fargo on Christmas Day.

That ripped it. No point in arguing with him. "All right then. Come home when you can, I guess. We'll just have to mail you the gun rack cozy that Grandma's made for you."

I handed the phone back to my mom then turned to Emily. "Let's ride."

Emily drove, Nola rode shotgun, and I sat in the back.

"Now, what is it exactly we're doing?" Nola asked.

"We're going to drive around town and look at Christmas lights," Emily said.

"What for?"

"Because it's tradition and because they're pretty, dammit, that's what for," I said, still mad about Clint and Izzy not being in town for the holidays.

"Jeepers! Excuse me for asking!"

"You've never done this before? What did you and your family do for Christmas when you were little?" Emily said.

"We went to visit my Aunt Helen and Uncle Pete and my cousins in Florida."

"Florida! That sounds like a blast! Where abouts?"

"Sarasota."

"Oooo, Sarasota, huh? Sarasota, Florida. Sounds exotic!"

It did, indeed. Of course, neither Emily nor I had any idea where Sarasota was. Nor were we aware that the average Sarasota citizen was about 128 years old.

"So, what did you do in Sarasota, darling?" Emily asked, attempting to sound like Mrs. Howell, the rich lady on *Gilligan's Island*. Or she could have been imitating Donald Penobscot on *M.A.S.H*. Hard to tell. Emily did terrible impressions.

"The usual stuff. We went to church and opened presents and had a big turkey dinner, you know. Laid on the beach if it was warm enough, that sort of thing."

"The beach! Oh, that sounds fantastic!"

"It was a good time. Sadly, my aunt and uncle are both gone now and we haven't been back there since they died. This year I'm going to my parents' and we'll have a quiet Christmas at their house."

"What about you and Travis? Are you two doing anything special?" Emily asked.

"I wish! I was really hoping we would do something together, but he went back to Arkansas for a couple of weeks. That's where his parents live. He'll be back on Thursday."

I said, "Arkansas, huh? Their unofficial state motto is 'Literacy Ain't Everything.' Did you know that?"

Nola ignored my comment, asking instead, "What was Christmas like for you guys when you were growing up?"

She asked, so I told.

All my grandparents lived in Roswell, and some aunts, uncles and cousins, too, so when I was a kid, that's usually where we gathered for Christmas. My parents piled Emily, Clint, and me loose in the back seat of our 1954 Buick, oblivious to the dangers of its lack of seat belts, airbags, safety glass, and childproof locks. The trip was a 200-mile stretch of godforsaken highway, devoid of anything remotely entertaining to even the most industrious child. A cluster of scrubby piñon trees and maybe a cow or two occasionally broke the monotony of the first twenty miles.

Once you got past those first twenty miles, the road became a sandblasted strip of unrelenting tedium with nothing to look at except the dirt, parched scrub grass, and barbwire fences.

My main diversion on these trips was Clint, and when he and I behaved (which was rarely), my mom might buy us a few comic books to read. As we careened south on US-285, my dad high on Valium and a Coors or three, Clint and I struggled to read *The Fantastic Four* through a cloud of Camel cigarette smoke. In the meantime, Emily flipped through a catalog of the latest McCall's dress patterns, straining to hear the music coming through the earphones of her transistor radio, its signal fading in and out.

We usually stopped for lunch at a rest stop, and by "rest stop" I mean a weathered wooden picnic table next to a rusted out trash barrel that was invariably overflowing. My mom pulled cheese and pimento sandwiches out of a grease-stained paper bag, along with some soft drinks and chips. We sat at the table and ate our meal in silence as we stared out over the desolate landscape. This was our idea of a fun family outing.

If the family budget allowed, we'd skip the rest stop and instead continue on to Vaughn, a railroad town that marked the halfway point between Santa Fe and Roswell. With a population of about 400 people, dining options were limited, so we always ended up at The Cactus Café for hamburgers. Some might find it odd that we got excited about having a hamburger in some tiny hick town, but going out to a restaurant—any restaurant—was a once- or twice-a-year event.

The Cactus was a big place (or so it seemed to a kid) with a lunch counter that wrapped all the way around a waitress station. The diner's perimeter was lined with booths covered in shiny red vinyl. The railroad station was across the street. Grizzled railroad men came in wearing their work clothes and blue-and-white-striped hats, their fingernails stained yellow from smoking hand-rolled cigarettes. Sometimes an honest-to-goodness cowboy dropped by, clomping through the place in his dusty, scuffed boots, holding his sweat-stained cowboy hat in his hand. Clint and I scanned every cowboy's hip, hoping to find a pistol there. Sadly, we never did.

Each table had a jukebox control, one of those metal boxes with song lists printed on laminated pages. You flip the pages until you find a song you like, insert your coins, and push the corresponding buttons to select the song. A5—"The Purple People Eater." Oh, how Clint and I loved that song.

Again, there were stipulations: if we behaved, we might get the five cents to play a song. But, as usual, we *hadn't* behaved, so we didn't get the five cents and had to be content with just flipping the little pages of songs back and forth, back and forth, until my mom got so annoyed, one of us kids got smacked. We also loved to sit at the counter, which also had the jukebox controls. You could play with the controls there, too, and as an added special bonus, you could spin and spin and spin on the counter stools, which also irritated the hell out of my mom, so whoever was closest to her would ultimately get a stinging slap to the back. Looking back on all this smacking and slapping, I'm beginning to wonder why we liked the place so much.

Traveling in the winter meant it would be dark by the time we got to Roswell. Often the kids (and occasionally the driver) would be asleep by then. When I was small, I liked to ride up on the rear deck of the back seat and drift off to sleep as I gazed at the stars. As we approached the northern edge of town, my mom woke us up so we wouldn't miss the city's Christmas lights along Main Street. Back then, I was convinced such beautiful lights must have cost a fortune. Basically, they consisted of tinsel and colored lights wrapped around the streetlight cables, with the tinsel occasionally punctuated by a big plastic medallion with a picture of Santa or candy canes or a reindeer on it. Tacky and gaudy by today's standards, they nevertheless mesmerized us as we rolled down Main. After all, in Santa Fe all we ever saw were dumb ol' bags of dirt called *farolitos*. These are sand-filled paper bags with a candle stuck down into each one. The sand is supposed to keep the bag from tipping over. Then you light the candle. A bag. Sand. A candle. Big smelly deal. No way could a bag of dirt compete with the sparkle of Roswell's Main Street.

Clint and I stood up to lean on the back of the front seat, our heads close together as we squirmed trying to get a good view of the lights as we passed under them. "Look, look! There's a sleigh on that one! . . . Oh, oh! There's an elf! Aww . . . " Emily had seen the same lights for years and knew them well, so she played tour guide. "Keep your eyes on the left side of the street. Sears always has polar bears in the window!"

On Christmas Eve, we kids were told to get out of the house for a while so Santa Claus could get an early start on delivering the presents. Some combination of relatives would cram into a car or two and drive around Grandma's neighborhood to see how the neighbors had decorated for the holidays. Typically, outdoor decorations consisted of a strand of lights around a few windows or maybe some lights on a tree. If a neighbor went all out, he might have a cardboard sleigh in the yard as well. We were hopped up on fudge and holiday cookies and ready to burst from the anticipation of the fabulous presents that would be awaiting us when we got back home, so even these modest lighting displays thrilled us.

I thought Nola and Emily had stopped paying attention some time ago, but Nola piped up, "And Christmas morning? What was that like?"

What was that like? Terrible, I thought. As far back as I could remember, I never got the present I'd asked for, or if I did get it, it was still somehow *wrong*. When I was eleven years old, for instance. Beatle Mania was rampant in my elementary school and "Beatle boots" were the rage. I liked the Beatles and I liked boots, too, so for Christmas I'd asked my mom for a pair of Beatle boots. She had bought me many terrible gifts over the years, so this year I was determined to break the curse. I described the sleek, black beauties to her, sparing no detail. Surely, given my thoroughness, I would at last get precisely that which I so coveted. Christmas morning, instead of finding the Beatle Boots under the tree, I found a pair of gold-colored fake lamé house slippers embellished with plastic multi-colored rhinestones around the top.

I despised them but was unsure of my fashion sense. Maybe they actually *were* cool. I mean they were sparkly, and what kid didn't like sparkly? So I wore them to school one day. Tillie Brandt, Goddess of All 6th Graders, smirked at them and said, "Where'd you get those? Off your dead grandma?" and laughed. I jabbed her in the sternum with my index finger and said, "Who cares what *you* think, dumbass!"

The slippers mysteriously disappeared that night. And from that day forward, if Tillie had any opinions about what I was wearing, she did not share them with me.

Over the years since, whenever I thought of those hideous slippers, I envisioned the nearby gravel pit front-loader operator unearthing them and, struck with terror over what little-girl-body-part he might discover next, quit his job on the spot.

Too bad. If he kept looking he might also uncover a crocheted vest (circa 1966), a flamboyant orange petticoat (circa 1967) and a startlingly itchy wool reindeer sweater (also circa 1967).

But let's not discuss that, I thought. Don't want to sully reality with what few precious childhood memories I have.

"Well, how was Christmas morning?" Nola asked again.

"It was all right, I suppose."

My story ended, and the three of us sat in silence for a moment as we drove past the New Mexico Highway Department building, its rooftop ablaze with hundreds of farolitos. Tiny snowflakes began to fall, dissolving on the windshield. Lights twinkled from houses nestled in the trees, plumes of fragrant piñon smoke rising from their chimneys. We gazed out the windows into the darkness of the foothills, lost in our thoughts. Maybe Nola and Emily were thinking about having children of their own someday and how they would keep the Christmas-light-touring tradition alive. And me? I was wishing I could still fit up in the car's rear window deck and do nothing more than gaze at the stars.

1977

18

It was March and the winds had been blowing for days, making us edgy. Albuquerque rarely experienced tornados, and when it did they were weak, so the high winds were more annoying than dangerous. I'd been in bed since 10:00, trying to get to sleep, but the wind was making the bushes scrape ominously against my bedroom window. I'd start to drop off, then hear that scratching sound and would jolt awake, thinking someone was breaking in. By midnight, I was too exhausted and irritated to be frightened by the creaking and scratching noises, so I just lay there waiting for the night to end.

My phone rang. It was Nola. She was sick. Emily was in Santa Fe, so would I please come over? I asked what was wrong—how sick was she? Did she need an ambulance? No, no, just please come over.

I threw on some clothes and headed out to my car, the wind whipping my hair around, blowing grit in my mouth and eyes as I crossed the parking lot. I opened my car door, and the wind caught it, flinging it violently back on its hinges. Now fully awake and safely in the car, I could gather my wits. Nola's not the alarmist type; if she said she felt sick, that meant she was *sick*. Why didn't I call an ambulance before I left the house? What's wrong with me? Why did I listen to her? What if I got to her place and she was already dead? What would her parents do when I had to admit to them that *I* was the one who had convinced Nola to stay in Albuquerque, alone and unprotected? After a few minutes of this line of thought, my guilt was replaced by defensiveness. What'd she have to go and call me for? I don't know anything about anything. What do I look like, a gastroenterologist?

I pulled into her parking lot. This time as I got out of the car, I held on tight to the door so my arm wouldn't get torn off. I ran for the protection of her stairwell and made my way up to her door. While I tried to smooth down my tangled rat's nest of hair, I rang her bell. It was taking her way too long to answer. I held my key chain up to the dim porch light, checking to see if I still had the spare key she had given me, my fingers trembling.

She opened the door, appearing haggard and unsteady on her feet.

"Are you OK? What's hurting?" I said, trying to convey just the right mix of concern and calm, instead of fear and ignorance.

"I have to lie down," she said, turning away, heading back to her bedroom. She was limping. I followed her, cursing my ignorance, swearing that I would take a first aid class, learn all about CPR, wrapping tourniquets and performing tracheotomies with ballpoint pens.

She got in bed, and I covered her up. The sheets were clammy. There were beads of sweat on her forehead.

"Does your stomach hurt?"

"Yes. And my back. My back hurts. A lot."

"Do you have a fever?"

"I . . . don't . . . know." She drew in a breath, and her face squinched up in pain.

"Do you think it's your appendix?" When I was a kid, the only time people had to go to the hospital was when they had appendicitis. Or when they'd been stabbed, which happened more often than one might think.

"No, I had my appendix out a long time ago."

"Food poisoning?"

"Maybe. I don't know. Damn, it hurts." Suddenly, she swung her legs out of the bed and made a dash for the bathroom. I sat on the edge of the bed waiting. Then I heard her vomiting. If I were a better friend, I would be in there with her. But I knew from experience that when it came to vomiting, it was monkey-see-monkey-do. I'd start vomiting, too. I was already gagging just from listening to her in there. Emily, why did you have to be in Santa Fe tonight, of all nights? And, hey—where's Travesty? Why hadn't she called him instead of me? God, that retching sound! I grabbed her pillow and gave it a furious fluffing.

She came back in the bedroom and lay down on the bed.

"Do you want me to call an ambulance?" I reached for the telephone.

"No, Sylvie, don't. No ambulance."

"Why not?"

"I'm not that sick," she said, then closed her eyes.

I went into the bathroom, stuffed a piece of toilet paper in each of my nostrils to keep out the stench, and got a washcloth. I ran it under hot water and went back to her bedside. Her eyes were still closed, so she didn't see my packed nostrils. I surreptitiously pulled out the wads and stuffed them in my pocket.

"Here, maybe this will make you feel a little better," I said, wiping her face and neck with the washcloth. "Do you want some water? Let me get you some water." She nodded. I went to the kitchen and got a glass of water and a straw, propping her up so she could drink.

"Did you take anything? Aspirin? Pepto-Bismol? Alka-Seltzer?"

"I took some Pepto-Bismol about two hours ago."

"Did it do any good?"

"Nooooo." She moaned and squirmed around under the covers, tried to get comfortable.

"That's it. Dammit, I'm calling an ambulance."

"No, no, don't do that."

"Why the hell not?"

"I don't know. Just don't. I'll be OK. Just sit here with me for a while. Please?"

I sighed, exasperated and more than a little afraid for her. "Don't worry, I'm not going anywhere." I sat on the bed next to her, adjusting the covers around her. "Did you call your mom? Or Travesty?"

"Will you STOP calling him that? Please?"

"Well, did you call him?"

"Yes, of course I called him. But he wasn't home."

"When? When did you call him?"

"Right before I called you."

It was midnight when she called me. So where was Travesty at midnight on a Tuesday night? I was going to ask her this, but then I saw her face: her eyes pinched shut, her jaw clenched, beads of sweat on her upper lip.

"Shut up," she said.

"I didn't say anything."

"No, but I know what you're thinking."

Damn, she was good.

I stayed another hour, asking her at least four more times to let me call an ambulance or let me drive her to the emergency room. There was no convincing her. "Go home," she told me, "I'm so exhausted, I think maybe I can get to sleep now."

On the drive home, the wind was still screaming down Lomas Street, the traffic lights whipping on their cables at the intersections like something out of *The Last Picture Show*. Tumbleweeds swirled across the road, and every once in a while one would fly up onto the hood of my car, scraping across the windshield; then the wind would grab it again and fling it up into the air, sending it on its way, destined to be trapped against a chain link fence somewhere. The wretched weather wasn't making me feel any better about having left Nola alone. She told me to leave her, but I shouldn't have listened. She was probably delirious from the pain. If anything happened to her . . .

After a fitful night, I got up and went to work the next morning. I called Nola's house at noon, figuring she'd taken a sick day from her job, but no one answered. I got scared then, really scared. I called her parents. Her mom answered the phone and told me that Nola was there with her, in Santa Fe. Thank God! I hadn't killed her after all.

Her mom told me that Nola had gotten up at about 5:00 that morning and driven herself to the emergency room. A blood test confirmed the doctor's suspicion—hepatitis. The doctor instructed her to lie flat on her back as much as possible for a few weeks so she wouldn't injure her liver. Nola didn't want to wake me up again, so she'd called her mom instead, asking her to pick her up.

Nola took a leave of absence from her job and stayed with her parents until she felt well enough to return to work. I went to Santa Fe to visit her while she was convalescing. Her mom greeted me at the door and then led me back to the den, where Nola lay on the couch watching TV. Her face and the whites of her eyes had a noticeably yellowish cast to them.

"Wow. You look yellow," I said.

"Nice to see you, too," she said.

"I mean, your eyes. Wow."

"Yeah. Wow. It's called jaundice. Lovely, isn't it?"

"Sorry, man. How are you feeling? Are you getting better yet?"

"I'm a lot better now. I was pretty scared, that's for sure. I've never felt like that before."

"Why didn't you let me take you to the hospital?"

"I don't know. I guess I thought I'd feel better in the morning. I didn't want to show up at the emergency room like some big sissy when all I had was an upset stomach. But I couldn't get to sleep, and about an hour after you left, I still hurt. So I decided I'd go and get it over with."

"How do you think you got it?"

"The hepatitis? No way to know for sure, but the doctor at the emergency room said that I likely got it from eating something that was contaminated. Maybe when I went to The Royal Trough last month." It wasn't actually called The Royal Trough, but that was our nickname for it. It was a cheap buffet restaurant, and we always ate like pigs when we went there, no matter how much we promised beforehand that we wouldn't.

"How does the food get contaminated?"

"From the employees at the restaurant, usually. Fecal-oral transmission."

"Gack! What the hell!"

"Somebody on the kitchen staff who is infected goes to the bathroom, doesn't wash his hands, and then mixes the salad for the salad bar."

It was difficult for Nola to wash up in a public bathroom. I always thought that was bad, because she might be spreading germs, but it occurred to me now that her fingers were never anywhere near any of the nasty bits. Other people were much more likely to infect her than the other way around.

"I just need to stay on my back for a couple of weeks," she said. "I went to the doctor a couple of days ago, and she said I'm doing fine. Oh, and the new nurse there was *very* confused about how to take my blood pressure. That was pretty funny."

"Yeah, I bet she did find that somewhat of a puzzle. But we all know you're *special*. You're my special friend. *Special*, can you say that?"

"Yes, Mr. Rogers, I can say that. *Special*." She tried to kick me. Luckily, I was too far away for her to reach.

"Speaking of special—what's going on with Travis?"

"I've talked to him a few times since I got here. He's going to come over next weekend and keep me company."

"That's nice," I said, when I wanted to say, "Whoopty-frickin'-do." But I had to ask, "Did you find out why he wasn't home that night you called?"

"Yes, I did. He had to go up to Embudo to try to collect on a loan, and he got home late. So he unplugged his phone so he could get some sleep because he had an early day the next day."

When I had first met Travis and he'd told me that he was a loan officer, I thought that meant he wore a suit and tie and was some sort of high-class bank executive. I'd since come to learn that a loan officer job was only a tiny bit better than being a bank teller, and I knew being a bank teller was a rotten job. I'd also learned that low-level loan officers had to do collection work from time to time, which meant driving to some ratty little town (like Embudo) out in the middle of nowhere and walking up to somebody's trailer and hoping the owner doesn't point a rifle at you or that their dog Rambo doesn't chase you down and maul you before you make it back to your car.

I started calculating. Embudo was between Santa Fe and Taos. From Albuquerque, it was no more than a few hours' drive.

Let's say Travesty left work at 3:00, got there maybe at 5:00, just in time to catch the "client" getting home from work. Let's be generous and say he talked to the client for an hour, trying to get him to make the payment on his 1972 Pontiac Grand Prix, which had blown a rod two months ago and was parked on blocks in the front yard. No matter how I calculated the time, it wasn't adding up. Clearly the bastard was lying and she should dump him immediately.

"He unplugged his phone?" was all I said.

"Yeah, that's what he told me."

I wanted to dazzle her with my powers of deduction, explain the timetable, win her over with my irrefutable logic, convince her to see things my way.

She grimaced as she shifted around trying to get comfortable. I studied her yellow face and the dark circles under her eyes.

For months, I'd complained about Travis every time his name came up. Travis is undependable. Travis is selfish. Travis is lazy. Travis is a sponge and he's taking advantage of you. Maybe today, for Nola's sake, Travis needed a pass.

I reached over and snugged her blanket around her shoulders. "Let's have some popcorn and watch a movie. I think that Jerry Lewis movie is on tonight—*The Nutty Professor.* Whaddaya say?"

19

Spring came and went. Travis did not. This was most unfortunate.

Luckily (for me anyway) his job frequently required him to travel on Saturdays. On this particular Saturday, he was working up in Tesuque, so Nola had the whole day to herself. Emily suggested the three of us ride to Santa Fe together. We'd have a quick visit with the parents and check out a new place on the west side that was selling house trailers. Looking at trailers, apartments, and model homes was one of our favorite pastimes because no matter where we lived, we wished we lived somewhere else.

Emily was going to drive us in her 1970 cherry-red two-door Monte Carlo coupe. The car was old and broke down every other month. But among the three cars we owned, it was the only one with air conditioning. It was early morning, and as we walked out to the car the temperature was already pushing ninety degrees. I got in first, climbing into the cramped back seat. Emily walked around to the passenger side so she could open the car door for Nola. Nola could open car doors by herself, but it was easier if somebody did it for her, especially if the door was particularly heavy. Emily opened the door and Nola slid into the black vinyl seat and immediately started screeching.

"Ow, ow! Hot, hot, hot!" she hollered. Unable to pull the hem of her dress down, she flung herself backwards, pushing her feet hard into the floorboards, trying to get her bare thighs up off the vinyl seat.

Emily grabbed the hem of Nola's dress and yanked. "Quit thrashing around for two seconds so I can get your dress underneath you."

"Hurry, hurry, hurry! Ay-yi-yi!"

Emily struggled with the hem, finally getting it pulled down under Nola's legs.

"Ahhh, whew. Damn. Jeez, Louise! Wow. That was hot."

"Sorry about that. I should have warned you or put a towel down or something. You OK now?"

"Yeah, I'm fine," she said, still fidgeting and cussing under her breath, trying to get the pressure off of the tender, scalded patches on the backs of her legs. "Fire up that air conditioning."

Fifteen minutes later, the radio was blasting "Green Onions" by Booker T. and the MGs as we bobbed our heads and I pretended to play organ on the back of Nola's seat. We headed northbound on I-25, barreling down the murderous 50-mile stretch of highway between Albuquerque and Santa Fe. The three of us had driven this route hundreds of times, alone and together, but sometimes it was difficult to relax and enjoy the ride. Just when you started to have fun, you'd spot skid marks tracking off the side of the road or see hunks of tire retreads scattered on the median or a pile of broken glass. Or worst of all, you'd spot a new roadside cross marking the site of a fatal car crash, placed there by friends or family of the deceased. Some crash sites were marked with plain wooden crosses, the name of the victim, and the date of death carved or burned into it. Other sites were more elaborate. One in particular always caught our attention because it was freshly decorated with each new season. During the Christmas holidays, a little artificial tree would appear at the site, wrapped with a red aluminum garland, a silver foil star at the top. Other times of the year, the site might be surrounded by pots of plastic flowers. Sometimes you'd see a large stuffed animal propped up on the cross. Whenever I saw the stuffed animals, I suppose I should have been thinking about the child who may have died there, but instead I found myself wondering if that big teddy bear smelled bad from having been left out in the rain and snow for weeks.

The highway between Santa Fe and Albuquerque was the most heavily traveled in the state. Everybody in Santa Fe knew someone who was injured or killed while travelling it. There were so many memorials on it that occasionally the highway department attempted to restrict them. They wanted to remove those they deemed too distracting or were in an unsafe location. On word of this, the Santa Fiends would fly into an indignant rage, demanding that they be allowed to grieve in whatever manner they wanted. If they wanted to put a giant, spangled crucifix up where Bobby was killed, it was their business. If it distracted drivers, so what? Bobby should be remembered! Even if he was drunk when he ran off the road, killing himself and his pregnant girlfriend. Deluged by criticism, the highway department would eventually be forced to back off.

We reached Santa Fe and turned onto Cerrillos Road, heading over to The Pantry, one of our favorite lunch spots. As we walked to our table, we left a small wake of whispering, staring diners behind us. Emily and I were aware of the commotion Nola caused wherever she went, but we'd been friends with her for fifteen years by now. We'd been out with her so many times, we'd relaxed into the routine. Only the most blatant gawking got a reaction out of us.

We each ordered stacked enchiladas with a fried egg on top. There was a sign on the table that I'd never seen in a restaurant before. It said, "We are not responsible for chile that is too hot." I took this to mean that if you ordered something with chile on it and it was too hot for you to eat, tough luck; they weren't going to bring you anything else unless you paid for it. Some enterprising restaurant owner must have gotten tired of tourists ordering food they couldn't eat and then demanding something milder. So the owner puts up a sign on every table, problem solved. "Next thing you know," Emily said, "every damn restaurant in town will be putting up a sign just like it."

Santa Fe businesses love to put up signs. There used to be a coffee cart at the mall with so many signs taped on it, it took fifteen minutes to read them all. "No bills larger than $20.00" "Cups are NOT free!" "One straw only!" "No checks or credit cards!" Usually at least one word would be misspelled and some other word would inexplicably have quotation marks around it. "No 'refills'!" Huh? All the exclamation marks, underlined words, and weird quoting would put me on edge, afraid that I might make a mistake and accidentally break one of the coffee-cart rules and The Coffee Lady would tackle me to the ground, choke me, and scream, "The sign says 'NO SUBSTITUTIONS' *puta!*"

We ridiculed the "too hot" sign and bragged to each other about rubbing green chile in our eyes. I silently prayed that I wouldn't later be cursing my bravado. Hot chile tastes fine going down, but can feel like battery acid coming out.

Our meals came. Of the three of us, Nola was the biggest sissy, so she took the first taste. If she could stand the heat, Emily and I knew we'd be fine. She took a bite. Her eyes squinted shut and her head jerked back. A bead of sweat sprang forth on her upper lip and her nose began to run.

"It's perfect," she declared.

We settled into interrogating Nola about Travis and The Big Red Truck. Had she loaned him the money to buy the truck?

No, she hadn't. She told him that she couldn't do it, that she was saving money to buy a house. She offered to help him with a budget, which would enable him to save the money himself.

"What did he say to that?" I said.

"Actually, he got pretty ticked off."

"Why? Because you wouldn't loan him the money or because he doesn't know what a budget is?' I said.

Nola squinted, pinched her lips together. I knew this meant "Knock it off."

"He got all irate, saying, 'Don't you trust me? How can you stay with me if you don't trust me? How can we ever move in together if you don't trust me?' It got rather annoying."

"What kind of whiny crap is that? Is he trying to make you feel guilty for not helping him?" Emily said.

"I don't know. I guess. He almost had me convinced that I was being unreasonable. That if I didn't trust him enough to give him the money, what was I doing with him? But . . . "

"But what?"

"But he didn't convince me. Dang it, it's my money. Seems to me if he knew how to manage money, he'd have some of his own, so why should I let him have mine? It probably sounds cold and bitchy, but hey, I've had to sacrifice a lot to save up that stash."

"So is he over it now? Or is he still mad?"

"I think he's still mad. I asked him if he wanted to come over after work today and he said he was going to be too tired."

"Phffft," I said, disgusted.

"Guess I'll just let him pout for a while. He'll get over it."

"Does he know we're scoping out trailers today?"

"Yeah, but I told him that we're just looking for decorating ideas."

Why, one might ask, would anyone go to a trailer park looking for decorating ideas? The only explanation I have for this is that we—and everyone we knew our age—lived in bad neighborhoods in World War II vintage apartments. We had no air conditioning, so we covered our windows with aluminum foil to keep out the punishing Albuquerque sun. Our furniture consisted primarily of hand-me-downs from our parents. I had my parents' massive 2,000-pound color console television that was so old it had vacuum tubes in it. Emily had their old sofa, which was upholstered in a hideous pattern of giant brown and gold zinnias. And Nola's furniture, though meticulously cared for by her parents, was 20-some years old. We were grateful for these antiquities because without them we'd be sitting on chairs we'd found abandoned in alleys, lighting our rooms with lamps dragged out of dumpsters, tattered library books our only form of entertainment. Everything but the clothes on our backs had been used before by somebody else, so we loved looking at anything that was new and modern.

We pulled into the Ortiz Mobile Homes' gravel lot and parked the Monte Carlo in front of the sales trailer. Before we had a chance to get out of the car, a salesman came out of the trailer and stood on its porch steps, grinning at us like we were his long lost daughters. When we got out of the car and he got a closer look at us, his face fell. Was it because of Nola? Was it because the three of us were so young and he couldn't believe we were serious buyers? Was it the way we were dressed? Emily and Nola weren't exactly dressed like they were going to church or to a job interview, but they were certainly presentable. I was in a t-shirt, jeans, and sneakers, and my sneakers were brand new, so what the heck was his problem?

"Can I help you ladies with something?" his tone of voice and guarded manner similar to that a Secret Service agent might use if you strayed too close to the president's motorcade.

"Why yes, thank you for asking," Nola said, using her extra perky voice. "We'd like to take a look at your models." She gestured with her tiny arm to a group of trailers opposite the office. "Are those the models over there?"

He studied us, appeared to be taking note of our jewelry, our shoes, the quality of our haircuts. Nola and Emily smiled pleasantly, while I tried my best not to look pissed off. In a matter of seconds, we were scrutinized, categorized, and dismissed as looky-loos but probably not petty thieves, either. His sales-guy-grin returned and he said, "Sure, those four over there are our model homes. Feel free to wander around as long as you like. If you have any questions, I'll be in the trailer."

He appraised the three of us one more time, then hitched up his pants over his paunch, turned and went back in the sales trailer. Nola shrugged and gave Emily a look that said, "Geez, what's his deal?" I muttered, "Asshole."

We headed over to the first model. Once inside, we were almost incapacitated by the smell of the out-gassing cheap polyester carpeting and the formaldehyde-soaked particleboard kitchen cabinetry, but everything in it, from the plastic flowers on the vinyl-covered wood grain veneer coffee table to the mauve colored La-Z-Boy recliner was new, new, new! It was difficult not to become intoxicated with the idea of waking up each morning and having your cereal at that cute little breakfast bar, coming home at the end of a hard day's work to cook on a stove that wasn't caked with grease from thirty years of use, taking a shower in a tub that hadn't been spit in and peed in and God-knows-what-in by scores of previous tenants.

"What do you think? Don't you love it?" Emily gushed.

"It's really cool! I can see myself living in one of these. I bet a trailer is a lot cheaper than a house. I could use the money I save to buy a new car or maybe go on a vacation some place with Travis," she said.

And probably have to pay his way, too, I thought.

"I wonder how much it is. I don't see the prices anywhere," she said. "Let's go in and talk to the sales guy."

When Emily and Kevin were married, Emily had spent some time shopping for trailers (long enough to learn they couldn't afford one), so Nola figured that made Emily the expert. Nola asked her to pretend that it was she who was interested in the trailer, not Nola, figuring that maybe the guy wouldn't try to give her a snow job.

We walked up the metal porch steps and into the sales trailer. Instead of living room furniture, there were two large sales desks. The room was open to the kitchen and coffee was brewing in the Mr. Coffee. I tried hard to ignore the open box of chocolate-glazed doughnuts on the breakfast bar, not wanting to be taken in by the sweet, delicious sales ploy.

The salesman we had met earlier was sitting at one of the desks, listening intently to whatever the person on the other end of the phone was saying. He held up a finger to us, indicating he'd be a minute, then waggled his finger at a couple of chairs, wanting us to take a seat. Emily pulled two chairs over next to his desk. I stood, knowing that standing would give me an advantage. What sort of advantage, I didn't know, but I'd read that sales people always wanted you seated lower than they were.

A blonde woman of about thirty sat at the other desk, jotting down apparently critical notes. Her work must have been urgent and gripping—she didn't acknowledge us in any way.

We waited. And waited. Emily's leg bounced up and down, getting anxious. Nola cleared her throat, loudly. I stared at the sales guy, deciding to be openly hostile. Making us wait while he blathered on the phone was clearly a power play, designed to intimidate and demean us, the schmuck! I was about to say, "Let's blow," when he hung up.

"Sorry about that, ladies, but I really had to take that call. Now, let's see . . . " He rifled around on his desk, searching for something. He found the papers he wanted and positioned them in front of him. Pen in hand, he was poised for action.

"My name is Dan, Dan Weber. And you lovely ladies are . . . ?"

"I'm Emily. I'm the one who is interested in buying."

"Well, what do you ladies think? Fabulous models, aren't they?"

"Yes, they certainly are."

"Which one are you interested in?"

"I really like 'The Cabernet' model. Is everything we see in it, except for the furnishings, of course, standard?"

"What, specifically are you interesting in knowing about?"

"Are all of the kitchen appliances in the model standard?"

"Not the microwave. Maybe the double door fridge is an upgrade. And I think instead of a gas stove, the standard stove is electric."

"And the dishwasher?"

"Mitzy?" he said to the blonde. "Mitzy, is the dishwasher in 'The Cabernet' optional?"

"Yes, I think so," she said, still not bothering to glance up from her fascinating paperwork.

"What about the bath—"

Dan cut her off. "Is your husband joining you today?"

"What?"

"Your husband. Will he be coming today to look at the models, too?"

"No, no my husband won't be coming."

"Will he be coming later this weekend?"

"No, he won't."

"Oh." He put his pen down on the desk, and then rolled his shoulders in small circles as if he was trying to get a kink out, looked forlornly out the window.

"How much is 'The Cabernet'?"

"How much?" He seemed startled by the question.

"Yes, how much?"

I sneered, trying to convey to Dan that I thought he was a moron. We're onto you, buster!

"That depends."

"On what?"

"What options you want."

"Let's say I didn't want any options. How much would it be?"

"Well, that's difficult to say, Emily. There are set-up costs, and so on, you have to take into account. Costs can vary." He picked his pen up again. "Would you have time to fill out this application today?"

"Application for what?"

"Your loan application."

"I don't want to fill out a loan application. I just want to get a rough idea of how much the trailer is."

"First, I'll need you to fill out this loan application." He offered his pen to her.

"I don't understand why I need to fill out anything. I just want to know the basic price, without options, without upgrades, without setup costs. Why can't you just give me a ballpark estimate? That's all I'm after."

He acted as if he hadn't heard her.

"If you'd like to take the application home with you, you and your husband can work on it and get it back to me later this week."

I noticed the part in Emily's hair, the scalp there bright red. I knew this meant she was preparing to detonate. I moved in closer so I could restrain her—if I chose to.

"I don't *want* to fill out an application. I'm not *going* to fill out an application. I just want to know—what is the BASIC PRICE?" she said, a tiny spray of spit coming out when she said "price."

"I can't give you that until you fill out the application." He sniffed a little and then tilted languidly back in his desk chair, as if that settled the matter.

Nola, who had been quiet up to this point, rocked her body up and out of the chair with surprising speed. Her expression was calm as she studied Dan's expectant face.

"Dan?" Nola said.

"Yes?"

"We appreciate you allowing us take a look at your models, and thank you so much for taking the time to explain the options and so forth. But, I have a question for you, if you wouldn't mind answering it."

"No, not at all. What is it?"

"Well, Dan, it's apparent you have all the brain power of a nematode. So I'd like to know how a man with your total disregard for customer service and ignorance of his products could delude himself into thinking he had a chance in hell of selling *anything* to us. Dan, I need to know—with whom do you think you are fucking?"

His face flushed and he opened his mouth to speak.

Before he could get the words out, Emily was on her feet, I had the door, and we were on our way down the steps to the car. Dan must have paused to say something to Mitzy because we were already in the car and backing out when Dan flung the trailer door open and took a step out onto the porch. His foot snagged on an upturned corner of the doormat and he stumbled. He lurched forward off the steps, arms flailing in the air, but then miraculously regained his balance. He shouted something at us, but we couldn't make out his words.

Emily laid a patch out of the dirt parking lot, the rear tires of the Monte Carlo flinging gravel behind us. She paused a split second to check both ways before turning onto Cerrillos Road, and then floored it. The V8 shuddered in its motor mounts as she whipped the steering wheel from side to side, barely controlling the vehicle as she made the turn. It took several minutes for her to get her temper under control and back off the gas. It was only then that Nola or I felt safe to speak.

"The Cabernet," I said, and snorted.

"What an arrogant dick head," Nola said.

"What a misogynistic piece of dog crap," I said.

"What's 'misogynistic'?" Emily asked.

"It means somebody who hates women."

"Leave it to you to use a three-dollar word when a fifty-cent one will do," she said.

"Hey, I didn't spend the last twenty years of my life in school for nothing. If I know a three-dollar word, I'm damn well going to work it into any conversation I can."

"Is that like saying 'with whom'?" Emily said to Nola, starting to giggle.

"'With *whom* do you think you are fucking?'" I said, loving the elegance of the expression. We made up sentences with "with whom" this and "with whom" that until our sides ached from laughing. After we beat it into the ground, the car grew quiet.

"Wanna go check out Zia Trailers over on Cortez Street?" Emily said.

Yes, yes we did.

20

Orlando was going to be housesitting for his parents in Santa Fe and had told me if I was in town, I should drop by. I'd never seen his parents' house before, so I was looking forward to seeing where he'd grown up.

I found his neighborhood easily enough but then drove around lost for fifteen minutes in a tangle of streets that twisted then merged then forked then wound around each other until you wanted to beat your head against your dash in despair. Eventually I found his street and turned down it. Like a lot of old streets in Santa Fe, it was so narrow that if any cars were parked along the side, you had to slow to a crawl and inch past them for fear of sideswiping them. After a nerve-wracking block, I spotted the house and parked at the curb. I hoped that my side mirror would be intact later when I left.

The first thing I noticed about his parents' house was that an adobe wall surrounded it. In Santa Fe you can tell a lot about a family's financial standing by how their house is separated from the neighbors. Poor people have nothing separating their property from their neighbors. If you have a little money, you'll surround your place with a chain-link fence. A nice wooden fence or cinder block wall marks the struggling middle class. More expensive homes have adobe walls. The higher the wall, the wealthier the inhabitants.

The wall around Orlando's parents' house was easily seven feet high. Adobe. Hand troweled. Every few feet or so, the wall had a little cutout with a custom wrought iron inset.

When I had first talked to Orlando in that second-grade cloakroom, I'd seen his oily lunch bag and was convinced his family was of modest means. We were equals. Now, seeing the grandeur of this wall, I knew either I was wrong way back then or something had changed. Was he the rich college kid, slumming it with the homely white-trash girl? I started to feel a little angry about it. *I went to college, too, dammit. I may be white, but I'm not trash!*

Suddenly I didn't want to get out of my car. I closed my eyes, tried to get a grip on myself.

When I was a kid, I thought everybody in the country walled themselves in. I never wondered about what we were trying to keep in (or out) with our fences and walls. In my neighborhood, every house had the backyard walled in by a five- or six-foot cinder block wall. Kids, dogs, and cats roamed at will, so maybe people wanted to keep us little hooligans and the animal doody out of their yards. In the summer there was nothing of interest to keep kids in the house, so we searched the neighborhood looking for something to do. We used the cinder block walls like our own private highways to each other's houses.

Clint was a year older than me, and when we were in grade school, he was several inches taller. I was too short to get up on the walls by myself, so he would boost me up and then pull himself up. The walls were narrow, so we walked them like a balance beam, with one foot in front of the other, arms outstretched to keep our balance. We'd walk the walls, peering down at the backyards on each side of us, looking to see if any of our friends were out playing, scoping out the swing sets and whatever toys might have been left out. We watched one house with particular interest; its backyard was essentially a giant hole in the ground. Our dad told us the owner was digging a bomb shelter. Why? I wanted to know. He just laughed and shrugged. Over the course of the summer, we watched the hole grow deeper and wider. Sometimes we'd walk on the wall and see a shirtless, dusty, red-faced man standing in the hole, leaning against his shovel, staring down at his handiwork, wiping the sweat off his face with a red bandana. Even though I was just a kid at the time, I'd dug a hole or two in my day, and I remember thinking the poor guy must have some hellacious blisters.

Clint and I often discussed what sorts of things would ultimately be in the bomb shelter. Jugs of water, big sacks of pinto beans, fifty-gallon drums of cooking oil, yes, certainly. But cookies, too, chocolate chip and the kind that look like little windmills. And Jiffy-Pop popcorn, that miracle of modern snack-food technology. Oh, and a snakebite kit. Neither of us had ever seen a snakebite kit, or a snake for that matter, but we'd seen plenty of shows on TV where you had to cut a guy's leg with a knife and suck the snake venom out of the wound. Neither of us wanted to be in charge of leg sucking, so we thought the snakebite kit might come in handy.

Sadly, our dream of getting invited over to tour the finished bomb shelter didn't materialize. Though the hole grew week by week, it remained merely a hole. One day the owner rented a backhoe, filled in the hole, sold the house, and our bomb shelter fantasies came to an abrupt end. The new owner was an old lady whose primary source of entertainment was sitting at a card table in her tiny living room, putting together jigsaw puzzles of Vermont's covered bridges or waterfalls. Nice as she was, she couldn't compete with the bomb-shelter guy.

When walking the walls, we frequently encountered obstacles. A wall too high to jump onto. A backyard with a mean dog. One homeowner had cemented pieces of broken, jagged glass onto the top of his walls, so whenever we got to that bastard's house, we had to jump off and make our way around it. Worst of all, we might run into that brat, Shep.

Shep's real first name was Shepherd. Kids made fun of his name, so he adopted "Shep" early in his elementary school career. Some of the non-Anglo kids had trouble pronouncing the "sh" sound—they pronounced it as a hard "ch," as in "cheese." So "Shep" became "Chep." It infuriated him to be called "Chep," but half his class pronounced it that way, so he had to live with it. Maybe that's what made him so cruel and selfish. He and Clint were in the same third grade class, but Clint wanted nothing to do with him.

Clint and I usually walked the walls together, but sometimes he would be off with his friends, playing "Army" or trying to set something on fire. One hot summer day, Clint was somewhere else, and I couldn't find anybody to play with, so I decided to seek adventure on my own. I went into my backyard and hopped up on the wall. The sky was stark blue and cloudless, and the brilliant New Mexico sunshine made the air shimmer in the distance. The warmth of the cinder block felt good on my bare feet. I'd been walking the walls for two years now so was confident in my balance. I could relax and enjoy the views down into the neighbors' yards, the smell of the lilac bushes, and the sounds of summer.

I'd been walking about ten minutes when I heard a noise a few houses up from me. It sounded like somebody throwing rocks at a trash barrel. Uh-oh. Shep! He must be in his backyard, indulging in some sort of despicable activity, maybe torturing cats. I stood still, listening, and considered turning back home. Then the noise stopped. I figured he must have gone back in the house, so I continued on my way.

When I neared his yard, I didn't see him, so I started to cross his section of the wall. The next thing I knew, a rock whizzed by my head. Crap! Shep's trying to get me! Now what do I do? I could jump off the wall. But if I jumped off on one side, it would be into dense weeds, full of goat-head thorns. Barefooted and bare legged, that didn't seem like a good option. Or I could jump off the other side into Shep's yard and take my chances that he meant me no real harm.

I decided to make a run for it. I scurried along the wall, my arms outstretched, teetering crazily from side to side. A couple more rocks flew by, narrowly missing my head. Terrified, I picked up speed, was practically running. I was almost at the end of his wall when out of the corner of my eye, I saw him turn on the garden hose.

He hit me with a spray of water. I lost my balance and tumbled off the wall into his yard, landing on my knees in a ragged patch of weeds, the impact causing a cloud of startled grasshoppers to swarm me as I pitched forward scraping my hands on the hard-packed dirt.

Shep put his thumb over the water coming out of the hose, increasing its range, and I was hit with a frigid spray to the side of my head. I staggered to my feet, made a dash for the wall, but he grabbed me by the back of my shirt, spun me around, and flung me to the ground.

He was on top of me in a flash, pinning my shoulders down with his knees. I squirmed and twisted underneath him, desperate to get away.

"Get off of me!" I hollered.

"What are you going to do about it?" He leaned his face directly over mine. His breath smelled like spoiled milk.

"I'm gonna tell!" I was trying to buck him off with my hips, but he was too heavy. The sharp rocks under me dug into my back.

"Who? Who are you going to tell?" He looked casually to his left, then his right. "I don't see nobody."

My skin began to itch and tingle with fear. I twisted harder, but his knees wouldn't budge. I cranked my head around and frantically searched the ground for something I could grab and hit him over the head with.

He started to make spit bubbles.

"No! No! Don't spit on me! Please don't spit on me!"

A long strand of saliva came down his chin, dangled and swung over my eyes.

An adrenaline surge rocked up my spine and I wrenched away from him with all my might. I got a shoulder and an arm free and took a wild swing at him, but missed. He tried to grab my arm and pin me again, but in the tangle of arms and elbows he hit me in the nose and a spray of blood came out, smearing across my cheek.

The sight of my blood must have scared him; he rolled off of me, his eyes wide with shock.

I stood up and a few drops of blood fell from my nose onto my shirt. I pinched my nostrils shut with my fingers, then bolted through his side yard, pushing the gate with my shoulder. I fled down the hot sidewalk, not bothering to look back to see if he was chasing me.

Back in my own front yard, I stood panting, tried to wipe the blood and tears off my face, figured I'd be in for a whipping once my mom found out I'd been on the walls.

What was I going to do?

I heard the screen door slam. It was Clint. He looked me up and down. My hair was a mad, wet tangle. Dirt and blood on my face and on my shirt. My legs and feet were scratched and dusty. One knee had squashed grasshopper guts on it, the other scraped raw. "What happened to you?"

I told him. I told him about the wall. About Shep. About the rocks and the thorns, the garden hose, the spitting.

"He was gonna *spit* on you?" His face was red now, his hands clenched.

"Yeah," I said, my voice quavering, fighting back the tears. I licked my fingers, then wiped them on my cheek, trying to get the dried blood off. "What am I gonna tell Mom?" I said, examining my stained shirt. "She told us to stay off the walls. I'm gonna get a whippin'!"

"Turn your shirt inside out and walk in the house like nothin' happened."

"But what do I do with the shirt? If I put it in the laundry basket, she'll see it."

"Wash up in the bathroom and put on a clean shirt. Then sneak the dirty one out to me. I'll get rid of it. Go—go on now."

My mom was busy in the kitchen, so she didn't see me come in or see me go back out to the front yard, where Clint waited. I gave him my bloody shirt; he wadded it up and started off down the street.

"Where ya going?" I called out to him.

"To see Shep," he said, without turning around.

I sat down on the porch step and waited for him. Thirty minutes later, he came walking up the sidewalk and I ran out to meet him. "What happened? Did you see Shep?"

In answer, he held up his right hand, made a fist, showed me his knuckles. They were scraped and two of the knuckles were bleeding a little.

In that moment, I loved my brother more than life itself.

"You won?"

"What do *you* think, pipsqueak?"

"And my shirt?"

"Gone."

"Gone where?"

"You ask too many questions," he said, giving my shoulder a little shove. I shoved back. "See, now that right there is your problem. You push like a girl."

"But I am a girl."

"That just means you gotta be smarter. If somebody wants to fight you, you should run if you can, but when you can't? Then you never let them take the first swing. Never. You take charge; you take that first swing and make sure it's a good one. Take a swing at me."

I swung at him, but he stepped back and I missed him.

"Not like that. You're too far away. Step in, get closer, make sure when you throw a punch it's gonna connect. Are you listening?"

Oh, I was listening, all right.

I heard the front door of Orlando's parents' house open, footsteps, and then the purple wooden gate in the adobe wall swung open. "What are you doing out there?" Orlando said. "Casing the joint?"

Startled, I couldn't think of a good excuse for having sat outside his house for the last five minutes. I sure didn't want to tell him about my "Economic Theory of Wall Height." Not yet, anyway.

"What am I doing? Oh, uh, nothing. I'm just trying to find my . . . my uh . . . " I rustled around the passenger seat, pretending to be searching for something.

"Well, get in here. The posolé is waiting," he said.

As we walked through the living room on our way to the kitchen, I surveyed the place. Overhead, *vigas* supported the ceiling. In the corner was a large Kiva-style fireplace. If you didn't know better, you might smirk. *Ha! Another victim of Santa Fe Style.* But you'd be wrong—this was the real deal. The house looked a hundred years old. Before this style of architecture became fashionable, the house would have sold for a modest sum. But in 1980, it was worth a small fortune.

I glanced down the hallway that I assumed led to the bedrooms. Family photos hung on the wall; Orlando's mom and dad on their wedding day; Orlando in his cap and gown, graduating from college; his older sister, Marie, smiling, proud, in her Army nursing uniform. In 1967, she'd gone to Vietnam, done her job, and come home. Six months later, she was killed in a car accident. She was only 23. I opened my mouth to say something about the picture but thought better of it. If Orlando was not thinking of Marie right now, I didn't want to make him start. Besides, Marie's picture had caused an awful catch in my throat.

We made our way back to the den. My eyes swept the room. No Mexican serapes thrown over the back of the sofa. On the fireplace mantel, no ceramic neckerchief-wearing howling coyotes or Kokopelli figurines. No paintings of nubile Indian maidens in traditional Hopi dress, wearing traditional eye shadow, mascara and lipstick. No cow skulls, no pressed tin, no beads, no feathers, no pottery, no spurs. Just comfortable looking, well-worn leather furniture and a wall with a floor-to-ceiling bookcase crammed with books.

"Ahhh, thank God," I said with a grateful sigh.

"Thank God what?"

"Oh, uh, I'm just relieved . . . that it's so cool in here. Very refreshing." It likely would have been rude to say I was relieved his parents weren't trendy bubble-headed dimwits.

"Yeah, my dad had central air put in a few years ago. Feels great, doesn't it?"

"Maybe someday I'll have central air," I said wistfully, as I gazed out the window at a lawn edged with brilliant purple coneflowers and hollyhocks.

"Hey, did I tell you I might get a summer internship at Digital?" I said. Digital Equipment Corporation manufactured superminicomputers, and working there would be computer geek nirvana.

"That's great news! When will you hear?"

"Probably not for months, so I'm trying not to think about it right now. I'll be pretty disappointed if I don't get it. How about you? How's your mom doing these days? Still working at the Highway Department?"

"Yup."

"And your Dad? Still commuting up to Los Alamos every day?" His dad worked at Los Alamos Scientific Labs: birthplace of the atomic bomb, home of some of the finest scientific minds in New Mexico, and—naturally—reviled by Santa Fiends as a hotbed of elitist, egg-headed weirdoes who thought they were better than everybody else. I wanted a job there. Desperately.

"Uh-huh, still making the drive," Orlando said.

"If Digital doesn't make me an offer, maybe you could ask him to put in a good word for me at the Labs."

"Yeah, sure, I'll get right on it."

The kitchen was cozy and filled with the smell of the posolé. Standing next to Orlando at the stove, I said, "You *made* this?"

"I'm insulted. Of course I made it. Where else could it have come from?"

"I thought maybe your mom made it for you so you'd have something to eat while you house-sat for them."

"I can do a lot of things you don't know anything about," he said, trying to give me a mysterious look. It didn't look mysterious at all; it looked goofy.

"Right."

"How about you stop being so sarcastic and heat up some tortillas."

"Where's the foil?"

"Why do you need foil?"

"To heat up the tortillas. Wrap them in foil and put them in the oven."

"You're such a *gringa*," he said, shaking his head with disgust. "You don't heat them up like that. Here, let me show you."

He turned on one of the gas burners and plopped a tortilla on top of the flames. With his hands, he scooted the tortilla back and forth and then flipped it over.

"How do you know when it's done?"

"When it starts to bubble up a little. See? Like this," he pointed to a blister on the tortilla.

"Got it. Let me do the rest."

We worked side by side in the kitchen until the posolé was done and the tortillas sufficiently charred by my inexpert hands. We took the food out to the patio and dug in.

The last time we'd had a chance to really talk was months ago, right after the Jackie incident. He'd told me then that he'd called her the next day, and to his surprise, she had released him from her talons without putting up much of a fight. Who knows? Maybe once she'd seen the kind of loonies Orlando hung out with, he'd lost some of his charm.

Right after that, Orlando made his move on Fiona. I'd seen them around town together and couldn't help but wonder what he saw in her. The hair on one side of her head was always matted, like she'd just rolled out of bed. No matter what the temperature, she wore a scroungy fleece jacket and sandals. If it was cold, she wore socks with the sandals. And those pants! Was I the only one who noticed they were always covered in cat hair?

When Orlando first introduced me to her, she said nothing for a minute but instead studied my face intently, as if she was trying to remember where she'd seen me before. I was starting to get uncomfortable under her gaze when at last she said, "You have beautiful high cheekbones. Are you part Indian?"

Everybody I knew used the word "Indian," though some said it was an offensive term. "Native American" was preferred, they said. Rarely would you hear the expression "indigenous peoples" or "first peoples." But nobody I knew referred to the big school in the middle of Santa Fe as "The Native American School" and nobody ate "first people's bread." It was The Indian School and Indian fry bread. I only knew a couple of Indian/Native American/indigenous kids and frankly, the topic of what to call them never came up. I just used their names: Pat and Leonard.

I squirmed under Fiona's attention—I hated people saying anything about the way I looked, whether it was flattering or not. "Yeah. I'm about one-eighth of a teaspoon of something."

"What tribe? Hopi? Navajo?" She was enraptured by the idea of it. A real live Indian! Native American. Indigenous person. Whatever.

"I don't know . . . it was a long time ago. Six or seven generations back," I said. I should have just told her I was a "mutt" and left it at that.

"How could you not *know*?!"

She couldn't get over the fact that I didn't care about my "heritage." She didn't understand that my "heritage" was Northern New Mexico Tract Home Dweller.

Next thing I knew, Fiona was on a tear, nattering on about Carlos Castaneda, shamans, spiritual quests, and peyote. I looked at Orlando, my eyes pleading *Help! Help me get away from this pendeja loca!* But he had only shrugged and smiled.

I took a bite of posolé. "Hey, this is delicious."

"Of course it is."

Now for my cunning segue into asking about Fiona without sounding unduly interested in their relationship.

"How're things going with you and Fiona?" So much for cunning. "Still going with that chi yoga flow?"

"Pretty good," he said, ignoring my snarky comment about her yoga fixation. "We did something a few weeks ago that you'll find entertaining. She forced me to take her up to El Santuario in Chimayo."

"Isn't that the place with the sacred dirt?"

"Uh-huh, that's the place."

Fiona had heard about El Santuario from a friend and wanted to see it for herself. She'd been told the shrine was full of crutches and canes left behind by those who were cured by its magical dirt. She wasn't sure if she believed in the powers of the dirt, but she wanted to get some of it anyway, just to be on the safe side. I guess the sex with her was pretty good, because Orlando agreed to take her there.

They drove up to Chimayo and found El Santuario's tiny chapel. The shrine (that is, the hole in the ground) is inside the chapel. Orlando waited at the chapel doorway while Fiona went in to investigate. Just inside the doorway, he saw a middle aged man kneeling on the dirt floor. The man's head was bowed and he held a rosary. Slowly, the man scooted across the dirt floor on his knees, muttering to himself.

"What was he saying?" I said.

"I don't know, Sylvie. He was speaking Spanish."

"Don't you speak Spanish?"

"Some, but not the sort of stuff you'd ever hear in a church."

Same as me, I thought. "Then what happened?"

Continuing on his knees, the man inched across the length of the room until he reached the hole, and then he took the sacred yellow plastic shovel that looked like it came out of a kid's sandbox and shoveled a little sacred dirt from the hole into what appeared to be a sacred empty Parkay Margarine tub. Then the man backed out of the shrine, still scooting on his knees, still muttering.

"Huh. So people come and take dirt out of the hole all the time, but the hole never gets any bigger. Right?"

"Right."

"Ah, very magical and mysterious indeed."

"Yes. Very."

"Did Fiona get some dirt?"

"Oh yeah, she got some dirt," he said, nodding slowly.

"What did she do with it?"

"She's got it in a bowl on her fireplace."

"I hope it's covered. She wouldn't want the cat getting into it."

"What cat?"

"She doesn't have a cat?"

"No, she doesn't have a cat. Why did you think that?"

"A dog—does she have a dog?"

"Nope, no dog."

What the . . . ? What the hell kind of hair is that on her pants?

"It sounds like you two had a pretty good time," I said. "What's next? A trip to Lake Arthur to see the face of Jesus on the Holy Tortilla?"

"I don't want to talk about it anymore."

Uh-oh. I had forgotten (for the jillionth time) one of Nola's rules: It's fine to poke fun at your own boyfriend (or girlfriend), but you didn't want to hear anybody else do it.

"I'm sorry. I was just kidding around. If you like her, she must be a pretty cool person."

"Forget it, it's all right." He changed the subject, asked about Nola and how things were going with Travis. At last, a topic I could safely speak my mind on. I told him how Travis traveled around northern New Mexico trying to get people to make their loan payments. He acted like he was such a tough guy. He loved to hear himself talk. He always had a beer in his hand. He watched NASCAR. He didn't like to read, wasn't interested in current affairs, didn't go to college, had horrible taste in music.

"I can't stand him."

"Yeah, I got that. Why do you think Nola likes him?"

Hmm, I'd never thought about that before. I was too busy thinking about all the reasons I detested him.

"He's pretty nice to her, I guess. I mean, it's not like he buys her stuff or takes her to fancy places or anything like that.

But every once in a while he drives her to the grocery store and helps her put groceries away. And sometimes he comes over and hangs around all weekend. She probably likes the company. And he's affectionate—he kisses her and hugs her a lot."

"Sounds like he's got a pretty good job, and he's nice to her and keeps her company. The guy doesn't sound half bad to me."

It was like having a bucket of cold water dumped on my head. Ever since I met Travis, I'd done nothing but find fault with him. But now, hearing myself describe him to Orlando, all those things I'd complained about sounded—well—petty. Am I an overprotective friend, needlessly worrying about ulterior motives? Am I simply jealous and so I don't like sharing Nola with him? Would it kill me to keep my opinions to myself?

After dinner, I headed back to Albuquerque. As I barreled up La Bajada Hill, Orlando's words gnawed at me. Maybe I needed to stop being so hard on Travis and instead think about how happy he made Nola. Maybe it was time I stopped being so self-centered and started acting like the kind of friend Nola deserved. Maybe it was time to make amends.

21

"**D**amn that Travis! What kind of stunt is he trying to pull!? Just how *stupid* does he think I am?" Nola snarled as she used her hip to slam the kitchen drawer closed.

Five minutes before, we had gone into her kitchen to make coffee. We were having a pleasant conversation about what she and Travis were going to do for her birthday, and I was trying extra-specially hard not to be snide, sarcastic, or mocking. I was mentally congratulating myself on how well I was doing, when suddenly she was yelling and hip-checking drawers, giving me a look like I was going to be next.

"What's wrong? What are you talking about?"

"Where is my goddamn Sweet-N-Low?!"

WHAM! Another drawer slammed shut.

"What is it? What's going on?"

"Arrrrrrrrrgghhh," she said, stomping back to her bedroom. A few minutes later she came back with a scrap of paper between her two fingers. "This. *This* is what I am talking about. Here—take it."

I took the paper from her, turning it over in my hands. "Is it some kind of receipt from Ruidoso Downs?" Ruidoso Downs was a horseracing track in a town three hours' drive south of Albuquerque. The old me would have blurted out, "Horse racing is for sadists! Gambling is for morons!" but the new, improved, sensitive me struggled to behave. "Maybe Travis actually did go to Ruidoso. What's wrong with that?"

"See that date on the receipt?"

"Yeah. So?"

"So? So? SO! We were *supposed* to get together that week-end and he told me he couldn't because he had to work. Last night I found this receipt on the floor by my bed. It must have fallen out of his pants pocket."

Damn! The guy wore the same pair of pants for a whole week?

"Maybe it's not his. Maybe he was just carrying it for a friend."

"Give me a break!" I flinched from the fury in her voice. I was glad to be at the far end of the kitchen, out of hip-checking range.

"He lied to me. He drove all the goddamn way down to Ruidoso to do what? To go to the goddamn racetrack! I can't *believe* he lied to me!" She plopped down on the couch and closed her eyes. The last time I'd heard her cuss this much, she was telling me how she'd gotten screwed in her divorce settlement and was going to have to pay off Todd's credit card bills. I knew to be quiet, to let her calm herself.

She took a few slow, deep breaths, and opened her eyes. "I did something, and I know when I tell you about it, you're going to think I'm like that demented stalker girl in *Play Misty for Me*."

"You mean you kidnapped his girlfriend and tried to kill her?"

"Don't be ridiculous. Besides, *I'm* his girlfriend, remember?"

"You're starting to scare me. What the heck did you do? Just tell me!"

"Travis told me he was going to play cards with his buddies this afternoon. I didn't believe him. I mean, who plays cards in the middle of the day, for Christ's sake? So I cruised by his trailer to see if he was home."

Big deal! What girl hasn't cruised her boyfriend's place? Multiple times. "Go on," I said, not ready to swap stalker stories just yet.

She told me his car wasn't in the driveway, so she drove around the block, thinking about her next move. Since his car was gone, maybe Travis had told the truth. She felt a little guilty about not trusting him. But not *too* guilty. She wanted him to know that she was nobody's fool and that if he tried to pull anything sneaky, she'd catch him. So she decided to leave a note on his door, write something like, "Was in the neighborhood, just dropped by to say 'Hi.' Sorry I missed you!"

This didn't make much sense to me. It sounded like Nola wanted him to know that she could drop by any time unannounced. Didn't that defeat the purpose? If he knew she might drop by, wouldn't he simply be more careful about covering his tracks? I didn't want that; I wanted him to be slipshod and reckless. If he was up to no good, I wanted him to get caught.

"New Me" told "Old Me" to keep my trap shut. So I said nothing, letting her continue her story.

She got a piece of paper and a pen out of her purse. She needed something firm to put the notepaper on when writing. She searched the car but didn't find anything that would work, so decided to put the paper down on the hood of her car, then she could lean down and write her note. She was starting to get out of her car when she saw a young woman come out of the trailer next door to Travis'. The woman was barefoot and carrying a Budweiser in one hand and a lit cigarette in the other. She made an unsteady trek across her yard to the gate in her chain link fence, placed a hand on the gate, but stopped. She was looking at something down the road. Nola turned to look, too.

Oh, damn! It was Travis' Oldsmobile 442 coming up the street. It was one thing to leave a note on his door and then flee, entirely another to look him in the eye and lie about why she was there. All that swagger earlier about her being nobody's fool faded in an instant. Panic took its place.

The woman with the Budweiser practically sprinted back to her porch. At her front door, she looked over her shoulder at Nola, and then disappeared inside.

Nola thought that was a little odd but didn't have time to cogitate on it. Before she had time to plan her attack or her apology or whatever, Travis was at her car door, leaning in to give her a peck on the cheek.

"Hi, sweet stuff. Whatcha doin' here?" he said.

"Oh, hi! I was in the neighborhood and thought I'd drop by. I was just getting ready to write you a note. " She waved the piece of paper at him. "See?"

"I told you I was playing cards today, hon." He was smiling when he said it, but there was something in his eyes that made the muscles in the back of her neck go tight.

"So how come you're home already? I thought you were going to be at Glenn's house till late tonight."

"I did too, but the game broke up early. We were just getting started when Marty's wife called and told him he needed to get home for some reason."

"Oh no! Is everything all right?"

"I don't know. He just grabbed his coat and ran out, said he'd catch us next time. He didn't look scared or nothin'. Maybe the washing machine overflowed or something like that."

"Well, lucky me, running into you! I'm here now, so how about inviting me in?"

"I'm the lucky one," he said, as he opened the door and helped her out of her car. As they walked up the sidewalk to his trailer, movement in the window of the trailer next door caught her eye. It was the woman with the beer, peering though the curtains of her kitchen window. Her eyes and Nola's met for an instant, and then the curtains fell closed.

I wanted to interrupt Nola's story here, give her some wild conjecture about the neighbor lady, try to make her snort or laugh. No, no. Behave. Now is not the time for my usual shenanigans.

"Huh. Weird," I said, proud of my restraint.

"It *was* weird! I think she wanted to talk to me."

"Why would she want to talk to you?"

"I don't know, but my feminine intuition is on full alert. I don't know if Travis lied about the card game or not, but he sure was covering up going to the racetrack. Maybe that neighbor lady is involved somehow."

"What are you going to do?"

"I'm going to ask him."

"Ask him what?"

"I'm going to ask him if he went to Ruidoso, and if he denies it, I'm going to show him the receipt. Then I'm going to dump his sorry ass."

The next few days crawled by. I stayed home on Friday night, wanting to be home in case Nola wanted to talk. I felt edgy and guilty, like I was to blame for things not working out between Nola and Travis, as if I had driven him to his sordid life of lies and gambling. I tried to figure out what I could say to comfort her. "You'll be better off without him." No, she won't believe that. "He doesn't deserve you." No, ridiculously trite, can't say that. "There's plenty more fish in the sea!" That's a load—if there's so many fish in the stupid sea why hadn't I been able to snag one?

Midnight came and went, and I had failed to come up with anything that I believed would make her feel better about splitting up with Travis. I trudged off to bed, my brain swollen with worthless clichés.

I fell into a fitful sleep and dreamt of Nola. She'd starred in my dreams before; usually we were doing something mundane, like walking down the street or driving somewhere. My sleeping brain must be incapable of reconstructing her properly, because in my dreams she always has normal arms. In some dreams, like the one this night, we were on a road trip, and I turned to her and was surprised to see her with arms. Surprised, but not shocked. I'd said to her, "Hey, where'd those come from?" She said, "I just got them!" like a kid with a new skateboard. Then she waggled her two hands at me as if to say, "Check it out! Palms! Neat, huh?"

The weekend passed without word from Nola. On Monday, I rode my bike to work. Pedaling down Oglala, I took in the smells of farm life, looked at the corn plants just starting to come out of the ground, and listened to the cows mooing off in the distance. As I rode by the blue farmhouse, my old friends Molly, Auckland, and Cupcake hurled themselves off the front porch and ran to me. I stopped at the fence for a moment, scratching each dog behind the ears, sticking my fingers through the chicken wire fence, letting them lick them.

As I rode off, the dogs ran along the fence line, following me until they reached the end of their yard. Why can't friendships with people be more like friendships with dogs? Uncomplicated. No drama. Predictable. But less saliva. I wiped the dog slobber off my hands onto my pants.

Since Nola had found the Ruidoso Downs receipt, I didn't know what to do or think. Orlando had said he didn't think Travis was such a bad guy. And, up till now anyway, Nola had been crazy about him. Did it make sense to put up with a guy who lied every now and again about something like a little gambling in exchange for companionship? Maybe the right thing to do was to tell Nola that I thought she and Travis were great together, that I was confident they could work things out. Perhaps I should watch some soap operas to pick up some pointers on how to say that sort of schlocky touchy-feely stuff with a straight face. Alternatively, I could do what I really wanted to do, which was to tell Travis, "The stagecoach leaves at noon; be under it."

Monday night, the call from Nola finally came.

22

"**G**uess what!" she said, not sounding devastated or furious or even mildly annoyed. "Travis bought me the most beautiful birthday present!"

Huh? What just happened? A few short days ago she was planning on steaming, reaming, and dry cleaning Travis, and now she sounded elated.

She launched into a detailed story of the night she got his present, when he got there, who cooked, who set the dinner table. After ten excruciating minutes of minutia, I could endure no more.

"For Christ's sake—just tell me what he said when you showed him the receipt!"

"Oh. Yeah. That."

"Yeah, that. Spill it."

She'd waited until after dinner and they settled on the sofa, all cozy-like. Then she whipped out the Ruidoso receipt. He looked rattled and asked her where she had found it. She told him she'd found it on the floor in the bedroom.

He launched into his own long-winded tale. He told her that he hadn't had enough money to get her the kind of birthday present she deserved, so he figured his only chance was to take what little money he had and go to the track. His buddy Glenn was driving down that weekend to Ruidoso, so he rode down with him. Travis didn't want to tell her any of this because he wanted to surprise her. So he'd made up the story about having to work that weekend.

I wondered how she could possibly believe such a ludicrous fabrication.

And the other day, the day Nola had cruised his place—well, he'd told her a teensy white lie about that, too. Instead of playing cards, he'd gone shopping.

Then Travis whipped out a little something of his own—a black velvet box. Inside was a silver chain with a tiny, heart-shaped pendant.

Heart-shaped? That does it, I thought. She's sunk!

Though my throat almost closed up from the strain of the lie, I told her I was relieved to hear her suspicions were unfounded. Before my throat could unclench, she said she'd decided to take my advice.

"You asked me once why I never went over to his house and it occurred to me I didn't have a very good answer to that. So I asked Travis if I could spend the night at his place next weekend. So there! I'm not as naïve as you think I am. And who knows? Maybe I'll even introduce myself to the mysterious neighbor lady, find out what her deal is."

True, I was disappointed that Travis had crafted an airtight alibi. But all was not lost. Nola getting to spend more time with Travis on his own turf might be just the thing to snap her out of the evil spell he had obviously cast on her. A man's house will tell you a lot about his character, more even than his dental hygiene. If, say, the toilet handle has been missing for six months, and you have to use a coat hanger that's hooked down into the tank to flush it—that tells you something. Or say the guy erupts in a fury because you accidentally screwed up his VCR settings—that tells you something too. What would Travis' house have to say?

Travis put her off the following weekend, saying he'd been so busy at work he hadn't had a chance to clean house. The weekend after that, he said he had to work. Tired of his excuses, Nola had to force the issue, throwing a hissy fit. He at last relented, and she'd spent the weekend there and been on her best behavior, not criticizing anything or telling him to move the sofa to a different wall so traffic would flow better around the coffee table or making him organize his spices alphabetically.

I guess she'd done a good job taming her bossiness; she was invited over again two weekends later, and several weekends in a row after that. We were sitting at Nola's kitchen table when she told me that things were going good. Fantastic, actually.

She told me that each time she stayed with him, she was a tiny bit bolder. Would he mind if she stashed a six-pack of diet Dr Pepper in his fridge so they'd be there when she came over? Did he realize how shabby his bath towels looked? Maybe she could buy him some new ones. Would it be too much trouble to move that rusty old hibachi off the front porch, perhaps putting it over by the trash barrel? He never used it anyway, and it was a potential hazard there on the porch. He was, she said, remarkably good-natured about taking most of her suggestions.

There was something, though, something she wanted to tell me about last Friday night.

She was over at Travis' trailer, and they'd had a nice dinner together—he'd made lasagna, which impressed her. Then they'd snuggled up on the couch and watched *Fantasy Island*. She wanted to tell me more about what went on that night, but I stopped her. Really, I told her, it's not necessary to tell me *everything*.

The next morning, a phone call interrupted their waffle making. That's not a euphemism, she wanted me to know. They actually were cooking waffles. It was Glenn. His Trans Am had broken down just north of Los Alamos and he had to have it towed to a repair shop. The shop needed to keep it for a few days, so he wanted Travis to pick him up and give him a ride back to Albuquerque. So Travis left for Los Alamos, leaving Nola alone at his trailer.

As soon as she heard his car leave the driveway, she went to work. First, she rooted around the kitchen until she found a dishrag that didn't smell mildewed, and then she set about organizing the refrigerator, throwing out old food, wiping down crusty bottles, making a mental note of the things she should bring over next time. She wanted to organize the canned goods, too, but they were placed too high in the cupboards for her to reach.

Then to the living room—an entire wall was devoted to Travis' *Lost in Space* collection. Three six-foot long shelves bulged with action figures and memorabilia. All the TV characters were there, starting with Will Robinson, that spoiled obnoxious little redheaded boy, and ending with that insipid sack of space poo, Dr. Smith. There were lunch boxes, key chains, and bottle openers, even a cigarette lighter with the Robinson family emblazoned on it.

She fantasized about pitching the whole dust-catching childish mess in the nearest dumpster, then thought better of it. Poor guy, he worked hard; he deserved to have a silly little hobby like this. It wasn't like he was snorting cocaine or collecting child pornography. They were just toys, after all.

She spotted the *Lost in Space* robot. Standing on tiptoe and using her two good fingers and her chin, she gingerly worked the robot to the front of the shelf, being careful not to knock over any of the other toys. She noticed the little button on its back.

She pushed it and the robot's arms waved as it croaked, "Danger, Danger Will Robinson!" She had to admit, that was sort of cool. Very retro.

Next she scoped out the bathroom. She hated cleaning bathrooms, but hated dirty bathrooms even more. The sink was in dire need of attention. She went back to the kitchen and found a long handled dish scrubber. Excellent. It would allow her to scrub the sink without having to stick her face right down into it. Nothing more nauseating than an up-close-and-personal look at a sink caked with chunks of toothpaste and shaving cream sprinkled with two week's worth of whiskers. She scrubbed it until it sparkled.

She pondered taking the shower curtain down, maybe run it a few times in a washing machine, bleach the hell out of it, but had no way to get it down by herself. It would have to wait till Travis got home.

She was getting pretty tired by the time she got to the bedroom, but she couldn't quit now—there was dusting to be done. She sat down on the waterbed, thinking she'd rest a minute before she tackled the dresser. As soon as she sat down, she regretted it. The bed sloshed back and forth and she fell backward on it. Old-style waterbeds were hard enough to get out of with two good arms; with no arms, it was going to be next to impossible. She squirmed back and forth on the bed, but it was like trying to get out of a horse trough. She started to get mad about it. She was going to be really embarrassed if Travis got home and found her stranded on the damn bed, like a helpless turtle on its back.

Fueled by frustration, she whipped her head violently forward, trying to get enough momentum to sit up. She succeeded in not only getting herself upright, but in flinging herself off the bed, stumbling ungracefully to the floor, and hitting her head on the door handle of the closet door, causing the door to swing open.

She lay there, stunned, waiting for the little shards of light to stop swimming in her eyes. The first clear thought she had was "Damn, this shag carpet could use a good shampooing!" She rolled over onto her back. The next thing she thought was "Hey, what's that box up there on the closet shelf?"

She got to her feet. Her head was still buzzing and she felt herself listing a little more to the left than usual, so she leaned against the wall for support. She stared at the box. It was pushed all the way to the end of the closet shelf, so only a little bit of it showed. When she'd been cleaning, she'd thought it odd she hadn't seen any mail on the counter, on the table, or on the dresser. No letters, no bills, no junk mail. Hell, not even a TV guide. Was that what was in the box?

She had to know.

She looked at me, and I saw in her face what I often saw. Steadfast resolve. "We're going to need Orlando."

23

"**Y**ou want to do WHAT?" Orlando said, looking at Nola and me like we had lost our minds.

Nola and I had him cornered. We had tricked him into letting us take him out to dinner. Now, with his stomach full of Tomasita's chile rellenos and two margaritas, we hoped he might be liquored up enough to go along with our plan. Actually, it wasn't "our" plan. It was Nola's plan. And it really wasn't much of a plan, per se. And it sounded like Orlando was the only person at the table with any common sense.

"What do you care what's in the box? It's probably a bunch of old electric bills or his baby pictures or something," he said.

"Even if it *is* bills or baby pictures, I want to see them," Nola said.

"Why don't you simply ask Travis what's in the box?" he said.

"I did. When he came home the day I found the box, he saw the big goose egg on my forehead and wanted to know what happened." Orlando and I both winced at this. The middle of her forehead still had a purplish-greenish-yellowish splotch of a bruise on it. "I told him I had accidentally fallen against his closet and that I'd seen the box and pretty please, wouldn't he tell me what's inside of it?"

"And?" Orlando said.

"And he told me that was where he kept his bills."

"Well, there's your answer. Mystery solved," he said.

"Who the hell keeps their old bills hidden in the bedroom closet?"

I started to raise my hand, but something in her eyes made me put it back in my lap.

"I need to *know* what's in it. Look, all I want you to do is drive. And if you don't want to drive, that's fine; just let Sylvie and me use your truck for an hour or two."

"Why can't you take your own car or Sylvie's car?"

"We need a vehicle that nobody in Travis' neighborhood will recognize. For an hour, that's all, one little hour. Please?"

Orlando studied my face, likely trying to judge if I had somehow been blackmailed into this or if I was actually dumb enough to think this was a good idea. "Nola, I want to say yes, but I don't understand. What could possibly be in that box that would matter?"

"Can't you just accept that I need to know?"

"I'm afraid not."

"Did Sylvie tell you that I'm divorced and that my ex-husband ran off with another woman?"

Orlando looked at me and I gave him a tiny nod. "Yes, she did," he said.

"And did she tell you anything about *who* he ran off with?"

He looked at me again. "Yes," I said. "I told Orlando about Todd and Sara."

"I've always been a student of human nature," Nola said. "I thought I *knew* Todd, knew him better than he knew himself. When he told me, 'till death do us part' at our wedding, I believed him."

Note to self: make sure "till death do us part" is not in my wedding vows. If I ever get married, which I probably won't, but if I do, scratch that stupid phrase.

"Maybe I got complacent about our marriage because when Todd left me, I was stunned. I was hurt, yes, but ashamed too. Surely there must have been clues along the way that indicated something was wrong between Todd and me. I can't tell you how many nights I lay awake pondering not just why I missed the signs, but what I would have done if I'd noticed the signs."

She shrugged one shoulder at me, her version of pointing. "She doesn't get this, I'm sure. She doesn't need anybody. If she was married to a guy and he left the cap off of the toothpaste, she'd give him the boot and not think twice about it. She'd rather be alone than put up with some guy's BS."

It was true. I hated a messy bathroom.

"But I'm not like Sylvie. I want companionship. I want love. And because of my disability, I know that I have to be willing to cut people some slack, because they sure as hell have to cut me some. I don't want to be an idiot about it, though. I pray, and I do mean *pray*, that Travis isn't up to something. But if he is, I need to know it, and the sooner the better."

Orlando clasped his hands behind his head and stared at the ristras hanging on the wall behind her. A long moment passed. Nola finally spoke.

"Well, will you do it?"

"No."

Nola's face fell.

"I mean no, I won't let you two take the truck. I'm driving." He hooked his thumb, indicating me. "I've seen Sylvie drive stick before. I don't want her trashing my clutch."

"I could hug you!" she said. No, she couldn't hug him. But her smile lit up the table, and I knew Orlando could feel it deep down in his stomach, warming his heart.

Or was it just the tequila?

Travis told Nola that he and Glenn were going to shoot pool Saturday night, so that was when we'd make our move. If Travis was lying and actually wasn't going to shoot pool, we'd have him on a technicality. But if he was telling the truth and he left the trailer for the night, we'd be able to get in. Win-win.

We waited until dark; even though the neighbors wouldn't recognize the pickup, they might recognize Nola, so we needed the cover of night. As we rolled into the trailer park, I heard my heart pounding, though it may have been Orlando's I heard. He and I were nervous wrecks.

"That's his place," Nola said, as we passed Travis' trailer. "Drive up the street a bit. Here . . . here's good."

Orlando stopped, killed the headlights. We sat in the darkness, surveying our surroundings. A few trailers down, a dog barked.

"Are you sure you want to do this?" Nola said.

"No, but I'm gonna do it anyway. I don't want to feel like we dragged Orlando all the way over here for nothing."

"Hey, don't do this on my account. I'm perfectly willing to turn around, go get a beer, and forget the whole thing," he said, his knee doing that sewing-machine thing, pumping nervously up and down.

"Are you sure I'll be able to find the box?"

"Positive. It's in the bedroom at the very end of the hallway. There's only one closet in the room. Look on the closet shelf. You'll see a brown cardboard box on the far right. You can't miss it."

"How can you be so sure he didn't move it? Maybe all your questions made him skittish," Orlando said.

"Nah, he knows there's no way in hell I could reach that shelf. And even if I managed to use a broomstick or something to knock it down, he knows I'd have no way to get it back up there."

"Enough chitchat," I said. "Gimme the key."

"What key?"

"The key. The key to the front door. Give it to me."

"I don't have a key."

"What? Are you telling me he never gave you a key?"

"His lock is all jacked up and I'm not strong enough to get it open. So he never bothered to give one to me."

"No. Nuh-uh. No, no, no," I said, squeezing my head between my hands.

Orlando bonked his forehead on the steering wheel a couple of times.

"How am I supposed to get in?"

"Just break in, you know, go through a window or something."

"What do you think this is, *The Rockford Files*? I don't know squat about breaking into a trailer."

"You'll figure out something." She leaned over and thwacked me with her two fingers. "Get going!"

"All right, all right, I'm going."

I hopped down out of the truck, quietly closing the door behind me. She leaned out the window, gave me her version of a thumbs-up. At least I think that's what she was doing. Because she didn't have a thumb, I couldn't be sure.

"If he drives up, I'll honk the horn three quick blasts," Orlando said.

"Got it." I took a deep breath and then trotted down the street back to Travis' place.

I stood on the sidewalk in front of his trailer, wondering how to get inside. I decided to try the easiest thing first: maybe he had left the door unlocked. I stumbled around his yard, peering into the darkness, arms outstretched like a zombie's, searching for his front door. Damn, didn't they believe in streetlights in this lousy neighborhood? Couldn't somebody at least turn on a stupid porch light? I stubbed my toe on something heavy on the ground, knocking it over.

"Ow, jeez, goddamn son-of-a . . . !" I hissed under my breath. I leaned down and turned the thing over. It was a hibachi. Great, now I had charcoal all over my hands. Where in the hell was the porch?

A dog barked again. A light came on in the trailer next door. I crouched low, fixated on the light, holding my breath. I thought I saw a sliver of a woman's face peeking out from behind the curtain; then the curtain fluttered, the light went out, and I breathed again.

I inched cautiously forward, but not cautiously enough, stumbling on the porch steps, lurching forward, saving myself from a face plant by clutching the porch railing. I tried the door handle. Locked. *Crap, crap, crap.*

The door had a glass panel in it. Maybe there was something in the yard that I could break it with. Maybe I could hurl that lousy hibachi through it.

No, no, that would make too much noise and leave a big mess. It would be best to get in, get on with it, and get out, nice and clean. I checked the windows, hoping to find an open one.

No luck. Then I saw it: the doggie door. If I could fit my heifer ass through that doggie door, I wouldn't have to break anything. I got down on my knees, lifted the flap, and started scooching my way through. This technique was working well, right up until I got my hips wedged in it. I twisted this way and that, raking my hip against the sharp end of a screw that was poking out. In a fit of angry exasperation, I violently wrenched myself the rest of the way in.

I sat up on the shag carpeting of the living room, my pulse racing, my face sweating, my four-inch-long screw-inflicted scratch oozing. Something glinted in the dim light. I whirled my head around and saw it was only the silver decal on the chest of the *Lost in Space* robot. "Stupid robot! You nearly gave me a heart attack!" I said.

I headed down the hallway, feeling my way back to the bedroom, and stopped at the last door. It was closed. My chest was squeezing my heart so tight, it hurt to inhale. The kitchen clock ticking, the water heater hissing, every creak of the vinyl-covered wood grain paneling sounded ominous. I stared at the closed door, imagining what I would do if I opened it and Travis was there, sitting on the waterbed, a Magnum, the largest hand-gun in the world, cocked in his hand.

Stop it! Nobody's in there! Just open the damn door!

Slowly I turned the handle and eased the door open. The moon was up now, shining through the slats of the aluminum blinds. I stood still, squinting, waiting for my eyes to adjust to the new level of light. I scanned the room, spotting a small turquoise-colored vase on the headboard. And what was that on it? Ugh—Kokopelli! That dumbass flute-playing nimrod! Is there no escape from Santa Fe Style?! I hoped this wasn't a bad omen.

I made my way over to the closet and opened its door. There—there was the box. I stood on tiptoe, reached for it, and noticed the charcoal mess on my hands. Annoyed, I wiped my hands on my jeans. Then I reached again, but couldn't get a grip on the box. I needed something to stand on.

I walked back to the kitchen, moving faster now that I knew my way, and grabbed a bentwood kitchen chair, took it back to the bedroom. I stood on it, got the box down, and then sat on the waterbed, angling myself to take advantage of the moonlight, waited for the wave action to settle down. I lifted the lid off the box. It was full of envelopes. On the top was a photograph of Travis and a woman who looked to be about the same age as him. Travis looked almost the same as he did now, except his mustache was longer, walrus-style. Bleh! They were sitting on a sofa, both smiling for the camera. His arm was around her. Both of them were wearing wedding rings. Huh, that must be his ex-wife.

I lifted up the picture and flipped through the envelopes. All but one had an Albuquerque return address from somebody named Janice. Janice Matthews. Matthews was Travis' last name.

The postmarks. They all were within the last year. The most recent one was only a month old. I considered taking just that letter. No, better to read it here, and then put it back. Don't want to leave—or take—any evidence.

As the waterbed gently sloshed me back and forth, I read the letter in the moonlight.

Dear Travis,

I've tried to be nice to you, tried to tell you every way I know how to tell you. But you just don't want to listen. I don't want to be married to you anymore. I've signed the papers and now I need you to sign them, too. It's time for both of us to move on, but I can't do that and neither can you until you sign.

You asked me for another chance and then another and then another and I'm just sick of it. You asked me in your last letter if I ever loved you. Yes, I suppose I did. But I don't love you now and I won't ever love you again. You lied to me, you cheated on me, and when I needed you the most, when Kylie was sick, you were nowhere to be found. I need a man I can depend on, and it's not you.

At first I thought maybe we could be friends, but now I know we can't do that. So please, just let Kylie and me get on with our lives. If you won't do it for me, at least do it for Kylie. Stop writing me, stop calling me and just sign the papers.

Janice

Underneath this letter was an envelope from two weeks ago. It was addressed to Janice, from Travis. It was unopened, the message "Return to Sender" scrawled across it.

I put Janice's letter back in its envelope. Travis is still married! He's been trying to get back with his ex for months. I flipped back through the letters. The oldest one was stamped six months before he'd met Nola. He's been lying to Nola from the very beginning!

I had to tell her.

Didn't I?

I heard the sound of car tires scrunching on gravel, and shot up off the waterbed. I stood on the chair and strained to put the box back on the shelf. I gave it a good push and started to step down. Suddenly the seat of the chair gave way, and my right leg rammed through the middle of it while my left leg raked down its side. I lost my balance, stumbled backwards; one leg still trapped in the chair, fell backwards onto the bed. On impact, a tidal wave surged through it, tossing me back and forth, savagely banging my elbow on the wooden headboard. The Kokopelli vase tumbled off the headboard, dumping its contents into my hair. What the? What *is* that? I thought, flailing at my hair with my hands. In the moonlight, I saw thick, yellowed slivers of something on the bedspread. Fingernails! Or were they toenails?! Gack!

I rolled off the bed, jerking and squirming around, whipping my hair back and forth like a madwoman, trying to fling the toenails out. Crap, they were all over the bedspread! *Quit freaking out! Get a grip, girl!* I stood listening for the car, not breathing, ears straining. Nothing. It must have driven past.

I wiped my hands on my pants again, trying to get more of the charcoal off, not wanting to smudge the bedspread. Choking back a gag, I scooped up the nails, put them back into the vase, and placed the vase back on the headboard.

Carrying the broken chair, I headed down the hall, paused in the kitchen. What was I going to do with it? I couldn't just put it back by the table or jam it in a closet or hurl it out in the yard.

A horn honked.

I flung the door of the trailer open, slammed it behind me. Carrying the chair under one arm and feeling my way in the dark with the other, I careened down the porch steps into the yard and broke into a dead run, heading down the street to Orlando's pickup truck.

Orlando must have heard me coming or seen me in his rearview mirror because the engine was running by the time I got there. I hurled the chair into the truck bed, jerked the door open, and scrambled in.

"Where'd you get that chair?" Orlando said.

"Yeah, what's with the chair?" Nola said, "And what the hell's all over your pants?"

"Just drive! Drive, man, drive!"

24

We were out of the trailer court, heading down San Pedro. Nola couldn't wait any longer. She wanted answers. Was I OK? Was I hurt?

No, I assured them both, I'm not hurt. Nothing a tetanus shot wouldn't take care of, anyway. And a vigorous hair brushing and shampooing.

Did I find the box? Did I open it?

Yes, I told them, I found the box.

And?

And nothing. The only thing I found was rent receipts for the trailer and utility bills.

Orlando heaved what I took to be a sigh of relief, but Nola was incredulous. She sounded almost disappointed. She and Orlando had sat in the pickup for a nail-biting half an hour, scared Travis would come home and catch us. Now, apparently, our expedition had been a complete waste of time.

"I need a drink," Nola said. "Let's get some daiquiri mix and go to my place." She got no argument.

Back at her apartment, we congregated in the kitchen and watched as Orlando whipped up some drinks in the blender. They wanted to hear the whole story. How did I get in? Why did I have the broken chair? What was all over my pants? I told them the story, demonstrated vividly how I shimmied through the doggie door, acted out how I had walked down the hallway trembling, exaggerated (but not by much) the drama and the fear, and told them I'd nearly pooped a pinecone when I heard the horn honking. They were both laughing.

I was about to tell them about falling on the waterbed and began in a grave tone, "Nola, I have to ask you something."

"What?"

"Why in the hell would anyone keep toenails in a vase on the headboard?"

"Uh-oh. You found them?"

"No, they found me."

Orlando wanted to be let in on the joke, so Nola had to confess to him that Travis liked to clip his nails in bed and put the clippings in the vase.

Orlando was appalled, but Nola simply shrugged as if to say, "That's my man! What can I do?"

Orlando wanted to know if Travis would notice the missing chair. I blasted out of the trailer in such a panic I hadn't considered that. Nola didn't think it would be a problem, that the only thing Travis seemed to care about was his *Lost in Space* collection. If the matter came up, she would say she broke the chair the last time she was there and so put it out by the dumpster and forgot to tell him about it. Sounded pretty weak to me, but because she so rarely lied—to me or to anyone else—I was pretty sure Travis would believe her. Besides, he was probably so worried about his own lies, it wouldn't occur to him that he might be the victim instead of the perpetrator.

We finished our drinks and I suggested we call it a night. At the door, Nola apologized to me for all I'd been through. Then she apologized to Orlando for making him an accessory to our crime. Orlando, gracious as ever, said that though he wouldn't want to do it again, he had to admit he enjoyed the thrill of it. A little.

He and I walked together down the stairs and got in his truck. It was almost midnight and maybe it was the daiquiri kicking in—all I could think about was getting to bed. I slouched down in the seat, rested my head against the doorframe, wrung out. Orlando looked me over. "Tired?"

"Oh yeah. Maybe a smidge drunk, too. When will I learn I can't handle liquor? Damn this ten-percent Indian liver." I yawned, closed my eyes.

"Did you lie to Nola?"

A shock of adrenaline zoomed through my brain, but I did not move. I kept my eyes closed.

"Did you hear me, Sylvie?"

"Yeah, I heard you."

He reached over and thwacked me on the arm with his finger, demanding my attention.

My first impulse was to lie to him, too. Like big brother Clint taught me so long ago. Keep the story consistent, Clint told me, so I won't have to keep track of which lie I told to whom. Besides, even if Orlando knew I was lying, he couldn't prove anything, so he would eventually have to accept the lie as the truth.

Dammit all to hell, I'd only told one lie tonight and I was already confusing myself.

This lie, if I told it again, would cause a festering doubt in Orlando's mind for now and forever. I'd convinced myself I had to lie to Nola to protect her. But lie to Orlando? No. If I did that, I was only trying to protect myself.

His eyes drilled into me until the traffic light changed, forcing him to look away.

I sat up straight, steeling myself to the task. The daiquiri, which had made my tummy feel so warm and happy ten minutes ago, was now making my gut spasm.

Then I told him. I told him about the letter I found, about how Travis was still married, about how he'd lied to Nola for months. As I talked, he stared straight ahead, focusing intently on his driving, spending an inordinate amount of time checking both ways as he entered intersections, thoughtfully flipping on his turn signals at every turn, seemingly absorbed with the task of getting me back to my apartment safely.

Then: "Who the hell's Kylie?"

"Damned if I know. Maybe she's his daughter."

"Didn't you say he didn't have any kids?"

"That's what he told us when we first met him."

Why, he wanted to know, did I want to keep this information from Nola? Why didn't I tell her the truth and let her make up her own mind about what she wanted to do about it? Wasn't it really her decision to make, not mine? Hadn't she said at Tomasita's that she didn't want to be blind-sided again?

Sure, that all sounds perfectly reasonable, I told him. But you weren't there when Todd ran off with Sara. You weren't there when Nola was in divorce court, explaining how he had abandoned her; you hadn't seen her humiliation, felt her pain. He'd never seen her cry—few people ever had. Believe me, I said, it isn't something you wanted to see.

And what about this? So far, she'd been lucky—there was always somebody there to help her when she needed it. But someday her parents would be gone and who knew where Emily and I would be in ten years, twenty? Then what would she do?

"I don't understand you. I thought you hated Travis. You should be thrilled to see them split up."

"Yeah, I used to think that way, but I changed my mind."

"I didn't think anybody could ever change your mind about anything. What happened?"

"You did it. You made me change my mind."

"Me? When?"

"When I was at your parents' house that day and you asked me about Travis. I told you about him and you said he sounded like he was a reasonable guy. You made me feel like a selfish bitch for always complaining about him."

"That was before I knew about this! The guy's *married* for fuck's sake!"

"Not for long. Now that he and Nola are tight, I bet he'll give up on Janice. In his own repugnant way, he probably really loves Nola. You don't know. Travis might be her last chance."

"Last chance for what? For love? You gotta be kidding me. How old is she, thirty?"

"She's twenty-eight."

"Whatever. I'm telling you, she's going to find out about the wife sooner or later."

"Maybe not. If I tell her now, she'll dump him for sure. And then what happens? If I keep my mouth shut, some day, Travis and Nola might get married and the two of them will live happily ever after and she'll never know a thing about Janice or Kylie and none of this stuff tonight will matter."

"You don't believe that," he said.

"When it comes to Nola, anything is possible."

25

At first, my lie kept me awake nights. Swallowing the lie was like swallowing a lit cigarette; its evil ember smoldered inside me. The night I had sat in the moonlight on Travis' bed, I was positive I shouldn't tell Nola about the letters. After the argument with Orlando, I wasn't so sure. I'd tried so hard to be the type of person he would respect and admire, hell, the type of person *I'd* respect and admire. I thought I'd understood what was required, but then he threw me a curveball. Why did people have to be so danged inscrutable?

As the days turned into weeks, the red-hot ember died down, and I found myself thinking about it less and less. Then Nola called, reigniting it.

She was doing well, she said. Travis hadn't been working on the weekends quite as much, so they'd been able to spend more time together. He was going off to play cards with his friends on Saturday night. Would I like to come over for dinner? She was willing to cook if I'd help her at the grocery store.

"What about Emily? Is she going to be there?"

"I asked her and she didn't want to. She's been going out with this new guy, Kirk, and it's like she's fallen off the face of the earth."

I knew what she meant. Nola had practically done the same thing herself when she met Travis.

The idea of it just being the two of us at dinner made me nervous. She'd have hours of uninterrupted time to interrogate me, and I worried I'd crack under the pressure. But if I told her

I couldn't come over, she'd want to know why, and then I'd be forced to stack lie upon lie until I was suffocated by a steaming pile of my own bullshit.

I told her yes—I'll come over.

That Saturday she drove us to Piggly Wiggly. She pulled into the lot and began maneuvering the Impala into a handicapped parking space.

"Uh, what are you doing?"

"What do you mean?" she said, leaning forward, pressing hard onto the steering wheel so she could reach the shift lever. She cut the engine.

"You can't park here."

"Why not?"

"It's a handicapped spot. Didn't you see the wheelchair painted on the pavement?"

"So?" she said.

"So? So, you can't park here. You can walk just fine."

"I defy anybody to tell me I'm not eligible to park here. Ha! So there!" She shot me an impish smile. As usual, her logic was unassailable. The car stayed where it was.

In the store, I pushed the cart as she called out items she wanted. As we turned into the canned meat aisle, a sense of foreboding came over me.

"Let's get a couple of cans of tuna fish," she said.

"Why? Why do you need tuna fish?" My eyes narrowed in dark suspicion.

"For tonight, for dinner."

"No tuna fish. No way."

"Oh, c'mon! My mom gave me this wonderful recipe for a tuna fish casserole. It's delicious! You take a can of cream of celery soup and—"

"No, no, no, oh hell no!"

"Shush! Everybody is looking at you!" she rasped, looking over her shoulder at the shoppers behind us.

"Can't we just have tacos?" I whispered.

"No, they're too difficult for me to handle."

"We'll make them open-faced."

"Doesn't that make them tostadas?"

I clasped my hands together, was almost down on one knee. "Please? Anything but tuna fish. Pretty please?"

Mercifully she backed off the casserole idea, and I left the canned meat aisle unscathed.

At the checkout stand, the cashier's face lit up at the sight of Nola. "Nola! How are you doing today? What have you been up to?" she said. "Is that a new haircut? It's *so* cute on you!"

They chatted amicably for a few minutes about haircuts and their plans for the weekend. Nola asked her how her kids were doing. The cashier asked her how work was going and blah, blah, blah. The cashier finally noticed me standing there and realized I was with Nola. "Oh. Hey," she said to me, then immediately turned her attention back to Nola.

As we walked out to the car, I asked Nola if she and the cashier were friends. Nope, not really, but she shopped at that store all the time, so she and Rhonda had gotten to know each other. *Rhonda?* What the—? I'd been going to that same grocery store for years, and the cashiers rarely made eye contact with me, and when they did, they seemed vaguely annoyed. I didn't know their names, and they sure as hell didn't know mine.

I found myself feeling peevish about getting snubbed by people I didn't even know, people I hadn't given a second thought to until today. Nola got the rock star treatment while I stood in the background like her balding, middle aged, paunchy roadie.

I was still puzzling over it when we pulled up to her apartment complex, but then my attention turned to schlepping grocery bags up three flights of stairs.

At last all the bags were in the apartment and we began to put the groceries away. The doorbell rang, startling us; unexpected company was almost never a good thing.

"Hey, little lady! How's it shaking?"

Travis. Ugh. What the hell was he doing here?

He stepped past me into the apartment. I recoiled as the noxious scent of his aftershave wafted over me. "Good lord, what is that? Is that *Hai Karate!* I smell?"

"Yeah, it is. Thanks for noticing!"

It's not a compliment, dumbass, I thought. "Gee, I didn't know they were still selling that stuff."

"Yeah, I found it at Walgreens. Got a good price, too." He tilted his chin up and used his hand to wave some of the stench in my direction. He turned away just in time to miss me pinching my nostrils shut. I followed him as he strutted into the kitchen.

"Hey hon! Just thought I'd pop in before going to the game. Whatcha gals doing tonight?" He kissed Nola on the cheek and gave her fingers a squeeze. Her eyes sparkled at the attention and she snuggled up to his chest.

I felt the ember in my stomach flare up.

I went back into the living room, wondering what I would do if she invited him to join us for dinner. Maybe I could feign appendicitis or some sort of epileptic seizure. I sat on the couch and practiced lolling my tongue out and rolling my eyes back in my skull.

Soft cooing came from the kitchen. I flipped the TV on. Eccch, now I heard slurping noises. I turned the TV volume up, trying to engross myself in a rerun of *CHiPS*. No go. The show was even more inane than I remembered. Since there was no TV remote, "channel surfing" meant I had to get up and walk over to the TV each time I switched stations. Even with all the hopping up and down off the couch, it didn't take long to see everything; there were only four channels. I turned the volume up again, this time loud enough to drown out whatever was going on in the kitchen.

Ten minutes later, Nola was walking him to the door, saying she'd see him the following week. He gave her a loud slippery sounding kiss on the mouth, during which I tried to stay focused on the motorcycle chase on *CHiPS*, hoping this would be the episode in which Paunch's luck at long last ran out.

"Awwwwmmmm," she sighed extravagantly, as she pushed the door shut behind her. She had seemingly forgotten about any transgressions, real or imagined, that he had perpetrated. I found myself still torn between wanting them to live happily ever after and wanting Travis to be abducted by aliens, who would roughly probe him and then take him to their planet in a galaxy far, far away, never to be seen again.

"Well, how's good ol' Travis doin'?" I asked, uncomfortably feigning interest.

She plopped down on the sofa next to me. "He said he won some money playing cards last night, so he was pretty excited about that."

"Did you ask him to stay for dinner?"

"I was going to, but before I could, he said Glenn was expecting him. I guess his buddies want a chance to win some of their money back."

"I hope they aren't going to be playing at his house—he might find he needs a fourth chair."

"You know, it's kind of peculiar—it's been almost a month and he hasn't mentioned that stupid chair. You'd think he would have noticed it missing by now."

"Maybe he has noticed it, but he thinks he's losing his mind. 'Say, didn't I use to have four kitchen chairs? Wow, man, I gotta cut back on the brewskis. And the reefer.'"

I expected to get a smack because of the reefer remark, but all she said was, "Usually it's just the two of us at dinner at his place, but it's his turn to host the next card game with his friends. He's definitely going to notice then. When I tell him that I broke it and threw it out, he'll be all right with it. I hope."

I told her that I didn't know exactly how our breaking-and-entering episode was going to bite us in our ample butts, but I had the feeling that somehow, someday, it would. "Well, I can't worry about stuff I can't do anything about," she said. "Besides, next week is our two-year anniversary!"

"Anniversary of what?"

"Our first date. It's hard to believe we've been together two whole years."

I'll say, I thought.

"I'm going to Santa Fe next weekend. I want to go down on the Plaza to find him a nice turquoise ring as a present."

Going to the Plaza to shop for jewelry means shopping from the Indians who sell their wares on the portal at the Palace of the Governors.

"What is it with people and jewelry? What a waste of money."

"He said he wants a ring, so *that's* what I'm getting him. Do you want to come with me or not?" Her right eyebrow arched, probably bracing herself for one of my Santa Fe tirades.

I imagined how such a trip might go. First, there was the hour-long hellish drive up I-25. Then we'd fight traffic all the way down Cerrillos Road to the Plaza. Next we'd drive around and around trying to find a place to park, maybe getting into a shouting match with another driver over a parking spot. Then we'd fight our way through throngs of tourists to the Palace of the Governors where the Indians lined the sidewalk, sitting on their blankets, hawking their wares. That's when the real trouble would start.

"Well?" she said.

"No, I don't want to go. I can't stand walking up and down the portal, looking down at all the Indians and having them looking up at me. It's embarrassing to be looking *down* on them. And I hate the way they stare at me like they're trying to figure out what I am. 'She could be Indian. See her cheekbones and her nose? Nah, look at her hair, too fine—maybe she's Mexican. No, her skin's too light,' trying to size me up to see if they should be snotty or friendly to me, trying to figure out whether I know the difference between a squash blossom and a squashed possum."

"Since when do you give a crap what anybody thinks?"

What *was* bothering me? Maybe reading *Little Big Man* and *Bury My Heart at Wounded Knee* had over-sensitized me to what The White Man had done. Watching the movie *Billy Jack* sure didn't help, and I felt terrible whenever I saw that commercial of the "American Indian" (who, as it turned out, was second-generation Italian) shedding a tear because of pollution. Damn! Had I succumbed to some diabolical Hollywood marketing campaign?

"Well?" Nola said.

"I just don't like all that scrutiny."

"Hmm," she said, tilting her head, pondering the problem. "I'll see what I can do to draw attention away from you."

She had a talent for bringing my whining to an abrupt halt. I'd be going to Santa Fe after all.

The day didn't start out great. Nola was supposed to drive, so I met her at her place. We were in her car, belted in and ready to go. She pushed the starter button. We heard something click, but the engine didn't turn over. I'd asked her if maybe the battery was shot, but she said no, her dad had replaced it the last time she'd had car trouble. She'd had a problem starting it a time or two since then.

I wanted to know if Travis had checked it out, looked under the hood. No, he's been too busy with work, she said. *Too busy?* What the heck does he have to do all weekend besides drink and gamble and shop flea markets for preposterous outfits for his stupid *Lost in Space* action figures? My face twitched, prepping for a sneer, but I fought it off, replacing it with a face I hoped showed only mild concern over our immediate difficulties. Things were so much easier back when I believed it was acceptable to blurt out whatever I was thinking.

"No problem, I'll drive," I said.

Once out on the highway, Nola asked me how Emily was doing. As usual, I didn't know. True, I'd just seen her at my parents' house, but that didn't mean much. I asked how she was doing. *Fine.* Whatcha up to? *Nothing.* Anything new? *Nope.* After trying to talk to Emily, I understood what it must be like to be the mother of a sulky teenager. The only good thing about the visit was that Clint was there. He'd come home from North

Dakota, sick of its brutal weather, burned out on small-town life, and (I surmised) bored with his most recent girlfriend. He was staying with my parents until he figured out what his next move was. While he was working in the oil fields, I often worried he'd be killed by an oil tank explosion or have his arm amputated while repairing an oil rig, but now he was home, safe and sound, all fingers and toes intact. Actually, I wasn't sure about the toes yet . . . I'd have to ask him about that. Toes or no toes, there was great comfort in having my big brother live in the same state I live in.

The tourists must have been sleeping in; the drive to Santa Fe wasn't as bad as it could have been. Only a few people cut me off and only one lady gave me the finger. Our good luck continued; it only took ten minutes of cruising around to find a parking spot instead of the twenty I had expected. It was fun walking over to the Plaza, too. It was a lovely warm summer day, the sky cloudless and blindingly blue. Bits of cotton fluff from nearby cottonwood trees drifted in the air like tiny white feathers. As we walked, I reached out, letting some of it waft into my open hands. Nola tried to do likewise, opening her two fingers, trying to will some of the fluff to come to her. It didn't work, so instead she lifted her face upward, letting it float down across her cheeks. Maybe this day would be non-hideous after all.

Given the ease of finding a parking space, we were surprised at the throngs of people that were already under the portal at the Palace of the Governors. Unlike us, most didn't seem to be searching for anything in particular, so they were taking their time, clogging the sidewalk, forcing us to step out into the street to get around them. Must they look at every single item in front of every single vendor?

As kids, Clint and I were fascinated by and scared of the Indians on the Plaza. They looked like "real" Indians then, the kind you saw on *Bonanza,* the kind who might scalp you and drag off your women-folk. They sat under the portal on colorful blankets with shawls draped around their shoulders. They wore moccasins and necklaces heavy with turquoise, coral, and silver. I don't know if they enjoyed dressing like that or if it was a calculated move to bring in more tourists.

An outsider might think one would see Indians all over Santa Fe, especially with the Indian School in the middle of town, but that was not the case. In high school, I knew only one Indian. Before that, I don't remember knowing any. Around town, the only time I saw anyone who was obviously Indian was at the grocery store. Typically, the scene would unfold as follows: Male Indian driver pulls into parking lot in dilapidated pickup truck, with two or three other people in the cab with him. Truck has camper shell. Indian woman in bed of pickup truck opens camper shell from inside. She and two or three other women, all in long, flowing skirts, crawl out over the tailgate of the pickup and head into the store. Upon seeing this, I would always think, (a) why in the hell are you women putting up with riding around in the bed of a pickup truck? and (b) if you insist on riding back there, why the hell don't you put the tailgate down when you want to get out?

Ten years ago, Indians on the plaza would talk to you, really try to sell you on a piece, insist you try something on, offer you a free sample of their cookies, bargain with you. In the 1980s, their outfits changed. Many wore Nike sneakers and cheap windbreakers from Kmart. T-shirts, jeans, baseball caps, and sunglasses were common. If they sensed you meant business, they would engage you, but otherwise they kept their heads down and continued to read their paperback books, knit, or rearrange their displays. Now that Santa Fe Style was sweeping the country, there would be no schmoozing, no bargaining, and by God, they would wear whatever the heck they felt like wearing.

Santa Fiends often passionately took sides on various Indian issues, and the local newspapers were awash in commentary about tribal issues such as water and mineral rights, suicide, alcoholism, education, taxation. The commentary was from Anglos. And Latinos. Not Indians. Never heard much about what they thought.

As Nola and I walked under the portal, I wondered if we were in for an hour's worth of nonstop stink-eye from the Indians. Two minutes later, it became obvious that nobody was judging my level of whitey-ness or fixating on my possible personal involvement in tribal issues. Instead, Nola became the focus of attention as she casually meandered along the portal, occasionally pausing to get a better look at a vendor's display of rings. I heard the tourists whispering behind us and saw the bewilderment on the face of any Indian who happened to glance up as Nola walked by. I felt a tension growing in my neck and shoulders, a tightness in my jaw. A few minutes ago, I was almost looking forward to strolling along, enjoying the weather, and hey, maybe buying a little something for myself. Now I was thinking, *Nola, dammit, just pick something and let's get out of here!*

I was lagging behind her, so when she came to a stop in front of one display, she had to call back to me. "C'mere!" she said, beckoning me, her fingers doing a little bounce up and down. I pushed through the crowd until I was next to her. The vendor was a chunky woman in a dark blue T-shirt, black sweatpants and sneakers. The only jewelry she wore was a beaded bracelet. She might have been fifty, but given the typical hard life on the reservation, she may have only been thirty-five.

She sat on a low campstool with her back to the wall. On one side of her was a Styrofoam ice chest, which I supposed held her lunch and drinks. On the other side were several well-worn brown grocery sacks. Sticking out of one sack was some kind of crochet work. Crochet struck me as very un-Indian-like. I wondered if this woman, like my grandma, crocheted little dresses for plastic dish soap bottles and Kleenex boxes.

On the blanket in front of her were several rows of blue velvet lined trays that held rings and bracelets made of silver, most with turquoise or coral inlays.

Nola said, "Can I see that ring right there on the third row, two down. Up one, no—up one more. There, that's it."

"Hand that up to me, will you?" she said to me.

I squatted down, eye level with the vendor. She plucked the ring out of its slot, eyed me suspiciously before handing it over, as if she believed there was a good chance I would run off with it.

I stood and held the ring up for Nola, turning it over in my hand a few times so she could inspect it.

Nola asked the woman, "How much for this one, please?"

"For you? Today, a special. Sixty dollars."

"Just for me, huh? Sixty bucks?" There was no sarcasm or accusation in her voice, only mild amusement.

"No, no. For you, I mean fifty. Only fifty dollars."

Amazing. If I had tried to bargain with the woman, she'd have shot me a look that said, "First you cheated us out of our land, and now you're trying to cheat us again on our jewelry! You should be ashamed of yourself!" I couldn't fathom why she had lowered her price for Nola, seemingly without any bargaining at all. It couldn't have been Nola's charming personality; she hadn't said much more than four sentences to the woman.

"I'll take it. Can you box it for me please?"

The vendor said yes and searched for a gift box. Nola asked me for help getting her money out. She would have been able to get it herself if she'd had a counter to put her purse on, but there wasn't even a card table handy. I took her purse off her shoulder and opened it, then delicately moved around items within, trying to find her wallet without disturbing anything. I tried to appear cavalier about it, like "No big deal, I'm her best friend; I rummage around in her stuff all the time." In truth, I'd only had to do it a few times before. The feeling I got from it was exactly the same as when I was a teenager and stole money out of my mom's purse so I could buy cigarettes—only worse, because here I had an audience. I had no reason to feel guilty or embarrassed, but I felt both. I had broached The Sanctity of the Purse.

The transaction done, we left the portal and made our way back to the car. The drive back to Albuquerque seemed especially long. Nola kept nattering on about Travis and how they were going to celebrate their anniversary. He was supposed to come over the following weekend and they were going to go out to a dinner theater. She thought the place was called The Barn or something like that and she wasn't sure what was going to be playing. *Roomies* or *My Roomie*—something with roommate or roomie in the title. Supposed to be a comedy. She'd heard they had delicious prime rib there, and she loved prime rib, especially with a good horseradish sauce. The sauce should be hot, but not too hot, you know, just creamy and spicy and . . .

Arrrrrggghh! Enough! I thought. *I don't care where you're going or what you're going to eat or whether or not the stinkin' horseradish sauce is too hot! Travis is a lying, conniving, low-life! He's using you! Why can't you see that? And I swear to you, if I have to listen to Rod Stewart sing "Do you think I'm sexy?" one more time, I'm going to open the car door and fling myself out on the pavement! For God's sake, change the channel!*

". . . I'm so lucky that I found Travis," she went on. "When Todd left me, I have to tell you, I was convinced I'd never find another man who would even date me, to say nothing of marry me! I was almost convinced I was going to wind up some frustrated, bitter spinster, you know, with like eighteen cats." Her voice broke off and she swallowed hard, struggling with a catch in her throat, and then regained her composure. "I'm doing my best not to get too excited. One has to be realistic about such things, you know." She paused, perhaps considering her odds. Then, in a sudden microburst of joy, she said, "Yay! I'm going to a dinner theater!" and started bobbing her head to good ol' Rod.

"Gee," I said, "Sounds like fun."

26

"Wake up!" Nola said, with entirely too much enthusiasm for 8:00 on a Saturday morning. I'd been asleep on her sofa, deep in a delicious dream about somebody, but who? Why the heck did she have to wake me up right in the middle of it?

I rubbed my eyes and untwisted myself from the blankets that tangled around my legs. We'd been up late the night before, talking about The Anniversary. I didn't mind hearing about the dinner theater and the play. I didn't even mind the vivid descriptions of each and every dish on the buffet. Unfortunately, had I been a researcher for The Kinsey Report, I would have been well satisfied with the end of her story.

"Aren't you going to ask me what time it is?" she said.

"Say what?"

"In the movies, whenever one actor wakes up another actor, they always ask what time it is."

I sat up and tried to blink the sticky stuff off of my eyeballs. "I don't give a—"

"Now, now, what have I told you about all that cussing?"

"That I sound like a sailor. Or a trollop. Or a trolloping sailor. I forget."

"I told you no man thinks a potty mouth is sexy. Now get up and let's go to the grocery store. I've got a terrible hankering for a waffle and I'm out of eggs."

Arrrrgh, the grocery store again? "Can't we just go out?"

"No! We're both saving money, remember? Me for my new house, you for your trip to New Zealand or wherever the heck it is you always say you want to run off to. We'll never get anywhere if we squander our money on frivolities. So get up!"

"I'm not going anywhere without a shower. Why don't you go down to Emily's? She's probably got some eggs."

She hadn't thought of that. "Good idea. Back in a flash."

"Take your time," I said as I opened the door for her and watched her head downstairs.

I went in the kitchen and started a pot of coffee. While it brewed, I busied myself sweeping the kitchen floor. Nola was a fastidious housekeeper, but chores that required elbow grease sometimes didn't get done. "No elbows, don'cha know," as she liked to say.

I heard a thump at the door and thought it was Nola kicking at it, unable to open it because she had a carton of eggs clutched under her chin. I opened the door.

Oh, bloody hell. Travis.

"Nola's not here," I said, as I attempted to close the door on him.

"Well, aren't you cute as a button, sleepyhead," he said, pushing his way in, his voice full of warmth and familiarity. It made me gag.

"Thanks for noticing," I said. Eddie Haskell, I wanted to add.

I was wearing what I'd slept in: sweatpants with dried paint on the knees and a T-shirt I'd picked up at a trade show.

"What's that say on your T-shirt?"

"DEC."

"Deck? What's that mean?"

"D-E-C. It stands for Digital Equipment Corporation."

"What kind of company is that?"

"They make computers, like the VAX 11/780. Minicomputers."

His blue eyes, pale and squirmy behind the thick lenses of his glasses, lingered on my crotch. "Minicomputers, huh? Is that what girls in miniskirts use?"

I opened my mouth to reply then snapped it closed. This "not cussing" thing was going to be tougher than I thought. This was the first time I'd been alone with Travis, and I doubted my ability to get through it without a sedative. Nola, help! What's taking you so long?

Civil, civil, be civil. Nola might actually marry this guy, so I'd better get used to the idea. I gritted my teeth. "Coffee?"

"You betcha," he said, following me back to the kitchen. As I poured the coffee, he stood too close and reached across me to get the sugar bowl on the counter top. "'Scuse my reach," he said, his forearm brushing against me. I flinched, but he seemed not to notice. He lifted the lid of the bowl. "Sugar's empty. Do you know where Nola keeps it?"

Oh yeah, I knew where it was. And the tuna fish and the cream of frickin' broccoli soup. The toilet paper, the shampoo. Vacuum cleaner bags, screwdriver, hammer. I knew her place as well as my own, maybe better. Why didn't *he* know where everything was? He'd spent more than enough time here to know something like that, the lazy bastard. I gave him a steely stare, and then bent over to get a bag of sugar out of the lower cabinet.

I reached for the bag and was startled when he rested his hand on my back, on the little band of bare skin that peeked out between my T-shirt and sweatpants. Instinct told me to twist around and slam my fist into his testicles. *Wait*, I thought. Perhaps that would be an overreaction. Perhaps there is no need to cripple him. Perhaps, just perhaps, this was merely a friendly gesture on his part. If he and Nola got married, he would be almost like a brother-in-law to me. Maybe this was just his way of saying, "Hey, sis!" No reason to get my knickers all in a bunch.

"You see it?" he asked, innocently.

I sucked in a long breath trying to calm myself and then lifted the bag, putting it on the counter with a little more force than I intended. I looked at him. He looked at me. The bag sat there. Oh, goddamn it, he wants *me* to open it and fill the bowl! What a worthless . . . arrrgh! No, no way. I will stand here staring at him until the solar system turns to dust before I fill that bowl! I stood motionless, like a cat watching a baby bird perched on a low branch, my eyes boring into his.

He opened the bag and filled the sugar bowl.

I didn't want to risk bending down again, so I turned my attention to the kitchen sink, leaving him to put the bag away. He left it on the counter.

He busied himself with his coffee, adding sugar, stirring, tasting, adding more sugar, tasting again. I wanted to shriek, "Just drink the damn stuff already!" and dump the sugar bowl on his head. He said nothing during his complicated coffee preparation ritual. Much as I hated to talk to him, the quiet was making me uncomfortable. I needed conversation.

"How's work going?" I asked, passionately apathetic about the subject.

"Same shit, different day. What about you, how's work going at that DEC place?"

"I don't work for DEC. I wish I did, but I don't. Maybe after I graduate."

"So, who do you work for?"

"I work for the state."

"Doing what?"

"I'm a warehouse clerk."

"Where?"

"You know where that big blue building is on the highway, a few miles past Oglala?"

"No."

"You know where Oglala is, don't you? That dirt road that connects Alvarez to Lopez Street? It's a shortcut between them; I take it all the time."

"Cool. I've always wished there was a faster way to get to Alvarez. So you're talking about that three-story building by the Chevy dealership?"

"Yeah, it's near there." His questions were making me jittery. The less he knew about my personal life the better. It was bad enough that he'd seen me in my PJs, so time to nip this in the bud. Let's talk about him, because Lord knows, he likes talking about him. "Are you working this weekend?"

"I was supposed to go out to Placitas but decided to hell with it. I just don't feel like going out there and dealing with those crazy assholes."

"Won't you get in trouble for skipping work today?"

"Ah, what they don't know won't hurt them."

"But don't you care—"

"Fuck that. They don't pay me enough to care." He smiled and gave me a wink, as if he had just revealed to me the secret to success in the workplace.

The guy likely made more money than me, and I cared about my job, cared a great deal, in fact. I was pretty sure that any further questions I might have about his work ethic would be unproductive.

"Placitas, huh?"

"Nobody but dumbass dog breeders and druggies live in that little hellhole."

"Dog breeders? Why would dog breeders live there?"

"Guess 'cause it's sort of out in the country. They probably figure nobody will complain about the dogs barking all day and half the night. I don't understand what it is with those people. Maybe you have to be crazy to think you can make a living breeding dogs, so all dog breeders are crazy. Or maybe only Placitas dog breeders are crazy."

"I had to go out to see this one woman," he continued. "Her place was a real dump, even without the three dog runs she had next to her trailer. I'd guess there were twenty dogs in those pens, barking their heads off, standing in their own filth. As soon as I opened my car door, I smelled the dog shit."

"What kind of dogs were they?" This was actually getting kind of interesting.

"I don't know—I think some kind of huskies maybe. Weird, though. Every single one of them was white."

"Samoyeds. I bet they were Samoyeds. They're sled dogs, you know. They make good sled dogs because they have a double-layered coat. What kind of lunatic would raise that kind of dog in the middle of the desert? The heat must be terrible for them!"

"Anyways . . . " he went on, crushingly indifferent to the dogs' misery. "I knock on the trailer door and this woman opens it and the damn trailer reeks of dog shit, too. She asks me to come in and man, oh man; I really did *not* want to do that. I saw a couple of bowls of petrified canned dog food on the kitchen floor. I hate the smell of canned dog food. Off in the corner of the living room was a filthy cage with a bunch of yapping puppies in it. There was even an open 50-pound bag of dog food on the damn couch!" He shook his head in disgust. "And dog hair on everything—her, the carpet, the furniture, everywhere. To top it off, it must have been 90 degrees inside that damn trailer. I was pretty sure if I went inside, I'd puke."

Breakfast was beginning to not sound so good to me.

"And over the couch, hanging on the wall, I remember this—I have a partially photographic memory, you know—were these certificates in gold frames."

I wanted to ask him what his definition of a "partially photographic memory" was but decided the question would likely trigger an argument.

"Must have been awards her dogs won at shows. They were printed with these snooty dog names, like 'Cerebrus Maximus Who-Gives-A-Flying-Crapus.'"

That actually got a little smile out of me. "Did you go in?"

"Nah. I lied and told her it was against bank policy for me to go in anybody's house. I handed her the paperwork and got the hell out of there."

"Sounds pretty awful."

"I had to go out there again awhile back." He seemed to be enjoying his captive audience. "The client lived in this rundown old adobe. Stinky, worn out green sofa on the porch with a broken washing machine sitting next to it. Couple of rusted out cars in the driveway, overflowing garbage cans next to the house. You know the type."

Indeed I did.

"I knocked on the door and nobody answered, so I peeked in the front window. Some old guys about fifty and some young kid, no more than thirteen or so, were sitting at the kitchen table, no shirts on. There was a big pile of mary-ju-wanna on the table and they were scraping handfuls of it into baggies."

"No kidding?" I was a stranger to the drug world, so my surprise was real. "What'd you do?"

"I knocked a few more times, but they never got up, just kept fillin' those baggies like they hadn't heard a thing. I can dig that, I guess. But I started thinking, hey, if the guy *did* answer the door, maybe thought I was a narc, came out waving a shotgun around, well, like I said before—they don't pay me enough to care. So, fuck it, I didn't even bother with the dude's paperwork, I just took off."

"Wow. Sounds scary."

He sniffed a manly sniff and took a slow sip of his coffee. "I deal with that kinda crap all the time. And worse."

Huh. Maybe his job wasn't as cushy as I had believed. And whaddaya know, we'd just had ourselves an almost pleasant conversation. Maybe his work ethic wasn't exactly the best, but at least he *had* a job.

I'd been looking at him during the druggie story, but now I turned back to the sink to finish washing up the dishes. I picked up a pie plate, started scrubbing it. "Sounds like you've had some interesting adventures."

His arms encircled my waist, and I felt his chest pressing against my back, his breath in my ear.

There was no rationalization, no conscious thought. There was only an instantaneous rush of rage-fueled adrenaline. In one smooth motion, my wet, soapy hands jammed down between my stomach and his arms and wrenched outward, breaking his grip on me. At the same time, I stepped back into him and savagely raked my foot down his shin, smashing my heel down into his instep. He fell away from me, hopping on one foot, his face flushed red. "Ow! Sunnuvabitch! Whadya do that for?"

I whirled around to face him. If his grope had not caught me by such surprise, I would have laughed at the ridiculousness of his question. As it was, I was coiled taut, ready to knock him to the floor and pummel his head into mush.

His expression changed from surprise to anger and he made a grab for my wrist, but I sidestepped his reach.

The front door flew open. It was Emily, carrying a bag of groceries. Nola was right behind her and said, "We're back!" She spotted Travis, who was now bent over, massaging his instep with his hand. "Hey, what happened?" Her eyes traveled to the damp spots on the front of my pants.

He stole a glance at me, must have decided to take his chances on me keeping quiet.

"Nothin' hon. I just tripped over the coffee table."

"Oh, poor baby! Are you OK? Need me to kiss it?"

"I'm fine," he snapped. Then, more gently, "It just stings a little bit."

"What the hell took you so long?" I said, with more venom in my voice than I meant to show.

"Emily didn't have any eggs, so she offered to take me to the store. We went to Piggly Wiggly, and I invited her to join us for breakfast. Now here we are." Her eyes went to Travis again, then to me, trying to read us. Then she smiled. "I brought cinnamon rolls," she said, in a lilting singsong way, the way you'd talk to obstinate toddlers. As if that would make everything all right.

It didn't hurt.

Travis hung around until the cinnamon rolls came out of the oven, then grabbed a couple for the road and left. Emily, Nola, and I sat down at the table for breakfast. Before I'd gotten down a bite, Nola said, "He's gone now. What gives?"

"What are you talking about?" I said.

"Yeah, what are you talking about?" Emily said, mystified.

"You looked positively deranged when we came in. What was going on? Did you two get in an argument?"

Crap, crap, crippity crap. She's going to call Travis and ask him the same thing. Of course, he'd lie. I could lie, too, but if I did, it would have to be the same lie as Travis' lie. If our stories weren't the same, there would be trouble. Should I just tell her? Yes. No. Maybe later when it's just the two of us. Dammit, I needed more time!

Nola waited.

I had to say something. Something not a lie. Maybe something vague.

"No, it wasn't an argument. Really, everything's fine. Sometimes I get all wound up over nothing. I don't even want to talk about it, it's just embarrassing—you know how I get." I studied my plate with intensity.

"Kids," she said, shaking her head.

"Ain't it the truth," Emily said.

The truth. Nola and Emily were constantly telling me to back off the truth. Sylvie, you're too blunt, they said. Stop giving unsolicited advice, they said. Think before you speak; you hurt people's feelings when you say things like that, even if it is the truth.

And now the truth was down on its knees pleading to be told.

I watched Nola happily butter her waffle, humming something I couldn't quite make out, something that sounded like "Raindrops Keep Falling on My Head."

The truth was going to have to wait.

27

Orlando would understand this. He would know how to handle the situation, how to talk to Nola, how to avoid driving a stake into her broken heart. Maybe she would be so mad at me for lying about Travis that she wouldn't want to be friends with me any more. What was I going to do? I'd made a mess of things, for sure. Now it was just a matter of minimizing the fuckage.

As soon as I got home, I called him. "I need to talk to you right away," I said. He had a baseball game that morning, so asked me to meet him at the field.

At the ball field, I found an isolated spot on the bleachers and sat. I spotted Orlando in the outfield. The batter hit one high that arced in his direction. Orlando was such a slow and deliberate guy, I was positive there was no way he'd get to the ball in time. He trotted at what appeared to be a leisurely pace, following the ball's trajectory. Odd—he covered a tremendous amount of ground without seeming to move much at all. Then he raised his mitt and the ball simply plunked into it.

I watched him field this way again and again, languidly moving across the field, looking as if he were accidentally in the right place at the right time to catch any ball that came his way. I had never seen him play any kind of sports before. I was stunned. What else was going on with this guy that I didn't know about?

The game dragged on. I'd forgotten my sunglasses. I could almost smell the refrying of my retinas. Sweat was pooling up in the back of my jeans. Salty rivulets of it were sliding down my forehead and into my eyes, stinging them. My swollen tongue lay parched on the dusty floor of my mouth. Water! Water! I must find wa-ter!

This *Treasure of the Sierra Madre* moment was abruptly halted by the end of the game and the sight of Orlando motioning me to come down to the field.

"Hey, man. *Qué tal?*" he said.

"Qué-a-whole-bunch-of-stuff, that's what."

"Let's talk at my place. I need a shower and I want to get out of these smelly clothes."

Me, too, I thought, but decided against suggesting it. "Do you have air conditioning?"

"Yeah."

"It's settled. Let's go."

Back at his place, he cranked up the air conditioning and told me to make myself at home while he got showered and changed. I sat in a big, comfy leather chair, and then it occurred to me I might be leaving a rim of salt on it from my sweaty clothes, so I leapt up and wiped the seat with the tail of my shirt.

I crossed the room to the air conditioner, a rattling old window unit, and turned my back to it, lifted up my shirt, reveling in the cool air on my skin. Ahhhh, blessed relief! I scanned the room. His apartment was a lot like mine. Small. Almost worn out. But his stuff looked good. He was obviously getting a better class of hand-me-downs from his parents than I was getting from mine.

I studied the spines of his books. He had lots of sci-fi like *Dune* and *Do Androids Dream of Electric Sheep?* There were classics too, Mark Twain and Dickens. He'd evidently hung onto many of his college textbooks as well. Was he ever going to need that *Principles of Watershed Management* or *Hydrologic Hazards* again?

Maybe so. After all, he did work for the New Mexico Department of Energy doing some sort of groundwater stuff that I didn't really understand.

"I'm starved," he said as he came into the living room, his hair still wet from his shower. "Let's go into the kitchen." I followed him.

"Want anything?" he said as he opened the door to his refrigerator.

"Just a Dr Pepper if you've got one."

"As it so happens, I do." He pulled one out, tossed it to me. He took more things out of the fridge and began to make himself a sandwich. "Let's get down to it. What happened?"

I told him about Nola leaving me in her apartment and Travis showing up. About how I'd forced myself to have a conversation with him. "That's progress!" Orlando said. "You know, I've been thinking about what you told me that night when we were at Travis' place. Maybe you were right. He's going to get divorced pretty soon. Besides, lots of guys are separated from their wives; it doesn't mean they're scumbags. So maybe we should all just relax and see what happens."

"He came on to me."

"He *what*?"

"He came up behind me while I was washing dishes at Nola's and put his arms around me."

"Like how?"

I told Orlando to turn around, face the sink. Then I circled my arms around his waist, pushed my hips into him. I held him this way a few seconds longer than strictly necessary, then let go.

"Oh," he said. "That's fucked up."

"Yeah. My sentiments exactly."

We sat down at his small kitchen table. He took a bite of his sandwich, chewed it slowly, drummed his fingers on the table. "You gotta tell her."

"I *know* I have to tell her. I'm not a nitwit!"

He shrugged, tilted his head, made a face that indicated that he believed the evidence was to the contrary.

"Quit that! I'm going to tell her—I'm going to tell her the next time I see her. I'm going to spill my guts and I'm probably going to cry like a sniveling five-year-old, and I'm going to tell her how sorry I am that I didn't tell her that Travis was married and . . . "

"Yes?"

"Arrrrgh! What I'm trying to get at is what *exactly* do I say? I was thinking about something like, 'Travis is a repugnant manipulative two-timing whore-boy, and he's been lying to you and making a fool out of you for two solid years and why the hell didn't you listen to me the first time I told you he was a waste of skin.' Which, by the bye, I thought was pretty good, but I really wanted to work in 'reptilian' somehow, too. What do you think?"

"I think something a tad more diplomatic, a bit less 'Sylvie' is in order."

"Can I keep 'whore-boy'?"

"No, probably not."

"Can I just tell her about Travis having a wife and a kid and leave out the part about him grabbing me?"

"I'm not sure."

An hour of deliberation left us exhausted and undecided. We couldn't come up with anything that wasn't going to cut Nola to the bone. Things had already gone too far. Yes, Nola should have listened to me, but *I* should have listened to Orlando when he'd advised me weeks ago to tell Nola what I'd found in the box. She was braced for bad news then, ready to hear the absolute worst. But now, after their *anniversary*, for Christ's sake . . . Why did she have to be so damn sentimental?

"We'll do it together," he said.

"What do you mean?"

"Tell Nola. You invite her over to your place and then we'll tell her. We'll say you wanted to tell her what was in the box but that I talked you out of it."

"Why should we tell her that?"

"So you don't sound like the bad guy."

"What the hell? I'm *not* the bad guy. *Travis* is the bad guy."

"What I mean is that if we say it was my idea, then maybe she won't think that it's your fault that—"

"My fault that what? I was trying to do the right thing for *her*, not for me. And a few minutes ago, before you knew he hit on me, you were agreeing with me, that I should keep my mouth shut."

"All right, all right, calm down. I'm not blaming you for anything, and I know you would never do anything intentionally to hurt Nola. We'll figure it out." He put his hands on my shoulders and gently pushed down. "C'mon now, sit."

Orlando knew my penchant for running scenarios, understood that when forced to speak off the cuff, my words usually left nothing but scorched earth behind, so it was critical I practice what I was going to say. We did a few dry runs. Orlando pretended to be Nola as I broke the news. The first run, he played Nola as angry and indignant. I was ready for her to be angry, but it never occurred to me that she wouldn't believe what I told her. It was good we practiced that one.

We ran the scenario again, except this time Orlando pretended to cry. "Why? Why would anyone treat me this way?"

he fake-sobbed. His performance was too credible, piercing my heart. I put my arm around him to comfort him. Her. Whatever.

One more run. This time, as Nola, he simply said, "Get out. Get the hell out of my house."

"But I was just trying to protect you. I was hoping he really did love you and that you two would— "

"Now. Get out. I never want to see you again."

Was it possible she would react that way? After all these years together, everything we'd been through? I told Orlando maybe we should reconsider; maybe we should let this thing play out. Sooner or later, Travis would slip up and Nola would discover for herself what a vile cretin he was.

"I can't believe you're waffling on this again. We're doing this for her, not for you. If you are really her friend, you'll risk your friendship to help her."

"Is that just some ludicrous platitude, or do you really believe that?" I wanted to know.

"Oh, I believe it," he said. "I definitely believe it. But I hope I never have to prove that to you."

28

Nola, Emily, and I sat on Nola's balcony surveying a sea of cheap apartment rooftops, reminiscing about the good old days when life was full of adventure, drama, and suspense. These days, we knew what each day would bring. We would get up. We would eat generic corn flakes out of black and white boxes printed with the slogan, "Suitable for everyday use." We would go to work. We'd come home, eat, sleep, do it all over again the next day. Who knew adulthood was so dull? At first, the reminiscing made us screech with laughter, but after the fourth or fifth story, I wondered out loud if we would still be reliving those same tired stories 30 years from now.

"No, dammit! We can't let that happen," Nola said. "We need new stories, new adventures!"

Emily rolled her eyes. "Like what? Find some guy, drive out to the toolies, and have sex with him in the back seat of the car?"

"Nah, that's what I did last weekend," I said. They shot me looks that said "Nuh-uh!" and "Really?" at the same time.

Our aspirations were high, but our funds were low. We needed to be creative. "How about going to the pool at the rec center? We could swim and lounge around, scope out the guys," Nola said.

I knew what Emily was thinking. No way would she want to be seen in public in her swimsuit. She had a perfectly acceptable looking body, nothing to be embarrassed about or ashamed of, but, as my grandma used to say, she wouldn't be "caught dead at a dog fight" in her swimsuit. Swimsuits were for sunning yourself in the privacy of your own backyard, not for strutting around in front of God and Everybody. If we went to the rec center, however, Nola would be on the receiving end of all the stares and hushed comments, not Emily, not me. This irony was not lost on me.

"Nah, let's think of something else," Emily said, and in truth, I was a little relieved that I wouldn't have to expose my soft underbelly, literally or figuratively.

"How about horseback riding? There's a stable out by Corrales we could try," I said.

Nola shook her head. "Nix on that. Falling off a bicycle is one thing; getting thrown off a thousand-pound horse is another."

"We could ride on the same horse. You sit in front of me and I'll hang onto you and the reins and steer the horse." I demonstrated how I would hold onto her.

She laughed. "Anybody who says 'steer the horse' isn't somebody I want to be riding with. How about something a little less life-threatening, say miniature golf?"

"No, I don't want to play stupid miniature golf."

"Why do we put up with you? You've turned into such a wet blanket," Emily said.

"Me?" I pointed to myself. "A wet blanket? Are you kidding? *Me?*"

"Allow me to remind you what you gave as Christmas gifts last year."

"What?"

"Smoke alarms. You gave every dad-blasted one of us smoke alarms. Ho, Ho, holy crap."

"You may thank me for that some day! Whenever you hear about a fire and some guy dies, don't you ever wonder why the dumb jerk didn't simply jump out the window? It's because smoke fills the room. Then that smoke actually *ignites*, setting the whole place on fire. And when you inhale that smoke"—I made a sizzling noise— "your lungs incinerate."

They looked at me placidly, unmoved by the ghastly scenario that I'd presented.

"Wet," Nola said.

"Blanket," Emily said.

"OK, OK, I'll go! Sheeesh!"

Consensus reached, we headed out to the golf course. This was the first time I'd been out with Nola since Travis hit on me. As Nola drove us to the golf course, I thought about "The Talk" that I was going to have with her tonight after Emily left. I sat in the backseat of the Impala, reviewing how I would break the news to her, psyching myself up for the wrath that was sure to come my way. I caught a glimpse of Nola's reflection in the rearview mirror. She was smiling, relaxed, looking forward to the delightful summer afternoon ahead of her.

She and Emily started a lively discussion about the sort of wedding they would want "the next time around." Nola said, "I got married in a church the first time. So I think the next time I'd like to get married somewhere exotic, maybe in a hot air balloon or something like that."

I felt that old familiar burning in my stomach.

I tried to ignore the front seat conversation, tune out all the talk of white gowns, flower girls, and color schemes. Ordinarily, I wouldn't be able to resist ridiculing their sappiness, but today I sat silent in the backseat, lost in dread.

I never thought the sight of a miniature golf course could fill me with such joy. I practically climbed over Emily in my rush to escape their wedding jabbering.

We walked up to the small rental booth, the three of us crowding close together. The clerk was a girl who looked about fifteen years old. Her nametag said "Tamara," a perky enough name for sure, but her posture told me all enthusiasm for her work was sucked out of her a very long time ago. As she glanced up from her *People* magazine, an exasperated sigh escaped her petulant, fruit-punch-colored lips.

Tom Selleck was on the cover of the magazine. Was it my imagination or was he *always* on the cover? Did *Magnum PI* have some magical power to which only I was immune? Or perhaps *People* had a high-ranking executive with a twisted fetish for overgrown mustaches and chest hair. I thought Nola and Emily might be interested in my speculation but then remembered that Travis had an overgrown mustache and chest hair.

The clerk stared at the three of us. After an unnaturally long pause, she said, "How many?"

"Three, please," Nola said.

At this, Tamara was immobilized, her eyes fixed upon Nola's tiny, two-fingered arm. You could almost see her teenage brain frantically scouring its neural pathways, unable to come up with a suitable response to what she must have considered a bewildering request.

"Tamara," Nola said. "Am I pronouncing your name correctly? 'Tam-uh-ruh'—is that right?"

"Uh-huh."

"That's an unusual name. I've never heard it before. It's lovely."

"Thanks." The girl was thawing, slowly.

"So Tamara, do you have any clubs that are really light-weight?"

"We have clubs for little kids," Tamara said, no doubt thankful for this guidance. She turned to the racks of clubs behind her, selected one, and showed it to us. It was about two feet long. I stifled a snort at the ridiculousness of it, picturing Nola practically standing on her head as she gripped the club with her two fingers.

"No, sorry, I don't think that one will work for me. It's a little too short. Got anything somewhat longer and lighter?"

This may have been the only real challenge Tamara's job ever presented. Surprisingly, she threw herself into the task, rummaging through multiple racks of clubs, turning to study Nola, then turning back to the clubs again. "Hey, how about this one?" she said, sliding it on top of the counter.

"Hand it to me, please, Emily."

Emily put the club's handle between Nola's two fingers. Nola bent over, pretending she was hitting a golf ball, swinging it gently back and forth. She lost her grip and it clattered to the sidewalk. "Ooopsie!" she said. "Let me try it again."

Emily picked up the club, handed it to her again. "Hang on to it a sec," Nola said. She situated her fingers this way, then that, until she was confident in her grip. Tamara looked on, her hands clasped together in front of her chest, her face expectant.

Nola took a few more practice swings, refining her grip each time. "Good, good—this one will be fine. Thank you for finding just the right one."

Tamara flashed a smile, perhaps feeling for the first time this summer that she'd done something worthwhile.

Off we went, with me carrying Nola's club as well as my own. The first hole was a replica of an adobe hacienda. The goal was to hit the ball through its front door. Emily went first. It took her nine strokes to knock the ball through. *Haha! Rookie!* I was next. Five strokes for me. *Eat that, Emily!*

Nola stood quietly next to us, observing our technique. Her turn. I placed the ball on the ground for her and then handed her the club. She pondered the hacienda, then studied the putting green, then looked back at the hacienda, then studied the green again. She squinted, like Eastwood in *A Fistful of Dollars*, bracing for a gunfight.

Emily shot me a look that said, "If she takes this long at every hole, we're going to be here all damn afternoon. Whose brilliant idea was this, anyways?"

Nola bent over, then almost imperceptibly rocked her shoulders. The sweet spot on the club's face made contact with the ball.

The three of us watched, astonished, as the ball rolled toward its target and came to a stop, two inches away from the hacienda's doorway. "You lying hussy! You've played this game before!" Emily said, putting her hands on her hips, the line between mock indignation and real indignation razor thin.

"Don't be silly," Nola said, "I've never played golf in my life. That was just beginner's luck."

"Right, sure it was. Luck. That's it."

The rest of the game went pretty much the same, Emily and I dueling it out for second place. Nola shellacked us, beating us on almost every hole.

On the way back to Emily's we had a good laugh about our day's adventure. We agreed that as adventures went, it wasn't much, but it was a decent break in the monotony. Maybe after the wounds of our defeat healed, Emily and I might be willing to go golfing again someday. Nola dropped Emily off at her apartment and we headed to my place.

While enjoying our golf game, I'd avoided thinking about how to tell Nola about Travis. I didn't have that diversion now; it was just the two of us in her car. And as much as I liked Orlando's idea about claiming it was he who had talked me out of telling her about what I'd found at Travis', I couldn't bring myself to add another lie on top of the pile I'd already told.

Maybe when she dropped me off at my apartment, I'd ask her to come in. Then I could slowly work up to it. No, that would be bad. If she got upset and started crying, then she'd have to drive home in that wretched state and I'd feel terrible. Better to tell her at her apartment, not mine. Then I could drop the bombshell on her, she could cry and get angry and throw me out, and *I* could be the one driving home in a wretched state. Yes. That's what I should do.

She drove past my street.

"Hey, you missed the turn. Where ya going?"

"I just remembered I've got my dad's belt sander in the back. He brought it up last week so Travis could borrow it. You don't mind if we run over there and drop it off, do you?"

"Go to Travis' house?" I said, with the same enthusiasm I'd have if she'd asked me to put on a tube top and join her at a monster truck rally.

"It'll only take a minute, I promise. If he's not there, I'll leave the sander under his porch and call him later to tell him where it is. If he is there, I promise we won't stay long."

This was ruining everything. I tried to regroup, figure out a Plan B, but all I could think about was now, no matter what, Nola's dad was never going to see his belt sander again.

"Promise?"

"Promise. Ten minutes, tops."

We pulled into the trailer court, parking across from Travis' place. I got out first, walked around to Nola's side of the car, opened her door, and unbuckled her from her seat belt. She got out and we walked across the street, stopping at Travis' chain link gate. I noticed his car was not in the driveway.

A woman called out from the porch of the trailer next door, the trailer where the light had gone on the night of the break-in. "Hey! Yoohoo! Hey!" Did she mean us? I made eye contact with her, pointed to myself. "Yes! You two!" she hollered.

"Who's that?" I said, subconsciously inching backwards to the Impala.

"That's the Budweiser lady—the one I told you about, the one who came out looking like she wanted to talk to me that day."

The woman got up from her lawn chair, a cigarette dangling from her lips. Next to her chair was an upside-down oak barrel she was using as a table. She leaned over and picked up her drink, took a swig. "Wait up!"

She steadied herself on the porch railing as she came down the steps and then teetered down the sidewalk toward us on red plastic platform shoes. As she walked, the crotch of her pink jogging shorts kept riding up, causing her to reach down with the hand that held her cigarette and give them a tug. She was, I surmised, oblivious to polyester's flammability.

She hadn't looked half-bad when she was sitting on the porch, but now that she was only a few feet away, it was clear that she did not now, nor likely had she ever, actually jogged. She fingered her bra strap, which was peeking out of her black tank top. The tank top had a gold sparkly crown silkscreened onto it that said "Budweiser, King of Beers." The top was too small, so her stretch-marked midsection spilled out over the top of her shorts.

"Hi," she said, tossing her cigarette to the ground and crushing it with her heel. "I'm Crystal." She smiled. I noticed one of her upper incisors was an unnatural shade of grey. Her breath reeked of beer and cigarettes.

"Hi, I'm Nola."

"I'm—" I started but was cut off.

"I live right there," she said, gesturing with her drink, which was tucked in a Day-Glo lime-colored cozy. "You looking for Travis?"

"Yes, we are. Do you happen to know when he left?"

"Nope, can't say as I do." She eyed Nola, searching her face for something. "You guys like dogs?"

"Huh?"

"Dogs. Do. You. Like. Dogs?" she said.

"Oh yeah, we like dogs," I said.

"Wanna see my dog?"

"Yeah, sure," I said, with marked enthusiasm.

Nola's eyes met mine. They said, *Have you lost your freakin' mind?*

We followed Crystal back to her front porch. She called out, "Maya! Come here, Maya!" A little brown and white terrier rocketed out of the trailer's doggie door, headed straight for us, and then sprang on Nola's bare leg, raking its rat-like toenails down her shin. "Ow! You little—" she said, jerking her leg, trying to get the dog away from her. I reached down and grabbed the dog, pulling it into my arms as it wriggled and licked me.

"Oh, shit, I'm sorry! I didn't think she'd do that! Did she hurt you? Oh, I am so sorry! Maya! You bad girl! Bad girl!" She shook her finger at the dog. "Bad, bad, bad!"

Maya kept licking me, not concerned in the least about being bad.

"You guys want a beer?"

"No thanks," Nola said. "We need to get going."

I sat down on one of the lawn chairs with Maya in my arms, adjusting the cushions, trenching in. "Do you have any Dr Pepper?"

"I've got some lemonade. It's not really lemonade though. It's Kool-Aid. Lemon Kool-Aid. You want some?"

"Sure, I'll take some," I said. Nola gave my foot a little kick as she cocked her head in the direction of her Impala.

"Gimme a minute," Crystal said, then went into the trailer.

"What are you *doing*?" Nola rasped. "Can't you tell she's smashed out of her gourd? Besides, I thought you wanted to get this over with as fast as possible."

I leisurely stroked the dog's back. "She's lonely. Can't you see it?" Crystal did in fact seem lonely, but that wasn't the reason for my procrastination. I saw this as a fantastic opportunity to avoid the "your-boyfriend-is-a-jackass" talk. At least for a while.

Crystal came out carrying a tray with two plastic margarita glasses full of ice and Kool-Aid. "Is this glass good for you, Nola?"

"Yeah, it's fine. Thanks."

She noticed her dog, calm now, almost asleep in my lap. "Maya likes you."

I said nothing, kept petting the dog, leaving it up to Nola to make conversation. She asked Crystal what kind of dog Maya was, how long she had had her, how long she'd lived in the trailer court. They chatted amiably for fifteen minutes. Then Nola asked her if she was married.

"I was. Once." She took a long drag off her Montclair, blew it out in a slow, sinister swirl.

"Divorced?" I said.

"You think it can never happen to you, but then it does," she said.

Nola nodded. "Don't I know it! I'm divorced, too."

"I'm not divorced." Crystal said.

Nola and I exchanged confused looks.

"You wanna know what happened? I don't like to talk about it, but you . . . " She jerked her chin at Nola. "You need to know."

"Me?" Nola said.

"Yeah, you. I've been trying to get you alone for I don't know how long, but Travis keeps showing up."

"So, what is it you need to get off your chest?" Her amiable tone had vanished. "Are you going to tell me that you slept with him or whatever? If so, there's no need."

Crystal snorted. "Slept with him? Hah! That's a good one! Fuckin' hilarious is what that is."

Nola said nothing, but I was pretty sure she didn't see any hilarity in the situation.

"You're Travis' girlfriend, right?"

"Yes, that's correct." There was an iciness in her voice that I was not accustomed to hearing.

Crystal studied Nola's face. "I'll be back in a minute." She went inside the trailer, and I heard her rummaging around in the kitchen cabinets, then the faucet turning on and off. She came back out, stumbling on the threshold.

I started to stand up to grab her arm and steady her, but she recovered her balance. "Are you all right?"

"No, but after the Valium kicks in, I'll be just fine. I didn't think I was going to need it, but this is going to be harder than I thought."

"Uh . . . " I eyed the five empty Bud cans that were on the table next to her chair. "I don't think you should be drinking and taking Valium. It's not safe."

Nola looked at me. "Sylvie." The exasperation in her tone said it all.

Crystal kicked off her platform shoes and lit a fresh cigarette. "I've been thinking about what I would tell you. How much and all that. I think I need to tell you about me first, see what you say. Then, if you believe me, I'll tell you the rest."

"Can't you just tell us 'the rest' now? We've got someplace to be," Nola said.

"No, it can't go like that. You need to know *me*."

From three feet away, I heard Nola's jaw socket pop as she gritted her teeth. "Well then, by all means, please go on."

Crystal pointed to her screen door. "See that? That aquarium?"

I peered through the screen into the dim light of her trailer and saw the aquarium on top of a bookcase. "Marcos, my ex-boyfriend, he liked snakes. And lizards. But mostly snakes. He kept them in tanks like that. That tank there—that's the only one left. I got rid of all the rest. When I first met him, he told me he liked snakes and lizards, and I thought that was kinda creepy. Then we moved in together and the tanks ended up everywhere: in the living room, in the kitchen, even in our damn bedroom."

I shuddered. I hated snakes.

"Every payday he brought home live crickets or mice or some damn something to feed them. We didn't have a lot of money, so it seemed crazy to me that he was spending so much money on them. Don't you think it's crazy?"

I nodded. "Oh, yeah. For sure."

"Seems unwise," Nola said, perhaps trying to remain uncommitted until she heard more.

"I never knew nobody into something the way Marcos was into snakes. At first it was interesting, kinda fun even. I liked learning how to take care of them, but of course he would never let me feed them or nothin' like that. Guess he thought I was too stupid to do it right. He didn't know when enough was enough, though. He kept getting more and more stuff. I was working my ass off and he was buying all this shit for himself, but whenever I wanted to buy something for me, he'd have a fit, tell me we couldn't afford it. One day I told him that I was tired of it, that I felt like I was living in a zoo and that he acted like he cared more about those goddamn snakes than he did for me."

"Good for you!" I said.

"That was the first time he hit me."

Oh no. Here we go.

"The next day I thought about it all day long. I made up my mind I was gonna leave, that I wasn't gonna let nobody treat me like that, ever. After work, I went out to the shed to get my suitcase. I was gonna pack up and get the hell of here, go back to my mom and dad. Then I hear Marcos drive up, and I brace myself for another argument. I turn around and there he is, getting out of his car, holding Maya." At the sound of her name, the dog looked up expectantly, wagged its tail.

"Of course, she was just a puppy then, really cute. He said he was really sorry for what happened the night before, that he didn't know what came over him, that it would never happen again. He told me he got the puppy to prove how sorry he was and how much he loved me. For a while after that, he was really sweet to me. On the weekends, we'd make popcorn and snuggle on the couch and watch movies, just like we used to before we moved in together."

I fought back the urge to scoff at his pathetic ploy. Crystal must have seen it on my face.

"You two went to college, I bet." We both nodded in an offhanded way, not wanting to appear unduly snooty. "I wanted to go to college too. You see me and think 'Yeah, right. You? In college? What a joke!'"

Damn! This girl was a mind reader.

"Believe it or not, I got good grades in high school. Like, I loved biology. I hoped maybe someday I could be a veterinarian. Then I moved in with Marcos and he told me I didn't need to go to school, that we were gonna get married and have kids." She smiled then, as if even she couldn't believe she'd fallen for it. "You're thinking I was stupid to stay, huh?"

"Well, I don't know about that," Nola said, her voice gentle again, squelching my need to say something defiant.

"That's what you always think before it happens to *you*. Something funny happens in your brain and you start thinking that it's your fault, that you said something wrong and that's why he got mad or that he had a bad day and then *you* went and got on his nerves.

"Next thing you know, you're wearing long sleeves to work in the middle of July, trying to hide your bruises. Your mom keeps calling you, asking why you don't come over no more and you lie. Your friends stop calling you 'cause you always tell them you're too busy. You got nobody to set you straight, nobody to tell you what a fucking idiot you are."

She studied us through a little cloud of cigarette smoke. "You." She pointed at me. "You wouldn't put up with it, would you?"

"No, no way in hell."

"I figured as much. But it's like this. If a guy like Marcos was in a bar and he saw a girl like you, he might talk to you, but he'd be able to tell right away you wouldn't put up with his bullshit. Then he'd move on. Move on to a girl like me."

Hmm, why would she think that? What was it she saw in me?

"I tried to go fifty-fifty with him at first. You know."

"A compromise," Nola said.

"Yeah, that's it. But it didn't make no difference. Everything was about *Marcos*. He'd come home from work with another snake and I'd say something about it, like how did he think we were going to come up with the money for the light bill if he kept buying stupid tanks and snakes and mice. Then it would happen." She made a fist, jabbed the air.

She sighed and her head slumped to her chest.

Nola and I exchanged alarmed looks. Was she unconscious? Just as I stood up to check her vitals, her head bobbed up and she rubbed her eyes.

"Where was I?" She yawned.

"You were talking about compromise," Nola said.

"I was?" she said, and jiggled her head a few times to clear the fog. "Well, anyways . . . after there was any trouble, Marcos was always super nice and would apologize and say he didn't mean it and he loved me. Loved me like nobody else would ever love me. And that shit worked. Worked for a long time, maybe a year."

She pointed to the fingers on her left hand. "See this?" She held the hand up close to Nola, wanting her to get a good look at it.

"Jesus," Nola said, flinching.

Then Crystal held her hand out to me. The flesh on the backs of her fingers was bright pink and rubbery looking. Her ring finger and her middle finger were partially fused together. My eyes went wide.

"After about a year, things changed. We didn't fight as much, but we didn't talk much either. We hardly went out anymore. And Marcos was lazy. He didn't mind cleaning the snake tanks, but he didn't like no other housework, like washing dishes or scrubbing the tub. He always left that up to me. Some nights I'd get home from work—I used to wait tables at the Sizzler—and I'd be dead on my feet. He'd be sitting on the couch with his feet up, drinking, watching TV. I'd lean over to give him a kiss and he'd say, 'Damn! You stink like a cheap steak!' then he'd laugh and say, 'Just kiddin', hon.' After he talked to me like that, say that mean shit, he'd expect me to make dinner and clean up while he sat on his butt watching TV all night.

"He started coming home late from work, especially on Fridays. Maybe he had a girlfriend, I don't know. He'd come in the trailer, wouldn't talk to me, even look at me. He'd go to the fridge, grab a beer or two, make a beeline for the bathroom. He'd lock the door and I'd hear him filling up the tub. He'd be in there for like two hours. Maybe he was reading his *Herpetology Today* magazines and beating off. Who knows?"

Nola snorted.

I figured I'd get slapped for asking, but I had to know. "What's *herpetology*?"

"It's the study of amphibians. Snakes, turtles, stuff like that." She took a drink of her beer, then pressed the back of her hand to the can, let it cool the damaged flesh.

"Anyways, he gets home one Friday night, grabs a beer and heads down the hall to the bathroom, like usual. I'd had to work the lunch and dinner shifts three days in a row, and all I wanted was to sit down and do nothing. Marcos gets home, looks in the fridge, and hollers, 'Why'd you get Budweiser again? I *told* you to get me Michelob! Where's my fucking Michelob?'"

"I told him, sorry, I forgot. So he grabs a beer and heads off down the hall to take his precious bath. No 'Hi,' no 'How was your day?' Just 'Where's my damn beer?' Not like all this was different from any other day with Marcos, but for some reason, that night it really pissed me off. So, he's going down the hall and I yell at him, 'As a matter of fact, I had a crappy day! Thanks for asking, asshole!'"

A rush of blood surged into my brain. I heard Nola suck in her breath; it sounded muffled and far away.

"He came down the hallway, man, it was like lightning, he was so fast. '*What* did you say?' His face was so red, on fucking fire, but I didn't care, I was sick of his bullshit and his sneaking around with his *puta* girlfriend and all his damn snakes. I got up off the couch and screamed, 'Yeah, you heard me! I said you're an ASSHOLE!' Then he hit me in the mouth with his beer bottle. That's how I got this." She curled up her lip, touched her finger to the grey tooth.

"I guess it's dead or something. I been thinking about getting it pulled." She ran her tongue over the tooth, seemed lost in thought for a moment, maybe contemplating how she'd look after it was pulled, the ugly gap yet another reminder of what she'd been through.

"My mouth hurt like hell, but I couldn't stop, couldn't shut up. It was like everything he ever said or did to me had been building up and I just couldn't hold it in no more. I screamed at him, told him I was leaving. He grabbed me and shoved me against the fridge and was choking me. Maya was barking her head off and then she bit Marcos, right here." She pointed at the back of her leg. "Thank God for Maya! I think he would have killed me if she hadn't done that, because after the bite, he let me go.

"But then Marcos turned around and kicked Maya clear across the living room. She just lay there on the rug. It scared me so bad, I swear, I thought she was dead!" Crystal's voice broke a little here, and I felt some tears coming. Mine, not hers.

"I tried to scream at him but nothing would come out. I guess something in here was messed up." She rubbed her throat, where his hands must have been when he was choking her. "That's when he grabbed my arm and dragged me over to the stove and turned on the burner. I tried to pull away, but he was too strong. He forced my hand to the stove and held it over the flame. The pain was horrible. I fell down on my knees and he lost his grip on me."

My hand went still on Maya's back. A slow, simmering heat started to build in my stomach.

"He leaned down, grabbed my hair, told me if I tried to leave him, he would kill me. He said 'I'll kill Maya, too!' I'd never seen him so mad. He even said he would go over to my Mom and Dad's house and kill them. Then he let me go, stood up like nothing happened, just grabbed a couple of beers out of the fridge and walked back to the bedroom and locked the door."

She picked up her pack of Montclairs, shook one out. The sun was almost down now, and though she was only a few feet away from me, she seemed to be receding into the twilight.

"I spent the night on the couch. I couldn't sleep. Poor Maya! I was so worried about her, but I guess Marcos had only knocked the wind out of her. And my hand, the pain—you can't imagine it. I put ice on it, but it still hurt. I curled up in a ball and I cried and cried. I felt trapped, like there was nowhere I could go, like this was going to be my life from now on, with the fighting and the beatings until someday Marcos loses it completely and stabs me to death or runs over me in the damn Sizzler parking lot."

Crystal went quiet, her hand hanging limp at her side, the Montclair burning down to the filter. She stared into the darkness, at what, I did not know. I reached over, took the cigarette from her and stubbed it out in the ashtray. Was it possible her beer and Valium cocktail might actually kill her? Should we call an ambulance or just make a good, stiff pot of coffee?

She squeezed her eyelids tight, as if trying to decide if she should go on. Her eyes were still closed when she spoke again in a voice so low that Nola and I had to lean in to hear it.

"The next day, he took off and was gone the whole weekend. I didn't see him again until Sunday night. When he finally got home, we ate dinner in front of the TV and he didn't say much the whole night. He left for work the next day without saying a word to me.

"As soon as he left, I took a bath. Then I put on some heavy rubber gloves, the kind you wear when you're scrubbing floors. I went around to each aquarium and got all the snakes and put them in the bathtub. I let them squirm around in there until I was ready to go to work. Then I took them out and put them back in their tanks."

That's weird. Why would she do that? I thought. I looked at Nola, but in the dimness, I couldn't read her expression.

"Marcos came home from work and took his bath. The next day, after he left for work, I scrubbed the tub with bleach and then took my bath. Then I put on my rubber gloves, took all of the turtles out of their tanks and put them in the tub and let them run around, then put them back in their tanks. Marcos came home, took his bath. The next day I did the same thing over again, snakes one day, turtles the next, lizards the next.

"About the third week of doing this, I added another step. I rinsed off the animals' feeding dishes in the tub, too, and let the rinse water pool up in the bottom of the tub. Especially on Friday nights."

Huh? I was starting to think she was as nutty as Marcos.

"One day I come home from work, and Marcos is in the bathroom on the toilet, moaning and whimpering. I leaned against the door and said, 'What's wrong, baby?' And he says, 'I've got diarrhea and I've been puking my guts out all afternoon.'

"I tell him, 'Oh, that's awful! Do you want me to take you to the emergency room?' No, he says, he's fine, just leave him the fuck alone. So I do. The next day, he's still sick, tells me through the bathroom door that he found blood in the toilet, but he still doesn't want to go to the emergency room. Tells me he thinks it's just food poisoning. He stayed home from work that day, and the day after that, spending most of the time in the bathroom puking and crapping. But like most stupid, stubborn men, he didn't wanna see no doctor.

"On the fourth day, I woke up in the morning, turned over to look at him, and he was stone cold dead."

Nola's head snapped back, as if she'd been slapped.

I jerked so hard, Maya was startled out of my lap. She scrambled over to Crystal.

"Salmonella poisoning. From the snakes," she said, then took a drag, blew a perfect little smoke ring. "Or maybe it was from the turtles. No way to know for sure. Marcos knew about snakes and reptiles, knew they carried disease; knew you had to be very careful to wash your hands every time after you touched them—wash them good, real good. Guess he never thought he might have caught something from the snakes. Not him. He knew everything there was to know about reptiles. Not like me—I'm just a stupid bitch. What would I know about it? Nothing, man, absolutely nothing."

29

Without the dog in my lap and my Kool-Aid glass empty, I felt twitchy and awkward in the silence. It was Nola who spoke up.

"You said something when we first sat down, something about how you wanted *me* to hear this story. Right?"

How she could possibly remember anything that was said before Crystal's story started I couldn't fathom. I was having trouble remembering exactly why we were even in this damn trailer park.

"Yeah. That's what I said."

"Why? I don't understand. I'm really sorry about everything that happened to you. It's awful, truly awful. Whatever may have happened to Marcos, well, you sure make it sound like he had it coming. But what's all this got to do with Travis or me?"

"Has Travis ever pushed you or hit you?"

"Don't be ridiculous! Of course not."

"Well, I've lived in this trailer court a long time. Me and him, we go way back. I've seen a lot of shit go down at his place."

"Like what?" Nola said. Even in the gloom of the porch, I sensed her irritation.

"Like people screaming at each other late on a Saturday night. Like the cops turning up and banging on his door. Like hollering and crying and throwing shit out in the front yard. And like Travis' sorry ass getting pushed into the back seat of a police cruiser."

"And *who* was he screaming at?"

"His wife."

"You mean his ex-wife."

"Is that what he told you?"

"Yes. He's divorced."

"I bet he told you he didn't have any kids, too. Right?"

Oh. My. God. Crystal's gonna spill it.

"Are you telling me he's still married and he has kids?"

"Yeah. That's exactly what I'm telling you. One kid, actually. Her name is Kylie."

"That's a lie."

"No lie. If you don't believe me, just ask him."

"Maybe I will."

"Maybe you should. But if you do, you better get ready to call the cops. And maybe an ambulance, too. That boy plays rough."

I didn't know if I should believe her. I didn't want to believe her. If Travis was a little teensy bit badass, yes, that's suboptimal, for sure. But it's not scary. I'd never been *afraid* of Travis or thought he might hurt Nola. I looked at Crystal's damaged hand and wondered how long it might take to get a permit for a snub-nosed .38.

"When is the last time you saw her, his ex-wife or wife or whatever she is?" Nola asked.

"Janice? I don't know, maybe two weeks ago."

Ay-yi-yi. This must have felt like a dagger in Nola's heart.

"Was the daughter with her?"

"No. Janice wouldn't bring Kylie back here. She's too good a mom to do that. It was just Janice, by herself. She wasn't at his place very long, maybe ten minutes. After she left, Travis came slamming out of the trailer and burned rubber out of the driveway. I was sitting right here when it happened."

I'd had enough. "Nola, let's get out of here before Travis gets back. C'mon. Let's go." I stood up.

Nola rocked her body, trying to get out of the lawn chair, but she'd sagged down too deeply in the frayed webbing to get up the necessary momentum. I leaned over her, put one hand behind her back, held onto her tiny arm with my other hand, then pulled her out of the chair.

Crystal stood up, steadying herself with one hand on the doorframe. "I'm sorry, Nola, I feel bad for you. I don't know you, but you seem like a nice lady. I don't want you to go through what I went through. What Janice went through. What half the fucking women in this trailer court have probably been through. So I hope you'll listen up, girl, and get the hell away from him."

"Thanks, Crystal. You've given me a lot to think about," Nola said, oddly impassive, sounding as if she were thanking an insurance agent for a quote.

There was an uncomfortable silence between Nola and me as we walked back to her car. I opened her door and buckled her seat belt, then got in on the passenger's side. I had to say something.

"Man, I feel like I'm in the middle of a soap opera! All we need now is for someone to come out of a coma and have amnesia. Then we'd have the whole package, get a spot on *Phil Donahue.* Maybe even a movie-of-the-week deal, don't you think?" I was trying to lighten the mood, but it wasn't working. Nola didn't so much as crack a smile.

"That was one heck of a story! Maybe her brain is shot from all the drinking and the tranquilizers and she's got Travis confused with the neighbor on the other side of her," I jabbered on.

"I doubt it. It's possible she's trying to get back at Travis for something. Like she had the hots for him and he wasn't interested."

Nola was focused on her driving, so missed my face's reflexive scrunch of revulsion. No way did that girl have the hots for Travis.

"Here's what I think," I said. "Don't go out with him anymore. Don't answer the phone when he calls. Maybe move to a new apartment. Get an unlisted number."

"Should I change my name, too?"

"Maybe."

"Now who's crazy? I'm not going to do any of that, Sylvie. I'm just going to talk to him, calmly. Rationally. Ask him about Janice and what's-her-name. See if he really is divorced."

"You mean force him to show you his divorce decree or what? Why bother? Why don't you just dump the guy?"

"You don't get it, do you? It's a lot easier for somebody like you to find a boyfriend than it is for somebody like me. I want to get married someday, have a family."

"I want to get married, too." Even I was surprised at the lack of conviction in my voice.

"I'm telling you, you don't understand. I don't just *want* to get married, I *need* to get married."

"No you don't, you're doing fine by yourself."

"But I don't *want* to be by myself! I'm not like you, I need to be around people, have companionship, feel like I belong somewhere, belong to *someone*. If people don't like you, don't want to be around you, you don't care. You're *you*, Sylvie. And you don't give a flying fuck what anybody thinks about you."

"Well, that's not exactly—"

"Forget it! I don't care what you say; I'm not going to dump Travis without talking to him. I want to know the truth."

There was that word again. Sitting on Crystal's porch, I was convinced I'd been saved, that I wasn't going to have to tell Nola anything about Travis; Crystal had done all the dirty work. Now I realized there was no way out of it; I must present my own evidence to the mounting case against Travis. If she screeched the car to a stop, kicked my ass out, no big deal—I've got a lot of experience with that sort of thing.

"Then here's the truth. Travis hit on me." Keep talking. Get it all out. "Remember when I spent the night at your place and you left me to get groceries with Emily? That's when he did it."

It took her so long to respond that I thought she hadn't heard me.

"Did what, exactly?" she said.

"I was washing dishes and he came up behind me and put his arms around me." For days, this secret had burrowed in my brain like a radioactive nematode. Now that I'd actually said it out loud, it seemed trivial. Not shocking in the least compared to Crystal's horror story.

She stopped at a light. "You aren't just yanking my chain, are you? I know you've never liked Travis." She turned to face me. "Look at me."

I looked at her.

"Truth?"

"Nothin' but."

"He's done," she said, then turned her eyes back to the road.

The quiet earlier had made me uncomfortable. The silence now was killing me.

30

After a night of fitful dreams, dreams of Nola fully armed, choking me, screaming at me that I had ruined everything, I woke, my jaw throbbing from clenching and teeth grinding. I biked to work, hoped the exercise and fresh air would clear my head, help me prepare for what was going to be a rough few weeks—maybe months—as Nola got over Travis.

It didn't work. The day crawled by, and at 4:30 p.m. the casual observer would have spotted me staring intently at my monitor, as if thoroughly engrossed in my code, when in fact my mind had dragged me back to Crystal's porch. Nola's getting off lucky, I thought. Unlike Crystal, there was a high probability Nola would end her relationship with her bank account, her dignity, and her teeth intact. *Lucky indeed!*

I was thinking about the aquarium on Crystal's bookcase, trying to decide if I had seen something moving in it or if it had been my imagination, when the phone rang, making me jump. It was Nola. She never called me at work. Hell, nobody ever called me at work. Which was just the way I liked it.

"You need to come get me," she said.

"Why? Where are you?"

"I'm at Travis' trailer. I need to leave, but my goddamn car won't start."

"What are you doing over there?"

"Never mind that. Just get over here!"

"Where's Travis?"

"He left. He's gone. How soon can you get here?"

"I rode my bike to work today."

"Fuck!"

"Hey, I'm sorry. I'll be there; I just have to go home first to get my car. It'll take me about a half hour to get home, then another fifteen minutes or so to drive over to the trailer."

"Fuck. Fuck, fuck, fuck!"

What the heck was her deal? "Maybe you should call Emily," I said. "She can probably get over there faster than me."

"All right, I'll call her too, but look, I don't want to get stranded here. Please, Sylvie, get here as fast as you can."

"I can be on the road in five minutes. But what will we do about your car?"

"We'll burn that bridge when we get to it," she said and hung up.

I sat for a moment, pondered our conversation, troubled over the inordinate amount of cussing. I had never, ever, heard Nola say "fuck" that much.

I better haul ass.

I usually changed out of my work clothes and into my biking clothes, but there was no time for that. I grabbed a couple of rubber bands out of my desk drawer and snugged them around the ankles of my jeans, got my bike, and was almost at a run as I wheeled it out of the building and into the parking lot.

I pedaled hard but found myself out of breath after a couple of miles. Why hadn't I taken better care of myself? What a dumbass I was for smoking all those years back in high school! And the breakfast burritos and biscochitos! Heart pounding, thighs aching, I had to rest. I pulled over and laid the bike down on a grassy strip next to the sidewalk. Once I got out away from the office buildings, there would be no grass, no trees, no shade. I cursed my long hair, which hung in a damp, ratted mass down my back. I lifted the hair off my neck, hoping to get a cool breeze, but felt only the blistering Albuquerque sun as it boiled the sweat off my skin. I squirted some water from my water bottle down the back of my shirt. There. Better.

Nola's voice had sounded urgent, but how urgent was it really? Was she merely irritated her car wouldn't start, or was she in some kind of real danger? Should I call the police? No, calm the hell down. If Nola was here, that's what she'd tell me. She'd say, "Stop catastrophizing, Sylvie, you're going to give yourself a heart attack. Get a grip!" Then she'd do her version of a slap, which was essentially just waving her arm in my general direction.

A car slowed as it passed me and its passenger launched a half-full Big Gulp out the window, but the trajectory was all wrong, so it landed ten feet ahead of me. Ice scattered on the grass, sparkling and cool, beckoned so much that I forgot to flip the guy off and instead considered scooping the ice into my water bottle or cramming it down the back of my shirt.

I picked my bike up off the grass. Eight more miles to go. No way to ride flat-out that distance. Gotta pace myself, not think about the fire in my knees, go easy on the water, make it last. I got back on the bike, pedaling slower now, but steady, forcing my thoughts away from my body, back to Nola.

Maybe all that happened was she told Travis, "I hear you're still married." Then what? Most likely he denied everything, but she eventually dug the truth out of him. He got mad, left in a huff. Her car wouldn't start, and she didn't want to wait for him to get over his little snit. And that, as they say, was that. Besides, Crystal had never come out and actually said that Travis beat his wife. She just said there was some screaming and the cops came. Routine shit for most neighborhoods I'd ever lived in, when it got right down to it. Lying two-timing jerks weren't exactly a rarity, after all. So, Nola might be in some sort of uncomfortable situation, but a crisis? Not likely.

For once, I was following Nola's advice; I'd beaten my frantic imagination into submission. Keep pedaling, I thought. You'll be home in half an hour, pick up Nola, and there will be tales to tell. I pictured Orlando and me on my patio, spinning him the story, him laughing when I told him about me seriously considering eating a stranger's Big Gulp ice off the ground.

Another mile of pavement rolled under me. I was in the rhythm of the bike now, the traffic noise drifting away, air gliding over my body and cooling my skin, slipping into the trance of the pedal crank.

31

Had I known then what I know now, I would have dumped my bike, stood in the middle of the road and screamed at the first car that came by to stop, stop, STOP.

The mystery would unravel but not at all the way I had imagined.

Nola had called Travis that morning, launching her sneak attack. She asked if she could come over, without giving him any indication of what she suspected. He'd had an edge to his voice, and she wondered if he somehow knew what Crystal had told her about Janice and Kylie and the cops coming over.

She wondered if Crystal, in some sort of alcohol- and Valium-induced delusionary state, had made it all up. Marcos, Janice, everything. What then? For a second, no more, Nola considered giving Travis another chance. Forget it; hitting on a woman's best friend is a Cardinal sin, isn't it? If not, it should be! All right, it's decided. No matter what happens now, her relationship with Travis is over.

Travis said he had the afternoon off and that she could come over around 4:00. Then he had hung up without any of his usual sweet farewells.

As Nola drove to the trailer court, she psyched herself up for the confrontation, playing out different conversations in her head. By the time she pulled up in front of his house, she felt confident she was ready for anything he might say to her.

She stood on his porch, tapped her car keys on the window in the door—her version of knocking. "Hello? Anybody home?" she called out.

"It's open," Travis said, his voice flat, betraying nothing.

Bastard! He knew she couldn't open the door herself, at least not without practically standing on her head and fumbling around with the knob for fifteen minutes. Was this some sort of twisted power play?

"Can't you open if for me, please?" She hated asking him for help, especially now, of all times. She waited on the porch, her resolve diminishing with each passing second.

It was a full minute before he opened the door. He did not look at her, instead wheeled around and plopped into his La-Z-Boy. The aluminum blinds were down, the slats louvered shut, making it darker than usual in the living room. It took a moment for her eyes to adjust.

"How 'bout we shed a little light on the subject?" she said.

"Suit yourself."

She crossed the room to the window behind his chair, struggled momentarily with the blind's cord, and finally managed to raise the blinds a few inches.

It was only mid-afternoon, but he was knocking back a cool one, a pyramid of empty cans in progress on the coffee table. His face was unshaven. His clothes looked slept in. He seemed irritated—no, more than that—full-fledged pissed off. But about what?

Wait just a damn minute, mister! she thought. *I'm supposed to be the one who's pissed off here, not you!* She sifted through the scenarios she'd played out on the way over, trying to find one that she could use now but came up empty.

"Well?" he said, taking a sip of his beer, solemnly setting it down on the table.

"Uh, well—there's something I want to talk to you about."

"I bet there is. Go ahead."

Why was he already in jackass mode? She couldn't stand it. "What the hell is *your* problem?"

He studied her, shaking his head, as if he couldn't believe she could be so foolish as to *pretend* she didn't know. He got out of his chair, walked over to his *Lost in Space* collection. His back to her, he picked up the robot, held it in his hand as if it was a rare and priceless artifact.

He turned to face her. "You know goddamn good and well what you did."

"What *I* did?"

She was indignant for a second. Then she thought *Uh oh!* Did he somehow find out about the night of the break-in? Maybe Crystal saw the whole thing and ratted them out. Maybe she really *was* obsessed with Travis and was trying to play both of them.

"Look, Travis. I don't know what you're talking about. I'm here to talk to you about what *you've* done, not what I've done. Now sit down a minute and let's try to have a civilized, adult, conversation."

"No, *you* look. I told you never to touch my stuff."

She felt her knees go wobbly. Holy hell, he did know about the break-in! If he was the man Crystal said he was, she was in big trouble. Abort the plan, abort, abort! Now is not the time for confrontation!

"Gee, I'm really sorry. I know it wasn't right," she said, determined to sound calming, sweet, conciliatory. "I just had to know what was in that—"

He shook the robot at her. "Did you think I wouldn't notice?" His face was scalded with rage.

"Well, no, actually. I didn't think you would."

"You stupid bitch! *Every* piece has a placard underneath it! *Every* piece dated and labeled! *Every* piece goes on top of its placard! Why in the *fuck* did you think I wouldn't notice you moved one of them?"

"Uh, I uh … I … what are you talking about?"

"Robot, dammit, ROBOT! You moved Robot! Don't bullshit me and tell me you didn't! He's supposed to be *here*," he said, placing it on the shelf, presumably on top of its precious placard. "Instead, I found it *here*!" He jabbed his finger at a spot near the front of the shelf.

What the? Was he talking about months ago, when she had cleaned his trailer and picked up that silly robot to look at it? Is *that* what he was so pissed off about? She was so flabbergasted, she almost laughed out loud. She sputtered in disbelief, no longer afraid.

"You think it's funny? Is that what you think?"

"Yeah, I guess I do. If you're going to get so upset over a stupid toy, how am I going to have a conversation with you about Janice and your daughter?"

Now it was his turn to be flabbergasted.

"I talked to one of your neighbors," she said, deciding to protect Crystal, make the story anonymous. Crystal had to live next door to the guy, after all. No reason to start World War III. "Seems some people think you are still married and that you in fact have a daughter. At this point, I don't think it matters. You and I are finished. I don't want to be in this relationship with you anymore." She searched to find words that were firm but not inflammatory. "We're just not clicking" was the most innocuous thing she could come up with.

"We're DONE when I say we're done," he said, taking a step closer to her.

Hadn't Marcos said pretty much the same thing to Crystal? Well, she wasn't Crystal. If Travis was trying to intimidate her with his absurd macho posturing, then he was in for a rude awakening. She said, "No, we're DONE now."

"What's this all about? Is it that psycho little bitch of a friend of yours? I suppose she lied and told you that I came on to her when I was at your house, right? Is that what Sylvie told you? Is it?"

He stepped closer to her. She forced her voice to be steady. "You need to calm down. Right. Now."

"Well, I got a little secret to tell you. That's not what happened. We were in the kitchen, and I was telling her about work. About my JOB. Trying to be sociable. *Trying* to be a fucking gentleman. Then *she* came on to *me*. I was sitting on the counter, then she starts rubbing my leg, starts telling me if we hurry, we can get it on before you come back. What do you think of your so-called 'friend' now?"

"I think she's my friend. And I think you are a liar. And an idiot, too, if you think I could ever believe such a preposterous story."

He pushed her. If she'd had arms, she might have caught herself as she lost her balance and tipped backwards, could have grabbed onto the arm of the sofa and stood her ground. Instead, she toppled over and landed hard on the linoleum floor.

"*You* calm down," he said, looking down at her. He turned, grabbed his car keys and went out the front door, yanking it closed behind him.

She pushed her back against the counter, working her way up to her feet. On the counter, she spotted an unopened letter addressed to Janice Matthews. The words "Addressee Unknown" were stamped on it. Maybe this is why Travis is on such a rampage! Nola wasted no time getting to the door. She struggled with its handle, finally managed to hold on to it long enough to twist it open. She got in her car, pulse racing, sweat beading up on her forehead, wondering if her tailbone was cracked. Damn, it hurt!

She pushed the starter button on the shift lever, and the engine started to turn over, but didn't catch. *No, no, please don't let me down now! Not now!* She pushed the button again. The engine turned over, but before she could say "Hallelujah!" it stalled. She pumped the gas pedal, tried again. Nothing. Not even a click.

She looked next door, at Crystal's place. Crystal's car was not under the carport and Maya, that tiny terror, was loose in the front yard.

She choked back the panic. She'd have to fight with that damn door handle again, get back inside the trailer, use the phone, call somebody, call somebody quick. She didn't want to be there when Travis got back.

32

Oglala was up ahead, and I was ready to be off the busy street, ride in peace, let my guard down. I'd forgotten it had rained the previous week, turning the road first into mud, then the sun beat down, petrifying the mud into a mile-long washboard. I bounced along in and out of the ruts, struggling to maintain control. At first I gripped the handles with all my strength, trying to force the bike to go in a straight line, but after a few minutes of getting pounded, my hands grew numb, and I discovered that a lighter touch made things easier. I loosened my grip and the bike stopped bucking so much.

I heard a car approaching from behind and glanced in my mirror, saw it gaining on me fast, flinging up a plume of dirt and rocks behind it. I'd seen this plenty of times before. Guys—and it was always a guy—seemed to get a thrill out of driving as close to me as possible without actually forcing me off the road. I braced myself, preparing to be enveloped in the inevitable choking, blinding cloud this testosterone-fueled Neanderthal was creating behind him. I worked my bike close to the edge of the road and narrowed my eyes like a lizard, ready now for the onslaught of flying debris.

I risked another glance in my mirror to get a better look at the car. It was a red Oldsmobile 442. The same kind of car Travis drove. I slowed down, squinted in my mirror, attempted to make out the driver's face. Then the Olds was next to me. Like a slow motion dream, I saw Nola in the passenger seat, her face turned to the side window, her skin like chalk, eyes wide, her face contorted in wordless terror. On impulse, I raised my hand to touch the glass.

The car's side mirror hit my handlebar grip. The handlebars jerked viciously sideways, and my fingers were torn away from them. I tried to stay upright, simply step off the bike, let it fall underneath me, but my left foot caught the edge of a rut, bending it backwards at an unnatural and startlingly painful angle. The bike and I fell together, the pedal crank raking a gouge down the side of my leg as I tumbled into the shallow irrigation ditch next to the road, striking my head on a protruding water pipe.

I lay there for a few seconds, dazed. Then I tried to stand up, but as soon as I put my weight on my foot, the ankle gave way and I crumpled back into the ditch. "That mother fucker!" I said, spitting dirt out of my mouth and rubbing the grit out of my eyes. As the dust cloud cleared, I saw the Olds stopped, about 100 yards away. Was Travis going to turn around, come back to see if I was OK? *Yeah, you just do that. You'll see how well I accept your apology, you bastard!*

Travis backed the car up. Through its rear window, I saw Nola rocking her body from side to side, as if she was trying to get loose from something. He was looking at her and, judging from his expression, saying something unpleasant.

He stopped the car a few yards from me and got out, then walked through the shimmering haze of heat and dust toward me. Beyond him, back in the car, Nola continued to rock back and forth. What the hell was she doing?

I couldn't stand, so I got to my knees, trying to get a better view over the edge of the ditch. Was she trying to get out of her seat belt? Maybe slide out from underneath it? Was that even possible?

Then Travis was standing in front of me, his smile tight, his face smug. He lingered there, seemingly amused with his handiwork. A scorching fury overtook me.

"You stupid jackass! You could have killed me!" My arms were cocked, my fists clenched.

He grabbed a fistful of my hair and yanked my head backward, nearly toppling me. He leaned his face down close to mine. The world around me disappeared. I saw only his face, inches from mine, grotesquely magnified, a sweaty, slippery florid mass. I saw the tiny, moist holes where each eyelash was inserted into his eyelids. His nose hairs were sticky; beads of dirt-dusted mucus clung to them. His pale lips were parched and scaly. I felt as if I could actually see the mist of his beer-sodden breath hanging between us.

From the direction of the car, I heard a muffled voice. It seemed to be coming from far away. My primal brain dismissed it as inconsequential.

"If you don't stay out of my business, you bitch, next time I *will* kill you," emphasizing his point by twisting my hair around his hand and giving it another brutal yank.

I do not like having my hair pulled. I do not like it one little bit.

I sucker punched him in the crotch and he fell to his knees. My hair was still wound around his hand, and as he went down, it felt like a piece of my scalp was ripped out. I was practically on top of him now, grabbing at his hand, madly trying to get it untangled from my hair.

He was still groaning and spitting when I broke free of him and stood up. I tried to run to the car, but could only hop and limp. I saw Nola's leg sticking out of the car. She must have opened the car door with her foot.

Travis recovered from my punch and was on me in a flash, hooked his arm around my neck, hurled me back to the ground. A boot, a very pointy boot, punctured the space between my ribs.

He crouched over me again. I swung wildly with both of my fists, landed a few solid punches to his head, and twisted to get out from under him. He crawled on top of me, pinning my shoulders with his knees, forcing my hands to the dirt, keeping me from swinging. I tried to buck him off with my hips, but he was no seven-year-old boy like Shep. The weight of him crushed my lungs and I felt like I was drowning. Each breath brought searing pain.

He punched me in the side of the head, causing a loud buzzing noise to reverberate in my skull.

There was nothing I could do now except scream. Scream like a girl.

"Help! Help me! Heeeeelllp!" I shrieked and kept on shrieking until Travis' hands closed around my throat. My head lolled to the side, my cheek pressed into the dirt. My tunnel vision contracted another notch. In the distance, like looking through a telescope, I saw the familiar blue farmhouse. The fence. The dogs.

Molly cleared the fence first, with Cupcake right behind her. That shrill and panicked voice in my head went silent. The dogs mesmerized me as I watched each paw kick off a cloud of dust and listened to their panting, ragged breath as they bolted down the road to us.

Travis apparently saw nothing, heard nothing. The shock of something unknown attacking him from behind and the nasty chomp on his calf made him let go of my throat. Cupcake jumped on his back and tried to bite his neck but Travis was too fast, rolled away, covered his face. Cupcake, undaunted, changed tactics and clamped down on his arm instead, whipping her head back and forth, tearing shirt, skin, muscle.

Now an old pickup truck was coming down the road. It slid to a stop, the door flew open, and a farmer jumped out. He ran to us, calling out the dogs' names, hollering at them, "Stop! Stop!" but they didn't let go of Travis until the farmer grabbed them by their collars and dragged them off of him.

"Are you all right?" the farmer said.

"Yeah, I think so," said Travis, clamping his hand down on his mangled forearm, trying to stop the bleeding.

"Not you, asshole! Her!" he said, jerking his chin in my direction.

Each breath made something in my chest cave in, scraping some delicate internal organ. "I'm . . . OK . . . " I said, clutching my side. "Ow. Goddamn."

Nola.

"My friend—she's in the car up there. Hurry! She might be hurt!"

"Are you sure?" He squinted at Travis. "I don't want to leave you alone here with him."

"It's fine. Just let the dogs stay." He let the dogs go, and they ran to me. "C'mere you guys! Good doggies! Good, good doggies!" They licked my face and hands, and I forgot for a moment about my ribs and my foot and the ringing in my ears.

The farmer gave Travis the once over. "You—get up. You're coming with me." Travis stood up, his hand still clamped on his arm. Blood was oozing through his shirtsleeve. He limped behind the farmer, muttering something I couldn't make out. His limp made me smile, filled me with pride in the aim and velocity of my sucker punch. Clint, dear brother, you taught me well.

I lay back in the ditch, feeling no pain at all now, wanting to close my eyes, to rest, if only for a moment. I felt a sloppy lick on my hand just before my eyelids fluttered and I sank down into a cool darkness.

I never put much stock in tales of near-death experiences, the kind where people describe drifting through a tunnel toward a golden light, that sort of pseudoscientific mumbo jumbo. Besides, I was nowhere near death, so maybe what happened next was the result of whatever concoction some EMT or doctor had injected into me. But damned if my life didn't flash before my eyes. And—this was weird—I saw Nola's life flash as well. Like some sort of TV split screen image, her life tracked next to mine.

Six-year-old Nola floated by, and though I didn't know her then, my brain held a vivid image of an Indian summer day, she and her friends pulling that little Red Flyer wagon with the fake arm in it, laughing. And me, six years old too, sitting on the cloakroom floor, indignant about my punishment, but glad to be out of the fray of the classroom.

Another image, a teenaged Nola singing in the choir, smiling at her family and friends in the audience. A teenaged me, ducking out of the line for yearbook pictures, hiding behind Building 12, content in the solitude.

Nola again, a young woman now, going out for drinks with the gang from work. Nola chatting up store clerks, charming waitresses, talking her way out of traffic tickets. Nola telling me how lucky she was that at every crisis in her life, miraculously, there was someone there to help her through it.

And me, very nearly mastering the art of needing nothing, depending on no one, but as the images flashed, for a fleeting moment I wondered what the attraction was.

In this split-screen movie, it was her story that had the happy ending. Not mine.

33

I woke three hours later at Lovelace Hospital. Something warm was dripping into my arm through an IV line, making my brain feel cozy and relaxed. My chest still hurt, but I breathed now without that searing pain. My ankle was in a cast.

Orlando and Nola were sitting in chairs next to each other, the conversation between them hushed, conspiratorial. There was a box of Kleenex on Orlando's lap.

"Bleeeeh! My mouth feels like a sandbox. Anybody got a breath mint?" I said, running my tongue over my sticky teeth.

"You've got a concussion, two broken ribs, and metal pins screwed into your ankle. Leave it to you to be worried about having minty fresh breath," Orlando said.

"And my floss, man, I need my floss," I pleaded. Orlando and Nola rolled their eyes.

Nola rocked forward in her chair while Orlando put his hand on her back, giving her a little push to get her to her feet, taking a wadded Kleenex from between her fingers. She stood next to my bed, studied my face. "How do you feel? Does your chest hurt?"

"Yeah, but not like before. The doctors must have repositioned the jagged, stabby pieces, pointing them away from my liver." I looked down at my skinned knuckles, bits of dried blood stuck to them. The fluff in my head was starting to dissolve, and I noticed her expression. "Have you been crying, Nola? What's wrong? Where's Travis?"

"You doofus! I'm crying because of you, not Travis. God, you can be so dense!"

My ankle felt like it was cracked in two with a pickaxe, but I said, "Why are you worried about me? What's the big deal? I'm OK. But then again, I haven't seen the doctor's bills yet . . ."

Nola shook her head and Orlando bonked my knee with the Kleenex box.

"Anyways . . . where's Travis?"

"I believe he is domiciled at The Gray Bar Hotel," Nola said.

There was a nasty raw patch of skin on the side of her neck. "What the hell happened to your neck?"

"Oh, that," she said, leaning her neck down to her fingers, rubbing it. "Stupid seat belt harnesses. I never realized just how hard it would be to get out of one without unlatching it."

"And now?"

"Forget it. Not possible."

"I'll keep that in mind. But what about Travis. Did he hurt you?"

"Maybe a slap or two. A little push. Nothing serious."

"No kidding? I always assumed a guy would have to at least give you a skull fracture before the law got interested. I can't believe they'd put him in jail for a slap or two."

"Well, there was that . . . and the fact that if those dogs hadn't attacked Travis when they did, you'd be on a different floor of the hospital."

"You mean in intensive care?"

"No, she means like downstairs. In the basement," Orlando said.

My eyes opened wide in surprise. I couldn't quite remember what had happened. There was some hair pulling. Yes, yes,

I remembered that perfectly. I massaged my scalp, checking for bare patches. And kicking. And punching. I most definitely remembered the punching. Was there more? Maybe it would come back to me later.

"Not that I'm not glad to see you, but what are you doing here, Orlando? How'd you find out about all this?"

"Nola asked the EMTs in the ambulance to let her ride with you to the hospital, and when she got here, she called everybody she could think of. Emily's here, too. She went downstairs to get some coffee. Your parents are on their way."

"My parents, too," Nola said.

"What about Clint? Did you call him?"

"Man, you really are out of it. Clint came already and left, said he had some hot date he didn't want to stand up."

"Oh." That hurt more than my ankle.

"He signed your cast, though. Look, right here."

"I can't see it. What's it say?"

"It says, 'You hit like a girl. Love, Clint.'"

I gave an appreciative nod, relieved he hadn't written a profanity on it or drawn something obscene.

"I gotta go downstairs for a minute," Orlando said. "I need to call Fiona. We were supposed to go out tonight, but I need to let her know I'm not going to make it." He gave my arm a squeeze. "I'll be back in a few minutes."

It might have been the narcotics talking, but I suddenly had this idea that next time Orlando was between girlfriends, I was going to tackle him to the ground and smother him with kisses.

After he left, Nola scooched her chair close to the bed, sat down, leaned in close. "I need to tell you something."

"Nooo! No heartfelt talks or gooey crap!"

"Shut up, stupid. I'm serious here. I want to tell you something. Orlando and I just had a very interesting conversation about what happened the night you—" She glanced over her shoulder at the doorway, then turned back to me and whispered, "The night you went on your little investigative mission and found the letters."

"You mean when I broke into Travis' trailer?"

"Shhhhhh!" She looked around nervously again. "Yes, that's what I mean. I want you to know that I'm sorry."

"What? Why are you sorry? I should have told you everything right away. I'm the one who screwed up. I'm the one who should apologize. I should have told you everything right away. But, I thought . . ."

"Forget all that, it doesn't matter. I know you and I've got a pretty good idea why you kept your mouth shut. I'm the one who got you involved in all this craziness. I shouldn't have asked you to break into Travis' house. That was wrong, wrong for a lot of reasons."

"Hey, I didn't have to do it. Nobody twisted my arm."

"I know. But you wouldn't have done it if I hadn't asked you to."

"Yeah, but—"

"Shush UP! Will you please be quiet and let me get through this?"

"Sorry. Sorry. Go ahead."

"I didn't listen to you when you told me not to trust Travis. Remember that night we went to see Zozobra with Orlando? You told me then to be careful, and I figured you were being your usual paranoid self."

Just because you're paranoid doesn't mean everybody isn't out to get you, I thought.

"You told me plenty of times that you thought he was lying to me, that he was using me, that he wasn't good enough for me. I should know by now that you have a sixth sense about people's characters. I don't understand how you do it or where it comes from. Sometimes it seems like you don't understand people or have any social graces at all. Maybe you do, maybe you don't, but I should have listened to you. I didn't, and because of that, you're in this damn hospital. I am so, so sorry."

I looked down at the sheets, fidgeted with the tape on my ribs.

"Please tell me you accept my apology."

I had a strangled feeling in my throat, a tightness in my chest that wasn't because of the cracked ribs. "Well, yeah. Of course I do. It's nothing. I mean, really . . . gee, I don't even know why you're worried about it."

"It was not *nothing*." She sniffed, looked ready to cry again. "Now listen to me. I want to take care of you for a few days. I already called my boss and took a few days off. I called your boss, too, and told him you wouldn't be in for a few days, that you'd had a bike accident and hurt your ankle."

"You what? Wait, no—I need to go to work. I'm in the middle of a big project."

"I know, I know. Your boss told me how tough it was going to be to get along without you, but that they'd manage somehow."

"Are you being sarcastic?"

"No, he actually said that. So you're coming home with me for the next few days. All right?"

I squirmed, adjusted the sheets, smoothed down the Band-aid on my IV, pondered the ceiling.

"Well? What is it now? What's the problem?" she said.

"Just promise you won't make any tuna casseroles."

Epilogue

In New Mexico, the wheels of justice move slowly, if at all. By the time Travis went to trial, my injuries were a dim memory. Even my armpits had healed up from being rubbed raw from those barbaric instruments of torture commonly known as crutches.

In the courtroom, I watched Nola approach the witness stand and chuckled to myself as I envisioned the bailiff telling her to place her hand on the Bible. The courtroom would fall quiet, and all eyes would be on her, wondering what she would do.

She did just what I knew she would do; she looked the bailiff in the eye, smiled, and asked him to come closer. Then she placed her two fingers on the Bible and said what anyone else would say. "I promise to tell the truth, the whole truth … "

For months, I worried nobody on a jury would give a damn about Travis running me off the road and trying to strangle me. When testifying, I knew I would be incapable of displaying any kind of delicate, feminine vulnerability, especially since the mere thought of Travis filled me with a dark urge to jab him in the eye with a screwdriver. The jury would no doubt pick up on that uppity, angry, unflinching vibe of mine and come to the conclusion that whatever he had done to me, I probably had it coming. Besides, it wasn't like women didn't get run off the road or punched in the head more or less routinely in this part of the state. I fretted that Travis would get off with no more than a token fine, perhaps a few weeks of community service.

Then Nola gave her testimony and described how Travis had pushed her down that day in the trailer. At this, there was an audible gasp from the jury and the spectators. Even the judge's professionalism escaped him for a fleeting instant as he flashed an expression of loathing in Travis' direction. I realized then, to my vast satisfaction, Travis was not going to get off so easy. The jury's opinion of me was irrelevant; they would want to punish Travis for what he did to Nola.

Nola's testimony was every prosecutor's dream; articulate, detailed, consistent. She described how he stormed out of the trailer, how her car wouldn't start, that she had called me. She was sitting in her car waiting for me when Travis pulled up. He hauled a case of beer out of the back seat of the Olds, and not giving Nola so much as a glance, carried it into the trailer.

She'd been relieved there hadn't been another confrontation with him, but five minutes later, he'd come back outside, carrying a beer. He walked over to her car, draped himself over the driver's side, stuck his head in the window and said, "What in the hell are you still doing here?"

"My car won't start, so I'm waiting for Sylvie. She's on her way."

He said he'd take her home. No way, she'd said, she'd wait for me. They argued about it for a few minutes, and then Travis practically tore the hinges off the door, yelling at her to get out of the car, *he* was taking her home, by God. When she refused, he put her in a headlock and dragged her out of her seat.

She was hollering up a storm by now, but if anybody in the trailer court heard her, they didn't bother to investigate. Travis shoved her into the Olds, yanked the seatbelt and harness across her body, latched her in, slammed the car door. She was trapped.

How it was they happened to drive down Oglala was pure coincidence. A road crew was working on Barcelona Drive, the street they normally would have taken to Nola's apartment, so Travis turned down Oglala to avoid the traffic, taking the very shortcut I'd been dumb enough to tell him about that day he tried to grope me in Nola's kitchen.

When she spotted me on Oglala, she knew it was me, even from behind. A young woman on a bicycle. On a dirt road in Albuquerque. On a blistering hot workday afternoon. Wearing a T-shirt that said on the back, "There are 10 kinds of people in this world—those who understand binary and those who don't." Who else could it be? Who, indeed.

She had kept quiet, hoped that Travis would not recognize me. But as they approached me on the road, she turned her head to look at me, and his gaze instinctively followed her own.

The rest, as they say, is mayhem.

Nola's testimony was the truth, but strictly speaking, it wasn't the whole truth. She didn't mention the night I broke into the trailer. Orlando's name never came up. Neither did Crystal's. It bothered me that she didn't tell everything, but when I was called to testify, I followed her lead; I answered the questions that were asked, volunteered nothing.

It itched at my ethics. Travis was on trial for assault, but what about me? Wasn't I guilty of breaking and entering (or entering anyway) and Nola and Orlando guilty of aiding and abetting?

I knew what Nola would have to say about this. She would say that she and I hadn't tried to maim or kill anyone. She'd say legal truth is important, yes, but moral truth is divine. Then I'd demand to know where she got that quote and she'd want to smack me.

That night after the trial, when we were alone together watching night fall on the valley, she would say something else, too. When Travis got out of jail, if he tried to hurt either of us . . . Well, neither of us knew anything about snakes, but we both knew his trailer did not have a smoke alarm.

THE END